FIRE ENGINE DEAD

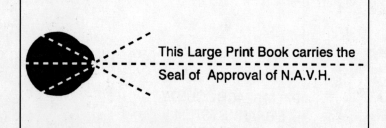

This Large Print Book carries the
Seal of Approval of N.A.V.H.

FIRE ENGINE DEAD

SHEILA CONNOLLY

WHEELER PUBLISHING
A part of Gale, Cengage Learning

GALE
CENGAGE Learning®

Detroit • New York • San Francisco • New Haven, Conn • Waterville, Maine • London

GALE
CENGAGE Learning·

LIBRARY OF CONGRESS CATALOGING-IN-PUBLICATION DATA

Connolly, Sheila.
    Fire engine dead / by Sheila Connolly. — Large print ed.
      p. cm. — (Wheeler Publishing large print cozy mystery) (A museum mystery)
    ISBN 978-1-4104-4935-1 (softcover) — ISBN 1-4104-4935-1 (softcover)
    1. Museums—Fiction. 2. Large type books. I. Title.
PS3601.T83F57 2012
813'.6—dc23   2012018605

Published in 2012 by arrangement with The Berkley Publishing Group, a member of Penguin Group (USA) Inc.

Printed in the United States of America
2 3 4 5 6   16 15 14 13 12
FD305

ACKNOWLEDGMENTS

Writing about firefighters can be challenging, because since 9/11 they have become national heroes, and rightly so. I hope that my depiction of the activities within the Philadelphia Fire Department in this book is generally accurate, and that no reader thinks that they are anything but outstanding citizens. Likewise, small-town volunteer fire departments deserve recognition, and I've known some members of those who were proud to give their services without compensation.

Among Philadelphia's wonderful array of museums is one devoted to firefighting equipment and paraphernalia, as befits the city where Benjamin Franklin organized the first fire company. While I have borrowed much of the history and organizational structure, I can assure you that Philadelphia's Fireman's Hall Museum collection is intact, and there are no arsonists on the payroll, to the best of my knowledge.

I owe a debt of gratitude to Dian Williams, Ph.D., author of the book *Understanding the Arsonist: From Assessment to Confession.* She is a specialist in firesetting psychology, and she teaches near Philadelphia, which made her an ideal resource for the information I needed. In her book she makes it clear that there are many reasons why people set fires. I hope she'll find that the motives I created in this book are credible.

Thanks as always to my perceptive editor, Shannon Jamieson Vazquez, who continues to ask gentle questions like "why would he do that?" and to my agent, Jessica Faust of BookEnds, who keeps this series moving forward. Carol Kersbergen is still my eyes and ears in the greater Philadelphia region. As always, Sisters in Crime and the Guppies chapter provide ongoing support and cheerleading — which every writer needs.

Soon after it [a fire] is seen and cry'd out, the Place is crowded by active Men of different Ages, Professions and Titles who, as of one Mind and Rank, apply themselves with all Vigilance and Resolution, according to their Abilities, to the hard Work of conquering the increasing fire.

— Benjamin Franklin
on firefighting in Philadelphia,
Pennsylvania Gazette, 1733

CHAPTER 1

I looked in both directions along the third-floor hallway. Good, nobody in sight. I pulled open the door to the library stacks only wide enough to slip through it, and closed it quietly behind me.

I was playing hooky. It had been only a few months since I had taken over as president of the Pennsylvania Antiquarian Society, shoved unceremoniously into the corner office from my nice, safe, lower-profile job as director of development. Don't get me wrong — I loved my new job. Or at least, parts of the job. But while the Society was a venerable and respected Philadelphia institution, it was now my responsibility to keep it solvent, intact, and open to the public. Not easy, especially since the current fundraising climate sucked; the hundred-plus-year-old building cried out for repairs and upgrades that we simply couldn't afford; and the salaries we offered were so uncompetitive that we had trouble hanging on to enough staff to cover the desks and retrieve and shelve items requested.

Hiding wasn't going to improve any one of those problems, but it was going to make me feel better. I'd first come to work at the Society more than five years ago because I loved Philadelphia and I loved local history. One of the unacknowledged perks of the job was the chance to prowl in the stacks. In the past I could claim that I was getting to know the collections so I could write grant proposals about them, but the truth was, I loved to handle original documents and memorabilia from everyone from William Penn to the most recent mayor of Philadelphia. I got a real rush from the heady smell of old leather and crumbling paper. I needed to revisit the stacks periodically to remind myself why I had accepted the job of president, especially when board members called every other hour to ask why I hadn't done A, B, or C. The answer usually was *because we can't afford it,* but they were getting tired of hearing that. Heck, *I* was getting tired of saying it. I needed some new lines — or preferably, more money.

I trod quietly along the dimly lit aisles, making as little noise as possible. Was I looking for anything in particular? Not really. I was certainly trying to avoid noticing the blue tarps spread over shelves here and there to divert the drips from the leaking roof, and the teetering piles of boxes that I knew were *not* acid-free archival quality, and which were slowly sinking under their own weight, doing who knows what damage to their precious contents. No shelves to put them on; no staff to shelve them. *Come on, Nell — you're supposed to be cheering yourself up!*

I found myself an old metal chair and took it to a corner, about as far from the door as I could get. I was surrounded by large ledgers from long-gone Philadelphia companies, and I knew if I opened any one of them I'd find some clerk's careful copperplate script in fading brown ink, recording the day-to-day transactions of daily life a century ago. I shut my eyes and breathed deep, waiting for the calm and quiet to do their work . . .

"Nell?" a male voice whispered.

I jumped a foot and opened my eyes. "Eric, how did you find me?" Eric was my administrative assistant. He'd only been in the job for two months, but I swear he had learned how to read my mind.

"I know you come up here when you get stressed out. I hate to bother you, but you told me to remind you about the luncheon today, and it's already eleven thirty."

Luncheon, luncheon . . . no wonder I'd told him to remind me, since I had no clue what he was talking about.

"The Greater Philadelphia Grantmakers Coalition?" he added.

Oh. I must have been trying hard to forget it. The coalition was a group of local funders who got together to talk about local philanthropy. What that meant, mainly, was that the area movers and shakers with money to give gathered together to divvy up the pot. To be fair, they also offered workshops, issued publications, and held conferences to encourage grant giving and teach effective proposal writing, all of which I had benefitted from in the past. I'd attended their events when I was a fundraiser, and it was now even more important that I have a presence among the group, to keep the lines of communication (and pocketbooks) open. This would be my first meeting with them since I'd ascended to the giddy heights of the Society's presidency. What's more, I'd promised to take along my relatively new director of development, Shelby Carver, so she could start figuring out who was who in the local funding community.

In short, I couldn't hide out. I sighed and

stood up. "Did you remind Shelby?"

"Sure did," Eric said. "She's waiting in your office. You want me to tell her I couldn't find you?"

I straightened my back. "Thanks, but I have to go. And I want to introduce Shelby to some people she needs to know. Thank you for finding me, Eric."

I led the way back to my office where Shelby was waiting. "Were you planning to duck out on me, lady?" she asked, her faint southern drawl softening her words.

"Believe me, I thought about it. You ready to go? You mind if we walk over?"

"Works for me. Looks like spring might actually get here sometime this year."

I pulled on my light raincoat, gathered up my bag, and said, "Let's go."

Once we were outside the building, I re-alized Shelby was right: I hadn't even noticed, but there were green buds peeping from the few spindly trees that could survive on city streets, and the air felt cool but pleasantly so. Shelby matched me stride for stride. I probably needed the exercise more than she did, since she usually walked to work from her home on the other side of Independence Hall, while I took a train from the suburb of Bryn Mawr. At least I walked from the train station to the Society, but that was about all the exercise I got.

"Where're we going?" she asked.

"The luncheon's at the Marriott. At least the food should be good."

"You want me to do anything in particular, or should I just sit there and soak up wisdom?"

I smiled. I enjoyed Shelby's slightly skewed humor, which matched mine. "I'll try to point out the important people, and the ones who have looked favorably upon us in the past. Unfortunately they aren't always one and the same."

The Marriott was a ten-minute walk from the Society, and we arrived in good time. I usually tried to arrive early for events like this, because it was a good opportunity to renew old contacts and make new ones. Besides, I was trying to set a good example for Shelby. When we walked in, people were standing around in clumps in the hallway, waiting for the doors to the luncheon to open. I greeted several by name — and so did Shelby, to my surprise. She hadn't lived in Philadelphia very long, but she'd certainly gotten to know a lot of people quickly — and influential ones, at that. I spotted Arabella Heffernan, my counterpart at the Let's Play Children's Museum in the city, when she bustled in. She saw me and made

14

a beeline over, and then we exchanged brief hugs.

"Hello, Nell! It's so nice to see you again."

"You, too, Arabella. How's the new exhibit doing?"

She twinkled — hard to believe, but Arabella could do that. "It's marvelous. The children love it, and our revenues are up. We're looking forward to the school vacation week."

"Sounds great. You remember Shelby, don't you?"

"Of course I do! Shelby, it's so good to see you. Are you settling in?"

"I am indeed, Arabella. Nell was kind enough to bring me along today so I can get to know people."

"I brought you along so you could take some of the load off of me!" I said in protest. "And for that, you have to know the players."

The doors to the main dining room opened, and the crowd surged toward them like water down a drain. You'd think that they hadn't eaten in days. Was a free meal really that exciting? In these tough times, maybe it was. We were separated from Arabella, and I guided Shelby toward a table of local CEOs I recognized, as well as other museum colleagues. "Hi, Arthur — do you have room for two more here?"

Arthur Mason, a man some twenty years older than me, stood up courteously and all but bowed. "Of course we do, for two such delightful companions. You're looking fine, Nell. And I don't believe I've made the acquaintance of this lovely lady?"

"Shelby, this is Arthur Mason. He's the CEO of the Waterfront Museum. Arthur, please meet Shelby Carver, who's replaced me as director of development."

Shelby turned on the charm. "We may not have met, but my ex-husband was positively addicted to your model ship collections. I swear, he was in there at least once a week."

"I'm delighted to hear that. Please, sit down."

We sat and were joined at the last minute by a young woman, about thirty years old, whom I didn't recognize. She seemed a bit breathless. "Can you fit in one more here?"

In fact there were several seats open, but I sympathized with anyone walking into an event like this and not knowing who was who. "Of course," I said warmly. "I'm Nell Pratt, and this is Shelby Carver. We're from the Pennsylvania Antiquarian Society. And you are — ?"

The woman sat and flashed an uncertain smile. "I'm Jennifer Phillips. I work at the

Fireman's Museum. My boss is here some-where, but we came separately."

"Haven't I read that you're currently undergoing renovations? Are you in fund-raising?" I asked.

"That and just about everything else," Jen-nifer said. "We've got a very small staff. And, yes, we're finishing up a renovation project right now, but we haven't started to reinstall the exhibits yet."

"Have you had much luck finding funding for the work?" I asked with sincere curios-ity. "This is a difficult time to go looking for outside support."

"We've done all right," Jennifer answered.

"I do hope you reopen soon. I've taken my grandchildren to your museum," Craig said. "They loved it." Conversation with Craig carried us through the appetizer course. When there was a lull, I leaned toward Shelby and pointed out several more members of the local institutional hierarchy, and with the next course came the requisite speeches from assorted coalition members, which in turn led to the keynote from a doddering local philanthropist whose name adorned several buildings in the city. Since he had a tendency to mumble, many mem-bers of the audience unconsciously leaned toward the podium where he stood speaking. I hoped they were only straining to hear, but I briefly entertained the suspicion that they were eagerly anticipating his demise: it was rumored that he had left some handsome bequests to several museums in his will, although nobody knew exactly which ones.

I was enjoying my more than adequate chicken dish when Jennifer jumped and fished under the table for her bag. It took me a moment to realize that the bag, or more precisely, the cell phone in her bag, was buzzing discreetly. She pulled it out and answered, politely turning away from the table, but it was hard to miss the intensity of her response. "What? Oh my God. Yes, he's here. We'll be right there." She turned back to the table. "Sorry, I've got a crisis. Nice to meet you all." She stood up, gathered her things, and headed for the nearest exit door, all the while scanning the crowd. She stopped at the door, her eyes fixed on someone halfway across the room, who had just pulled a cell phone from his pocket and answered it. Clearly he didn't like what he was hearing. He hung up quickly, then looked around until he spotted Jennifer near the door. She waved him over. He stood and made his excuses to the people at his table, then wove his way around several tables before stopping to lean close to Jennifer. He said a sentence or two, and she nodded before they both turned and went through the door at a brisk clip.

Who was he? Fortyish, slender, and nicely dressed but rather washed out in coloring, he looked vaguely familiar, but he wasn't anyone I knew personally. Most likely Jennifer's boss, whose name escaped me at the moment. They'd both seemed extraordinarily upset, and I wondered what kind of museum crisis could inspire that strong a response. But it wasn't really my business, so I turned my attention back to the droning speaker and tried to keep my eyelids up until the coffee was served.

After dessert and the accompanying platitudes, Shelby and I found our way out to the sidewalk. The fresh air felt good after being cooped up in the ballroom for a couple of hours.

"A little stuffy in there, wasn't it?" Shelby asked as we waited for the light to change so we could cross Market Street.

"The air or the speeches?" I smiled at her. "You'd better get used to it. A lot of these people made their money the old-fashioned way: they inherited it."

"Not so much of that these days, is there?"

I sighed. "Sad to say, no. Gather ye rosebuds while ye may, as the saying goes. You'd better sharpen up your grant-writing tools."

"I'm ready and willing. But you've got to tell me what we should focus on first."

"I know, I know." Our needs were many and the resources few. It was hard to set priorities when what we needed to do was everything. "You've seen the shopping list, and now you've heard what the funders are looking for. See if you can match them up, and I'll run the options by the board at our next meeting and see if they have any connections with the funders."

Shoptalk took us back to the Society. We went up to the administrative floor and parted ways, to our respective offices. When I settled myself at my desk, I realized that it was indeed time to set Shelby to hunting for funds. She'd been at the Society long enough to get to know us, and outside money was drying up fast, thanks to the current financial markets. I pulled out a pad and started making a list.

CHAPTER 2

As guardian of a building full of millions of documents on paper, I consider it my duty to support printed newspapers like the *Philadelphia Inquirer.* Plus reading the paper gives me something to do while I ride the train from Bryn Mawr to the city every day. This morning's lead story, above the fold, was about a major warehouse fire that had occurred the day before and had resulted in the death of at least one person. After fire companies from Philadelphia and several surrounding communities had put out the fire, the body of the warehouse watchman had been found among the ruins.

The watchman had left no close family. No firefighters had been hurt in fighting the fire, which was the only bright note. The warehouse was not a total loss, but it would take time to assess the damage. Arson was suspected, but authorities would not say whether they had any leads, only that the investigation was ongoing. The article mentioned that a string of similar fires had occurred recently in various parts of the city, although none quite as spectacular as this one — and no one had died in those earlier fires. There was a sad footnote: the late watchman, Allan Brigham, had been a retired firefighter himself.

As the train pulled into Suburban Station, I folded up the paper and tucked it in my bag. I enjoyed the brief walk to the Society, especially now that the weather was improving, and I stopped to pick up a cappuccino along the way. As far as I knew, my calendar was clear for the day, and even for the week. The next Society institutional event was still several months off, although planning was already under way; the next board meeting loomed, but it was still a couple of weeks distant. This would be Eric's first exposure to the full board. He already knew the members by name, and more important, knew which ones required special handling. I was trying to ease him slowly into the process of gathering information and distributing it to board members in a timely fashion. Not that they'd read it until the day before the meeting, but at least we in administration were holding up our end. Eric had proven to be a quick learner. In spite of his youth and lack of experience, he had shown good judgment about what to pass on to me and what to divert to other departments, for which I was grateful. And he was discreet. I was glad I had taken a chance on hiring him.

He was, as usual, at his desk when I arrived. "Mornin', Nell."

"Good morning, Eric. Anything I need to know about?"

"Only one change to your schedule. A Mr. Peter Ingersoll from the Fireman's Museum called and asked to see you, and I penciled him in for eleven. That work for you?"

I couldn't recall having met anyone named Peter Ingersoll — but I could hazard a guess that he was the man who Jennifer had huddled with at the luncheon yesterday. They had both looked upset then, and I had to wonder if whatever he wanted to talk to me about was related to those frantic phone calls yesterday afternoon. "That's fine. I'll be in my office."

I managed to accomplish quite a bit before Eric stuck his head in my door to say, "Mr. Ingersoll's here. You want me to go down and bring him upstairs?"

The third floor, where our administrative offices were located, was off-limits to the public, although they could circulate freely

23

in the reading rooms on the first and second floors. It wasn't much in terms of security, but it was the best we could afford for the time being. "Please."

Eric disappeared and returned quickly, followed by Peter, who was indeed the man I'd seen the day before. I mentally patted myself on the back for identifying him correctly. But yesterday he had looked concerned; today he looked strained. He strode into my office and extended his hand. "Peter Ingersoll. Thank you for agreeing to meet with me on such short notice. I'm so sorry to barge in on you like this, but there's something that I hope you can help me with."

I rose to shake his hand. "I hope I can help, Mr. Ingersoll. Please, sit down. Would you like some coffee?" I noticed Eric was still hovering in the door.

"It's Peter, please. No, caffeine is the last thing I need right now, I'm so wired." He dropped into a chair in front of my desk.

I sat in my own chair and nodded at Eric, who closed the door quietly behind him. "And I'm Nell. What can I do for you?"

"As I told your assistant, I'm the president of the Fireman's Museum. Do you know it?"

I smiled. "Indeed I do — I went to an

event there, what, two years ago now? It must have been around the time of the Ben Franklin bicentennial." I tried to remember details about the museum. I knew it was housed in a former firehouse, and I remembered the collections — what could be seen through the substantial crowd at that event — as a charming assemblage of equipment, emblems, and old photographs.

"Ah, yes — I hope you had an enjoyable evening."

"I did. I'd heard you're closed for renovations at the moment?"

He nodded. "We are. We're almost through. We'd hoped to link the opening of the refurbished museum with some sort of tribute to the firefighters of 9/11, but between permits and planning — and, of course, fundraising — we fell behind. We're scheduled to open shortly. Or we were."

I watched in dismay as Peter struggled to control his emotions. "Are you all right? You sure you wouldn't like a cup of tea or something?" Or maybe a Scotch, straight up?

He waved a hand. "No, I'm fine. It's just so new, I'm having trouble getting my head around it. Give me a moment." He looked down at his lap, his eyes closed, for maybe thirty seconds, before facing me again with a much calmer expression. "I apologize — you have no idea what I'm talking about, of course. Did you hear about the warehouse fire yesterday?"

"Yes, I read about it in the paper this morning."

Peter glanced around the office, as if to confirm that we were alone. "Please don't spread this around, but . . ." He swallowed. "That warehouse was where we were storing the museum collections during renovations."

I felt as though someone had punched me in the gut. Questions tumbled through my head, and I waited to speak, trying to sort out which to ask first. "Are they all gone?"

He shook his head. "We don't know yet. Parts of the warehouse were spared from the fire, although there may be secondary damage to the stored items that survived — smoke, water. But we don't know where our particular collections were. I'm still hoping for the best."

Some small hope, at least. Then the practical side of me took over. "What were you thinking? This was a public warehouse, right? No climate control? What about security? What kind of safety record does the warehouse management have? How could you have put the collections at risk like that?"

If possible, Peter looked even more distraught than he had originally, and I immediately felt guilty. "Don't you think I've asked myself the same questions?" he said. "You're absolutely right: those collections should have been in a safe and secure location. But it all came down to money. The better the storage, the more expensive it is. We just didn't have the money, not with all the construction costs and the lost income while we were closed. Surely you can understand that?"

Unfortunately I did understand, only too well. A limited budget could stretch only so far, and corners got cut. "I'm sorry — it's rude of me to second-guess you now." Especially since the worst had happened. "You thought the collections would be there for only a short time, right?"

"Exactly," he said, somewhat relieved. "We thought they'd be in and out just a few months at most, but then the whole process kept dragging on and on and our reopening kept being postponed. There's nothing you can say that I haven't already said to myself. I feel terrible about this. I feel I've let the museum down, and the fire department, not to mention the city."

We both fell silent for a moment, in

mourning for the lost collections. Then I gathered myself up. "So, what brings you here, Peter?"

Peter gave himself a shake and straightened his tie. "I'm hoping you have some records about the museum, its founding and its collections, here at the Society."

"Ah," I said. "I see. But don't you have those records?"

"Some of them. The older, archived ones . . ."

I completed his sentence. "Were sent to the warehouse along with all the other stuff."

Peter held up his hand. "I know, you don't have to tell me how stupid that was. But I was overruled by my board. They were looking at the bottom line, period. They're firemen and bureaucrats mostly — not collectors or museum people."

"May I ask why you want this, right now?"

"Because we need to get a handle on what we've lost, and what we should look for, if anything in the warehouse survived. I have to report to the board."

A task I didn't envy him. "What about insurance?"

"You mean, did we insure the collections? Only minimally. I'll admit a lot of items weren't worth much on the open market —

you know, antique fire axes and old helmets and the like. It was the collection as a whole that was valuable, at least to us. So much of it was donated by local firefighters — things they had collected or salvaged over the years. Again, the board balked at the premiums. If I recall, a few of the key pieces were covered, although I haven't had time to check to see for how much. No doubt it's well below replacement value. And certainly those items are irreplaceable in any case."

"What is it you think I can provide?"

"As much information as you have about the individual items, I guess. That would help us to file a claim, and it would also enable us to drum up sympathy from the public when we try to rebuild the collections. Or maybe I should say, *if* we try. For all I know the board may decide to scrap the place."

He looked so miserable I scrambled to find something positive to say. "Well, until someone has been through the warehouse, you don't know how much you've lost, right? Maybe you'll be lucky. And in the meantime, I can ask our librarians to see what we've got on the collections. I'd hate to see the museum fold — it's a gem of its kind."

"I certainly think so." Peter stood up.

"Thank you, Nell. I appreciate your willingness to help, even if you don't find anything. I feel just sick about the whole thing."

"I'm happy to help — that's what we're here for, as a repository of local archives. Let me walk you out." I guided him back to the elevator and down to the lobby. Peter said little along the way, apparently sunk in his own misery, and I couldn't blame him. At the door I said, "I'll give you a call as soon as I know anything. Try not to take it too hard." I watched him stumble down our stone steps and pause at the bottom, as if he'd lost his way.

He really did seem like a man in shock. I wondered how I would feel in his shoes. Of course, our collections were much more extensive, and probably more valuable than his. Not to mention far more vulnerable to fire — all those tons of paper, hanging over my head. I resolved to check the state of our fire suppression systems. As far as I knew, no one had looked at them for a while.

Back upstairs, Eric looked up when I walked past his desk, questions in his eyes. I debated whether to share with him what Peter had told me about the behind-the-scenes mess but decided against it, so I just shook my head slightly. "Eric, I'll fill you in when

I can, but right now I've got to keep what Peter Ingersoll told me in confidence." I checked my watch — almost lunchtime. "I'm going to go out to get some lunch, and then you can go eat. I need to talk to Felicity after lunch, and maybe Latoya." Felicity Soames was our all-seeing, all-knowing head librarian, who could lay hands on anything that was in the building, as she had demonstrated on more than one occasion. Latoya Anderson was our vice president of collections; her knowledge of our records was less encyclopedic than Felicity's, but I thought I should keep her in the loop, since this was an outside request for items in our collections. Latoya and I had a slightly rocky professional relationship, but I knew she could be closemouthed about things and wouldn't let this go beyond the walls of the Society. "I don't have anything else scheduled for today, do I?"

"No, you're clear."

As I left the building in search of a quick sandwich down the block, I realized that Peter hadn't said anything about whether the fire had actually been a case of arson, although the newspaper article had clearly indicated it most likely was. Not that it would make a difference to Peter, since the collections were gone either way, whether the cause was arson or an act of God.

CHAPTER 3

Once I'd eaten lunch, I went looking for Felicity. I was caught up on my administrative responsibilities for the day, and I always enjoyed the librarian's company. She'd been at the Society forever; her love for information in any form was obvious, and she was unfailingly thrilled to pass it on. Any hapless visitor who approached her with a simple question usually walked away with a stack of references and photocopies an hour later.

Felicity was, as usual, behind her desk, which sat on a raised dais so that she could observe activity in the reading room. I took a quick census: the room was moderately filled, and nobody was asleep. That made it a good day. Felicity raised a hand in greeting when she saw me. "What brings you to my lair, Madame President?" she asked in a hushed voice.

"I have a boon to ask of thee," I replied.

Two could play that game. "Can we go somewhere private?"

She scanned the room and motioned one of the shelvers over. "Keep an eye on the room for a bit, please." It always struck me as a tad absurd that we had to keep an eagle eye on our library patrons, most of whom were eager researchers with limited time. But that in itself was a problem. All too many thought that they had the right to make off with the pieces they needed for their work — individual documents, pages sliced from books, even books themselves. Since we had no electronic surveillance, and we couldn't do body searches when people left the building (and I'd seen some pretty creative concealment of purloined items in my day), we had to rely on our staff's human observation. "I'll try not to keep you long," I promised.

We made our way to a quiet room tucked under the handsome stone and mahogany staircase in the front. When we had settled ourselves, Felicity asked, "What can I do for you?"

I checked to see that the door to the room was closed. "Did you hear about that warehouse fire?"

"Yes, where the watchman died. Sad thing. Not the first fire recently, was it?

Maybe there's a firebug on the loose."

"That's the one. The thing is, the director of the Fireman's Museum, Peter Ingersoll, came by this morning and told me — and this is way, *way* off the record for now — that the museum had been storing its collections there while they remodeled."

Felicity looked appropriately horrified. "Oh no! How awful." Then her mouth twitched. "And what an ironic thing — the fire collection going up in flames. Are they a complete loss?"

"He doesn't know yet, but it doesn't look good. And worse, his collections files were housed there, too." I hesitated before adding, "What makes it even worse is that the watchman was a fireman. Retired."

"Oh dear — I saw that in the paper. And what kind of idiot is Ingersoll?" Felicity snorted. "What was he thinking, keeping everything there?"

"He told me he was overruled by his board, who wanted to do things on the cheap. Don't worry, he already knows it was a stupid decision, but there's nothing to be done now. Apparently they never anticipated the stuff being in the warehouse for long — but renovations got delayed and dragged on and on."

"So what did he want from us?"

"He wants to know if we have any records of the founding of the Fireman's Museum, and for the collections. And failing that, I think he'd be happy to have any kind of information about Philadelphia firefighting, particularly images, in the event he has to try to reassemble a collection. For fundraising purposes."

"Ah." Felicity thought for a few moments. "That's not my area of expertise, but I'll see what I can pull together. How soon?"

"He didn't set a deadline. I think the poor man is in shock. I'm sure I would be, under the circumstances. A day or two, maybe?"

"I think I can manage that," Felicity said. "I know I've seen several folders . . . Well, let me take a look and I'll get back to you."

"Thank you. Everything else going well?"

"About average. We could use another shelver or two — it's hard to juggle schedules to maintain consistent coverage on the floor. Maybe by summer, when we get more vacation visitors?"

"No promises, but at least things should have stabilized by then. Have you seen Barney lately?" Barney was a local electrician with a passion for Philadelphia baseball history — and an apparent interest in Felicity. I'd made him an honorary member after he'd helped us with some electrical issues in our aging building.

"He's come by a few times," Felicity said primly. "He certainly is enthusiastic."

"I'm glad to hear that. Well, I'll let you get back to your desk. Let me know what you find."

We departed and went our separate ways. Upstairs I debated about my next step. I should probably talk with Latoya, although I didn't relish the prospect. Latoya, a tall, stately black woman close to my age, had been with the Society for several years, although not as long as I had; she had been hired by my predecessor. She was extremely well qualified for her position as vice president of collections for the Society, but she had never quite bonded with most of the staff, and I knew little about her other than her professional credentials. For most of her tenure she had seemingly considered herself higher up the administrative chart than I, although we had both been nominal department heads. My sudden and unexpected elevation to the presidency had unsettled her a bit, and we were still negotiating our new working relationship. Still, protocol dictated that I should consult her about this problem, and there was a good chance that she would have some relevant information about the Fireman's Museum. So I marched down the hall to her office.

"Do you have a minute, Latoya?"

She looked up from whatever she was working on at her scrupulously neat desk and said, without smiling, "Of course. Please come in." A faint startled expression crossed her face as I pulled shut the door behind me, and when I took a chair, she asked warily, "What can I do for you?"

"Did you hear about that warehouse fire yesterday?"

She shook her head slightly. "I don't pay a lot of attention to local news. What about it?"

I filled her in on the news about the warehouse fire and the Fireman's Museum, and Peter Ingersoll's request. Latoya appeared appropriately distressed at learning of their loss. "What an awful thing. Were they insured?"

"Peter was kind of vague about that, but probably not fully. After all, it's a small place, and I think their budget is pretty slim. He implied that they had skimped a bit on the insurance coverage, particularly since most of the items in their collection aren't intrinsically valuable."

I reluctantly acknowledged to myself that I should take a look at our own insurance situation. I'd had little to do with that when

I was director of development — after all, nobody offered grants to pay for insurance. I knew the broad outlines of our coverage, but that was all. As a public institution, we had to maintain liability and property coverage, and for all I knew, coverage for floods, earthquakes, and sewer backups, but collections were another matter. Since it was hard to get a handle on collections that had been accruing for over a hundred years, and harder still to assign a dollar value to them, I could well imagine that my predecessors had stuck with the most vanilla — and least expensive — options in that area.

Latoya agreed to see what she could find for me, and I felt more hopeful now that I had both Felicity and Latoya, with their varying expertise, working on this. Latoya could give me any information we had on the lost collections, although I didn't expect her to find a lot; on the other hand, Felicity could ferret out the entire history of the institution and the people involved. As I stood to leave, I asked, "By the way, any progress on hiring a new registrar?" We had lost our long-term registrar last year, and whoever filled the position would report to Latoya. But between the internal changes in administration, the holidays, and the ridiculously low salary we had originally offered, we hadn't seen a lot of applications, even in the current lousy economy.

"I'm interviewing several qualified candidates this week. Please thank Marty again for finding a way to enhance the salary."

"Will do — and I'll be happy to talk with anyone you think is appropriate."

As I walked back toward my office down the hall, Eric looked up and whispered, "Ms. Terwilliger is in your office."

"Thank you, Eric." I marched in to find Marty sprawled on my gracious antique settee, reading a document. "Hello, Marty. What brings you here?"

"Peter Ingersoll and his disaster."

I sat down behind my desk and sighed. Why was I not surprised? Marty — Society board member, ally, and friend — knew everyone in Philadelphia and the surrounding counties and was related to half of them; her family had been among the movers and shakers in Philadelphia for a couple of centuries. "Let me guess — Peter is a third cousin, twice removed?"

Marty snorted. "My brother Elwyn was at prep school with him."

"How'd you hear about Peter's disaster, as you so aptly put it?"

"Elwyn is in the insurance business."

"You mean the Fireman's Museum has

already been in touch?"

Marty shrugged. "I don't know, but the insurers have been checking their liability. Why do you know anything about it?"

"Because Peter was here this morning, asking for help to find records of their collections for the insurance claim. I've put Felicity and Latoya on it. By the way, Latoya says she's talked to some candidates for the registrar position and thanks you for the added financial support."

"I want to be sure whoever we hire is good — and will stick around for a while. We really need to tighten up our collections management."

"All it takes is money, as you know very well. But I'll be glad to get that position filled, too. Back to you, though — why would your brother think you wanted to know about Peter Ingersoll's problems?"

"You know that fire engine that was the centerpiece of their collection?"

I tried to recall anything like that from my one visit to the museum and came up blank, although it was hard to imagine missing something as large as a fire engine, no matter how big the crowd. "Not offhand. I was only there once."

"My grandfather donated it."

"Your grandfather collected antique fire

engines?"

"Just the one, although he had some other fire stuff as well. The cousins and I used to play with the buckets and helmets when we got together there. I'm pretty sure we trashed some collector's items, though Grampy never said a word. But he wouldn't let us go near the fire engine, even though of course we wanted to. Made in Philadelphia around 1825. Horse drawn, hand pump. Gorgeous piece, in good condition — even the paint and gilding. Real fancy. It would break his heart to think that went up in flames. Luckily he's dead. And pretty ironic, don't you think?"

"A fire engine burning up? Yes. Let's hope it escaped the fire. Was that all you wanted to talk about?"

Marty slouched against the elegant curves of the settee. "What, you want to get rid of me already, Ms. High and Mighty? Position going to your head?"

I checked to make sure Marty was joking; she was. "Of course not, Marty. I'm always glad to see you."

"Yeah, right. But I do have some business — it's about the Terwilliger Collection."

Of course. The Terwilliger Collection consisted of the Society's vast collection of Terwilliger family papers — records going

42

back to the original Terwilliger settler, in the early eighteenth century, and included those of one of the great leaders of the Revolution, Major Jonathan Terwilliger, as well as a host of lesser dignitaries of Philadelphia political, economic, and social life. Marty's father had bequeathed the collection to the Society years earlier, and Marty had immersed herself in their cataloging. She'd even cobbled together enough money to hire someone to help.

The huge collection was housed in our so-called fireproof vault, a sturdy chamber built in 1895 with a special endowment from a then-board member who was concerned about the vulnerability of the Society's largely paper-based collections to fire and theft. At the time, the room had been state-of-the-art. Now it was just a closely sealed room with metal doors, which made it only marginally safer than the rest of the building. The Terwilliger Collection took up approximately half the room, some four hundred linear feet of books, folders, boxes, and miscellaneous bundles.

"What about it?" I asked, even though I didn't really want to hear her new idea. "Aren't you happy with Rich's work?"

"He's doing fine, don't worry. But I'm thinking that when you hire your new registrar, it might be a good test to hand him the collection and see what he makes of it. With Rich's and my help, of course."

"Or *her,*" I said automatically. "Interesting idea." And not unfair, considering that Marty and her extended family were chipping in a healthy sum of money to endow the registrar's position. "But do we need to do something now?"

Marty, as usual, went straight to the point. "I want to move the whole collection upstairs, at least temporarily. I know Rich has been working hard on it, but this one-box-at-a-time approach is taking too long. And since the registrar's position has been vacant for a few months, most of the other projects have been cleared, so there's room right now."

"You're thinking of the third-floor room?"

"Yup, with all those big tables. Rich and I can shuttle the stuff up there. All I need is your permission to move forward."

The request was purely pro forma: what Marty wanted, Marty usually got. But it was her collection, she was putting up the money, and the space was available. Why not? "Make it so," I said grandly. "And since moving the collection out will open up the fireproof vault, we can take the opportunity to do a thorough overhaul in there, maybe shuffle some other collections around to improve our use of space."

"Sounds like a plan. I'll go talk to Rich." Marty bounded up and headed for the door.

"Right now?" Her energy never ceased to amaze me.

"Sure, why not?"

"Okay, go for it."

Before exiting, she turned back and said, "Heard anything from Jimmy lately?"

Jimmy was James Morrison, one of Marty's many cousins and a special agent in the local FBI office. He was in charge of the disposition of a chunk of recently recovered items that had been stolen from our collections, including a number from the Terwilliger Collection, as soon as the FBI sorted out the legal aspects of the case.

We'd also been kind of seeing each other for a few months. "Now and then," I said evasively, then hastened to add, "Which works fine for us. Don't do anything, please."

"Who, me?" Marty said, and went on her way.

CHAPTER 4

The next morning the warehouse fire story in the *Inquirer* had slipped to page two, but the reporter had made the connection to the Fireman's Museum, and this time there were pictures, including a large one of the charred ruins. In the midst of one almost self-consciously artsy photograph, I could make out the ruins of a vehicle, the twisted remains of the piece looking like a tortured skeleton. My fears about what it was were confirmed by the caption: *Prized antique fire engine consumed in warehouse fire.* It saddened me, both for the museum's sake and for Marty's, since for her it was a piece of her family's history as well as a Philadelphia artifact.

When I arrived at the station, I stuffed the newspaper into my bag and strode briskly to the Society. Once again Eric had beaten me to his desk. "Mornin', Nell. Can I get you some coffee?"

"I'd love some, Eric — thank you." I hesitated a second, then asked, "Did you see the paper today?"

"You mean about the fire and the collection? I did. So that's why Mr. Ingersoll was here?" I nodded, and he stood up quickly. "Oh, Agent Morrison called a few minutes ago." Eric handed me a phone slip and went down the hall to the break room.

I went into my office and hung up my coat — I'd eagerly retired my winter one for the season, but the mornings were still nippy enough to require some sort of jacket. Had Marty prodded James once again? I really didn't need her interfering with my love life, such as it was, and I was pretty sure James could manage on his own as well. I sighed, then picked up the phone and dialed.

"Nell." James, sounding rather grave, answered on the second ring.

"James," I replied. So much for the niceties. James could be brusque. "You called?"

"I did. Can we meet for lunch?"

From his tone I inferred that either this was business or someone could overhear him. "Sure. When?"

"Noon, at that Italian place around the corner?"

"See you then." We hung up simultaneously. Not exactly romantic, but I'd be

47

glad to see him anyway.

When Eric came back bearing my coffee, I said, "I'll be out for lunch. With Agent Morrison."

"I'll put it on your calendar," Eric said, with no further comment. Definitely discreet.

Half an hour later Rich Girard knocked on my door. He was one of our part-timers, a lanky young man who was trying to figure out what he wanted to do with the rest of his life while learning some useful skills for collections management, in case he wanted to go to library school or get an advanced degree in history. Marty had quickly put him to work on the Terwilliger Collection. I gestured him into my office. "Let me guess — Marty talked to you?"

He threw himself in a chair and nodded. "She told me what she wanted to do. I just wanted to make sure that you knew about it and approved. I mean, I work for you, right?"

"That you do — well, more directly for Latoya — but I thought Marty's idea made sense, so you go right ahead. Unless it's too much work?"

"It may take a couple of days to switch things around, but it's probably a good idea to clear stuff out of the vault anyway. Actually I like the idea of having the whole collection in the workroom rather than having to bring up one box at a time. It'll make my job easier."

"Will there be enough room in the workroom on this floor, do you think?"

"Probably. And maybe we could take a look at what else should go in the old vault, while we have it opened up?"

"My thought exactly," I replied, and we launched into a discussion of which collections would complement the Terwilliger Collection, in terms of both period and frequency of use. Marty's focus was her family papers, but I had to look at the bigger picture. Luckily we could serve both with this project. "Just don't forget to maintain good records of what you've moved where, and keep Latoya updated. I know that's usually the registrar's job, but we've got to keep things current until we find one."

"I'm on it."

"Thanks, Rich. Of course, I'm sure Marty wants this to happen like yesterday. Use the freight elevator to haul the stuff upstairs, please — we don't want to tie up the elevator out front." We had only the one for patrons to use, and quite a few of them were elderly and needed it.

"Gotcha. I'll get started getting space ready up here."

After Rich left, I busied myself with minor administrative details. I was pleased that we had actually launched a new project, even if it was something as simple as reorganizing. For the last few months the Society had been in turmoil. When I'd been asked to take over, the board had given me a grace period to settle in — and I was aware that they were watching and waiting, since the position wasn't permanent yet. But it was time to start moving forward. We'd hired Shelby and Eric to fill two of our staff vacancies, and we were actively looking for a registrar now. I had every confidence that we would find one in the next month or two. And as far as I could tell, based on attendance and membership renewals, the problems behind the scenes had gone largely unnoticed by our patrons — and that was good news.

At ten of twelve I pulled on my coat and headed out for my lunch meeting. Not a date, nope. James and I arrived at the door to the restaurant at the same time. Every time I saw him, I was amused at how well he filled the role of FBI agent. He looked well tailored, strong, and decisive. And he was in fact every one of those things. I had to admit, the combination was really quite sexy.

He held the door for me. "Thank you for meeting me on such short notice, Nell."

"I assume you wouldn't have asked unless it was important, James." My, weren't we formal? I sneaked a peek: yes, he was smiling, as was I. Business as usual.

We waited until the maitre d' had escorted us to a table and handed us menus before resuming our conversation. "So, what's this all about?" I asked. "Can you release the items from the Terwilliger Collection yet?"

"It's not that, it's about that warehouse fire. You know about it?"

That was not what I expected to hear. "I do. Don't tell me there's terrorism involved?"

"No, but we do consult with the police on a variety of issues. We're interested in this particular investigation for several reasons. One, it was a major fire event, and there were materials from a range of owners involved. Two, someone died. Three, we have facilities for arson investigation that the local authorities may lack."

I held up a hand. "That's plenty, thank you. So it is officially arson?"

He nodded. "Yes, that much was established early, as soon as the local investigators could get into the building."

"So why do you need to talk to me?"

"I understand that the collections from the Fireman's Museum were housed there temporarily."

I saw a glimmer of logic. "Yes, I was told that. By the museum's president, actually, yesterday morning."

"Peter Ingersoll," James said.

"Yes. I assume you know him?"

James's mouth twitched. "You mean, through Marty? No, I did not know him before the fire. Did *you* know him?"

"Not until yesterday." I didn't mention that I'd seen him at the luncheon a day earlier; we hadn't actually met then anyway. I had forgotten to ask Peter, but it seemed likely that the phone call he had taken there might have been his first notice of the fire. "He came to me to ask for documentation about the museum's collection, since apparently his records burned in the fire. Bad planning, no? When I saw him, I think he was still hoping that something had survived, but that picture in the paper this morning . . ."

"The Terwilliger fire engine? That I do remember — we thought it was really neat, when we were kids, and naturally we wanted to climb all over it, but we weren't allowed

— in theory. Of course, we did when none of the grown-ups was looking."

Marty had told me about the gang of cousins who'd roamed the various family estates years ago, and I knew that James had been one of them. Sometimes I wondered how much that family network had helped him in local investigations, although I knew he regarded Marty as something of a loose cannon. But then, Marty didn't have to follow FBI rules.

"It looks like a total loss, which is really a shame. Does your personal connection to the fire engine mean you have to recuse yourself or whatever?"

"No, nothing like that. It's just a fluke."

"So, apart from the pleasure of my company, why am I here?"

"Because you're officially part of the local museum community, and I appreciate your insights. And any information you might happen to hear. For example, what you find out from Peter Ingersoll."

"It sounds as though you don't trust him. When I spoke with him yesterday, he seemed devastated by what's happened. Is there something I need to know about the dead man, that wasn't in the papers?"

"He was a retired firefighter named Allan Brigham. He retired early — rumor was that he had a drinking problem, but other than that, nobody's had anything bad to say about him. At least, not yet. He was collecting a pension from the fire department and also working as the night watchman at the warehouse."

"Do you think he had anything to do with the fire?" I asked.

"Nothing jumps out. But the investigation has just begun. By the way, his funeral will be on Thursday. Have you ever seen a fireman's funeral around here?" When I shook my head, he went on. "It's a major event — firefighters from the city and even other states show up, and streets are closed for the procession. The department honors its dead, even those no longer active with them."

We had to take a break to order our meals, during which time I found I was growing increasingly uncomfortable with what James was saying — or not saying. When the waiter had left, I said carefully, "What is it I'm supposed to find out from Peter Ingersoll? Like, am I supposed to guess if Peter Ingersoll was upset because someone died, or about the destruction of the museum's collections?" I noticed that James had never answered my question about whether he trusted Peter, and I was sensing that he didn't.

James sat back in his chair. "You tell me."

I sat back, too, and stared at him. "I don't know the man, so I can't tell you that. Are you suggesting that he had some involvement in destroying the collection? Why would he do that? I mean, who stands to benefit?"

James shrugged, which I found unhelpful. "How much do you know about the financial standing of the Fireman's Museum?"

"Not much — why would I? Peter said they had gotten some outside funding for revamping the space and the exhibits, but he still wasn't sure about their insurance status. James, we're talking in circles here. Why don't you just tell me what you're looking for?"

I was flattered that he'd actually asked for my help, but at the same time troubled that he was asking me to snoop on my colleagues. The Philadelphia cultural community wasn't all that big, and I was still the new kid, at least among the upper ranks. I needed to keep them as friends, not alienate them. My impression of Peter Ingersoll, albeit based on a brief interaction, was that he wasn't the type to engage in murder and mayhem, but I'd been wrong about people before. Was there an honor code among administrators? Where did I put that manual? In any event, I didn't think it extended to covering for a colleague who engaged in major crimes.

Once again James had ignored my direct question. Was this standard FBI procedure? "Look, I can probably give you some qualitative info on how that particular museum is structured and operates. But I don't want to sniff around for gossip about whether someone on the inside at the Fireman's Museum is up to something shady."

"Nell, that's really all I'm asking. Nothing devious."

"Don't you guys have an art theft unit? Why can't they do it?"

"We do, and they're good, but they're a small group and spread kind of thin. And they don't know the local scene as well as you do. You know the players, the relationships, the history of the institutions around here. You don't have to snoop — just tell me what you know, and what's in your files. Is that fair?"

It seemed simple enough. And I did want to help. "All right, that I can do. And I can let you know what records we have about their collections, especially since Peter has already asked that I pull them for him. Now can we just enjoy lunch?"

"Of course."

It was, in fact, an enjoyable lunch. It was hard to look on my sporadic meetings with James as dates, but clearly we enjoyed each other's company. And since we weren't in the first flush of youth, we weren't rushing anything. I was glad he had asked for my help, but was that because he respected my professional expertise or because he wanted an excuse to see me again? I wasn't about to ask. And I was kind of tickled to have access to the machinations of the FBI, even if only a little.

After we'd eaten, we strolled out of the restaurant onto Broad Street. "Thank you for lunch, James," I said demurely.

"Thank you for agreeing to join me on short notice. I appreciate your assistance."

"I'm happy to be of service." I couldn't take it any longer and burst out laughing. "Okay, which nineteenth-century novel are we imitating? Good to see you, James. I'll let you know if I find anything interesting. And I'll tell Marty to stop prodding us."

"Like that'll work. Thanks, Nell."

And we went our separate ways. I walked back to the Society feeling, for once, a small sense of control over circumstances. I was still feeling good when I got back to my office.

"Have you eaten yet, Eric?" I asked.

"No, I was waiting for you to get back." He handed me my sheaf of messages. "And Felicity left some stuff on your desk for you."

"You go ahead and find lunch. I'll deal with this stuff." I waved the messages. Maybe my elevated status dictated that I should have an underling place calls for me, but I thought that was nonsense: I was perfectly capable of dialing a phone by myself.

Felicity had deposited a stack of folders and documents maybe an inch thick in the center of the desk. I wondered briefly if this was everything we had or only as much as she could find in an hour — I suspected the latter. I settled into my chair and began reading. Much of the information consisted of clippings about Philadelphia firefighting history, going back to Benjamin Franklin, and articles about fire insignias and insurance company charters. Felicity had made some annotations about which of those might have found a place in the Fireman's Museum collections. All that was straightforward. A second folder moved on to non-paper items, like buckets and fire axes and helmets. A third, slimmer folder included images, both pre and post the invention of photography, of fire engines. The early models were endearingly primitive, and I had to wonder if they were really much better than a line of guys passing buckets. But they quickly grew in size and elaboration, and morphed from horse-drawn hand pumpers to steam-belching monsters. The file stopped short of modern engines, as expected.

Felicity had added some clippings about the acquisition of the showpiece engine that had perished in the fire, mainly because of the mention of the Terwilliger name. We even had some eight-by-ten press photos. It might have been an early model, but it was unquestionably elegant, down to the lush detailing of the decorative images on the sides. What a lovely thing it had been, and what a waste its loss was for the historical community.

But . . . something was not right. On a hunch I pulled out the paper I had read in the morning, and opened it to the page with the warehouse spread, including pictures. I laid the two images side by side.

I heard Eric return. "Eric, can you come in here a moment?"

"Sure, Nell. What is it?"

I gestured him closer. "Take a look at these two pictures and tell me if I'm crazy."

He came around to my side of the desk

and looked at the pictures. "That's from the warehouse fire, right? What a mess. And this other one's what it looked like before? But . . ." His eyes met mine. "It's not the same one?"

I nodded solemnly. "That's what I thought. Even allowing for shrinkage and warping and whatever, the burnt one is simply the wrong shape. I think somebody pulled a switch."

"Oh my," Eric breathed.

"Exactly."

"What're you going to do?" he whispered.

"I'm not sure. But I think I'd better call Agent Morrison again."

CHAPTER 5

Maybe I was seeing things, or maybe I was looking for problems where none existed. Could there have been two engines in the collection? I tried to recall the one visit I'd made to the museum, and I was pretty sure there wasn't room for more than one in the tiny space they had. But I knew I'd feel better if I passed my suspicion on to James, who would either tell me I was hallucinating, or he'd take it and run with it, letting me wash my hands of it. I dialed his office number.

"Morrison," he barked when we finally connected.

"It's Nell," I said.

"Oh," he said in a milder tone. "You've got something already?"

"I'm not really sure, but I have something I think you need to see. Can you stop by my office?"

"I'm tied up this afternoon, but I can

make it later. After five okay?"

"Sure." That would give me time to do a little more digging. If the picture in the paper showed what I thought it did, I needed to find out more details about the museum and its collections. Latoya would be more useful than Felicity in that arena. Heck, maybe Shelby, too — the files in the development office probably had organizational information for the place; hadn't we held some sort of joint event with the Fireman's Museum at the Society a few years back? Before my time, but I remembered checking the file for the promotional materials and table arrangements for the event when I was planning a later event here. So I'd talk to Latoya first, then Shelby. I'd have to bring Shelby up to speed about what was going on — or what I suspected might be — but I trusted her, and she had a good sense of social connections. And Eric already knew — I hadn't considered all the implications when I showed him the pictures, but now the cat was out of the bag. I didn't think either of them would blab, but I shouldn't spread my suspicion any further. I felt a pang of guilt about keeping Latoya in the dark, but James might need this information kept quiet, and I'd have done enough in telling Eric and Shelby.

I carefully marked the photos with sticky tabs, added my newspaper to the file (making a mental note to myself to ask Eric to see if he could print out a higher-quality photo online), neatly stacked the pile — and slid it into my drawer. Then I stood up and went down the hall to Latoya's office again.

She looked up from whatever she was working on, reading glasses perched on her nose, clearly not happy to see me. "You wanted something else, Nell? Apart from your request yesterday? I'm working on that."

"Yes," I said, sitting down across from her before she could invite me. "Tell me what you know about the Fireman's Museum."

"Can it wait, Nell? I'd really like to finish this."

I was getting kind of tired of her superior attitude. I had a work-related question, and damn it, I was her boss. "No, it can't wait. This is part of a criminal investigation, and the FBI has asked for our help."

She gave me a long, unreadable stare before she folded the journal in front of her. "What do you need to know?"

"If I remember correctly, there's something unusual about the organizational structure of the museum. What can you tell me?"

She leaned back and stared at the wall over my head. "As I recall — and don't hold me to it — the Fireman's Museum was first suggested by a bunch of fire buffs in the 1960s, in advance of the 1971 centennial of the Philadelphia Fire Department. They put together the core collections from fire stations all over the city. The fire commissioner at the time offered them the use of a retired firehouse, but it took a couple of years of work before it could open as a museum. The original staffing came from the fire department and volunteers. Still does, more or less — members of the fire department still volunteer time to provide tours, which saves a lot in staff salaries.

"They've gotten some funding from the city and from local insurance companies. They created a nonprofit corporation to manage it, with a volunteer board of directors."

I was impressed by her knowledge. "Interesting," I said. "I hadn't realized it was such a homegrown institution. Thank you, Latoya, that's exactly what I needed to know. How do you know so much about the place?"

"I used to date a fireman." She didn't elaborate.

"Do you know if they've continued collecting, after that first effort? I know it's not a large place, so space for exhibits must be limited."

"In a small way, as I understand it. And of course, there was that fire engine, given by the Terwilligers."

"Of course. Marty filled me in on that. Was that the only one they had?" She nodded. I stood up. "Well, I'll let you get back to what you were doing."

As I was leaving, she said, "Nell, what's the FBI's interest in this? I thought it was a case of arson, according to the press."

"The FBI has a lot of arson resources, and there is a lot of information to wade through regarding whatever was stored at the warehouse. Plus the Fireman's Museum is a public institution." I didn't think I should say any more, and I didn't want to voice my suspicions about the fire engine to Latoya. "Thanks."

While I was at it, I decided I might as well dot my i's and cross my t's, and sought out Shelby, stopping by my office first to retrieve the file of photographs.

"Hey, lady. You need me?" She greeted me.

I dropped into a chair in front of her desk. "I need to pick your brain, and your files. Do we have any Terwilliger wills or inventories in our files?"

"Like who gave what to whom?" Shelby asked. "Wouldn't that be in collections?"

"Probably, but we would have copies, too, in the personal files." I didn't want to keep going back to Latoya. I wrestled for a moment with the ethics of telling Shelby the whole story while giving Latoya the edited version, but I trusted Shelby more than Latoya. Plus I had a feeling the answers lay somewhere in the development files rather than the collections files.

"And might this have something to do with that real nice fire engine that went up in smoke?"

"Can't get a thing past you, can I?" I smiled. "It would. I understand Marty's grandfather gave it to the Fireman's Museum, in the seventies, maybe? I've already got some pictures, but I wondered if any additional information had sneaked into the development files. Uh, about that fire engine . . ." I pulled out the two photos and laid them on Shelby's desk, side by side. She looked confused at first, and then I could see the light dawning in her expression.

"Something funny going on here?" she asked.

I nodded. "I'm thinking insurance fraud

gone wrong. Keep this quiet, will you?"

"Of course I will. So why don't we take a look at those files? You going to help? Because you've got to know the records better than I do."

"Sure."

It took us a couple of hours to wade through the extensive Terwilliger files, since Marty was the third generation of the family to be involved with the Society. It appeared that all members of that family had been exceedingly thorough in their documentation, which shouldn't have surprised me after what I'd seen of the historical collections. It was almost as though they knew that future generations would be looking at them. For all of that, we didn't come up with much more than I already knew. Since the Society had not been the recipient of the fire engine, most references to it were tangential. There was, however, a copy of Marty's grandfather's will (which included substantial bequests to the Society) and inventory, which described the fire engine in broad terms. It confirmed the story but didn't provide much more information.

When I looked at my watch, I realized that it was nearly five and James might be arriving at any moment. "Thanks, Shelby. I think we've found whatever there is to find here.

I'm sorry to leave you with all the mess, but I'm expecting someone at five."

She laughed, unruffled. "That's right, leave it for me to clean up. But to tell the truth, I was glad of the chance to go through it all. The Terwilligers really were something, weren't they? The best kind of mix — wealthy but not pushy about it, and definitely civic-minded."

"The current generation isn't too shabby, either, if Marty's any indication. You can leave it until tomorrow if you want."

"I might as well finish up now." Shelby began gathering up the scattered files, and I left her to it.

At five fifteen Front Desk Bob, a former police officer who manned our reception desk while providing a small measure of security, called to say that a Mr. Morrison was in the lobby. I went down to escort James upstairs, and we maintained a professional demeanor as we took the elevator to the third floor and then walked to my office. Shelby looked up as we passed, and gave me a thumbs-up, which I ignored. Eric looked startled by James's unheralded appearance after hours, but I gave him what I hoped was a reassuring smile and told him he could go home. Finally I closed the door behind us and pointed to the chair in front of my desk.

"So, what's this about, Nell?" he asked.

"There's something I think you should see. I'm not going to say anything more — you can make your own judgment."

I retrieved the folder with the pictures and, with a show of ceremony, pulled out, first, the high-quality black-and-white photo of the Fireman's Museum engine from the Society's files. I laid it in front of him. Then I pulled out that day's newspaper, still folded open to the story of the fire, and laid that alongside. I sat down silently and waited.

He looked at me, then at the photos, clearly bewildered. And then I enjoyed watching the light dawn as he compared the two, once, then again, his eyes darting back and forth. Then he sat back and exhaled. "They aren't the same," he said flatly.

"That's what I thought."

"The one that burned was not the Terwilliger engine."

"Nope."

He rubbed his eyes. "Damn. How? When?"

"They moved the collections into storage, what, eighteen months ago? It could have been then, or any time since."

"Somebody would have to have paid off

somebody else to get it out of there. Nights, there was only the one watchman around — Allan Brigham, the one who died. Hell, could be the swap was made the night before the fire, and Brigham was killed because he was in on it and knew too much."

Clearly James was thinking out loud and didn't expect an answer from me. I was content to cheer him on. "Maybe."

His eyes focused on me. "Inside or outside job? What're these things worth?"

"How would I know? You'll notice we don't have anything quite that big here, and I don't follow that market. But I'll remind you that to a true collector, price is no object — he'll pay what it's worth to him." And I was willing to bet that there were a lot of people who were passionate about firefighting, including some collectors with money.

"Thanks a lot. I know I asked you to help, but I really didn't think you'd open a can of worms like this. Now we've got to look at fraud and murder, in addition to arson. And art theft."

"I do my best. After all, my tax dollars pay your salary."

"Does Marty know any of this?"

"Not from me — I just figured it out this

70

afternoon. I don't know what she's going to think when and if she sees the news photo. She did seem to know the original pretty well, as you did, so it's possible she might come to the same conclusion. What's more to the point is, what would she be likely to do about it?"

"I'll talk to her. I don't need her muddling this up." He stood up. "I guess I'm going back to my office. Can I get copies of that stuff?" He pointed toward the pictures.

"Sure. Follow me." I led him down the hall to the communal copy machines and made copies. "There you go. I'll have to let you out — Bob should have left by now."

"Fine." He trailed obligingly down the hall to the elevator, and then I led him to the now-dark lobby. Before he left he turned to me and said, "Nell, I'll take it from here. You don't have to do anything more."

"My, that sounds familiar. You do know I'll be talking to Peter, right?"

"Just give him what he asked for about the collections, okay?"

"No problem. But what do I do if Marty comes tearing in and starts demanding action?"

"Send her to me. Period. All right?"

"Yes, sir. Certainly, sir." I refrained from saluting.

"Nell, I'm serious. One man is dead, and now I'm not so sure that was an accident."

My flippant mood evaporated. "I know. You take care, too, James."

"I will. Good night, Nell."

CHAPTER 6

When Marty came stomping into my office
the next morning, brushing past Eric without even looking at him, I had a pretty good
idea what she was mad about. Of course,
the crumpled copy of the *Inquirer* crushed
in her fist was a solid clue. She threw herself
into a chair, her face flushed. "Somebody
pulled a fast one!" She glared at me.

James had told me not to talk to her about
this, but as I had anticipated, she'd figured
it out all by herself. At this rate, it was going to be difficult to keep a lid on things,
but luckily I didn't think many people
would look very hard at the picture and put
two and two together. I thought briefly
about playing dumb, but Marty deserved
better, and I wasn't very good at it anyway.

"Shut the door, please, Marty." I waited
until she had complied. "I think you're
right. But think of it this way — that means
the Terwilliger fire truck is probably alive

and well somewhere."

"Yeah, but my grandfather gave that to the museum so people could enjoy it! And now some jerk has made off with it and destroyed the museum's collection at the same time."

"And possibly killed somebody in the process," I added quietly.

Marty seemed to shrink just a bit. "Right. Sorry. I'm being selfish." She stopped ranting long enough to realize what I'd said. "Wait — you knew? When did you figure this out?"

"Yesterday." I waited for her wrath to descend and was not disappointed.

"*Yesterday?* When were you planning to tell me?"

"I haven't seen you since then. And it's not as though you're responsible for doing something about it. That's up to the police."

She eyed me critically. "Does Jimmy know?"

I nodded mutely.

She jumped out of her chair. "What? You told him before you told me?"

"Marty, he's law enforcement. This is arson and maybe murder and fraud. What do you think you can do that he and the police can't do a whole lot better?"

She deflated again and dropped back into

her chair. I was getting exhausted just watching her. "I know, you're right. Official business and all that crap. What's Jimmy's take?"

I shrugged. "He didn't tell me. Since he only just found out himself" — I thought I wouldn't mention that I was the one who had pointed it out to him — "I don't know if he's had any time to get balls rolling or wheels turning or whatever it takes. At least the police were smart enough to ask the FBI for help."

"Yeah, for once." She thought for a few moments. "What do you think the point was? Money? Or maybe the fire was the main purpose, to cripple the museum, and whoever set the fire couldn't bear to destroy the engine? Oh, but that would mean the person had to know it was there, which points to an inside job."

I sat back and stared at her. "Marty, why are you assuming that the museum and its collection was the primary target? It was a big warehouse, and there were others involved. James said they had to look at everybody."

"Unless this was one of those creepy arson-for-fun crimes, do you know of anything else there worth destroying? The fact that the prize fire engine has gone missing kind of points straight at the museum, don't you think?"

She had a point — trust Marty to connect the dots. Interesting that she'd gone straight to motive. "At the museum, or at the warehouse? The night watchman knew it was there — it's kind of hard to miss an antique fire engine. It's not small."

"And the night watchman is dead. Was he careless, or did somebody else make sure he ended up that way? You know anything about him?"

"Just that he was a retired firefighter, so he shouldn't have been careless. The police don't talk to me, and there's no reason they should. James came to me to ask what I knew about the museum and their collections. Period."

"He didn't come to me?" Marty grumbled. "I probably know more than you do about who's who and what's what around here."

She was right about that, but I wasn't about to tell her that her cousin didn't trust her to keep her mouth shut. "Granted. But this investigation has just begun, and things are changing fast. It started out as a simple fire, and then the firemen found the body. The death could have been an accident, or it could have been deliberate, but the police have to investigate both the arson *and* a possible murder. Now it looks like there's also been a theft, which complicates things. The FBI were already involved informally, and they're just waiting to be invited to the party. Who knows where things will go from here?"

"Hey, don't forget that the Fireman's Museum has ties to the city. We could throw municipal corruption into the mix while we're at it." Marty's usual good humor appeared to have been restored. She had little respect for the current administration.

"Yes, there is that." I'd have to understand that connection a bit better before I could guess how the city would benefit from any of this. "But none of it is really our business, is it?" I waited to see how she would respond. Based on her long and intricate history with the city and its citizens, Marty seemed to feel entitled to meddle in affairs at all levels.

She cocked her head at me curiously. "Why not? You're part of the collections community, and so am I. You've said it before: what harms one local institution reflects on all of us. If it's proved that somebody died because of whatever might be going on at the Fireman's Museum, then we all suffer — we don't need those kinds of headlines. And you and I, we have insights that the police and even the mighty FBI lack. I don't know about you, but I'm not going to sit on the sidelines and watch, not if I can do something."

I sighed. That was exactly what James had been worried about. In some ways Marty was right. But James was also right, about keeping civilians out of the mix. I was caught in the middle. "Okay, I'll give you that. But I don't know what to do next."

Marty sprang up. "I'm going to go give Jimmy a piece of my mind." When she saw the look of dismay on my face, she said, "Don't worry, I'll leave you out of this. I figured out the switch all by myself, didn't I? And I can find out if there's anything new today, like autopsy results. See you!" And with that she was gone, leaving me feeling drained.

Eric peered cautiously around the door. "All clear? What was that all about?"

"Come in and shut the door," I said wearily. When he had, I said, "You might as well know this, because there's a chance you might get some phone calls from the press or the police, and you should be prepared. That warehouse fire? Remember the pictures I showed you? Both Agent Morrison and Marty believe that there was a robbery involved — the fire engine that Marty's family gave the Fireman's Museum seems to have been removed before the fire and a different one put in its place. Which means that the fire may have been deliberate, and it's not clear whether the death was related. And we shouldn't be talking about any of this."

"Wow," Eric said. "And here I thought the museum world was supposed to be kind of stuffy."

Poor Eric — he was learning fast. "All this is off the record. James has asked what I know about the museum and their collections, and the director, who I had never met until this week. Look, if you do get any calls, pass them on to me. But I hope it won't come to that."

I managed to get some more work done before Latoya knocked on my door frame. "A moment, Nell?"

"Sure. Come on in." This was unusual. Somehow Latoya always made me come to her.

She sat gracefully, tucking her long legs under the chair before beginning. "I've found a candidate for registrar that I'm rather excited about, and I wondered if you'd have time for an interview?"

"Of course." I knew how important the

position was to the smooth running of the Society, and how badly we needed to fill the vacancy. "Tell me about . . . him? Her?"

"Him. His name is Nicholas Naylor. He brings an interesting mix of skills — he was a history major as an undergraduate, but he's also done a lot of software development, particularly for cultural applications."

I settled back in my chair. "That does sound interesting, not that I know much about that side of things. What brings him to us?"

"It's not that he needs the job — currently he's working at Penn. But he'd like more autonomy to work on his software programs. I've told him what Alfred was using as software, and he said he could improve on it. And it wouldn't cost us anything above his salary. I see it as a win-win situation."

I wasn't so sure. We'd paid dearly for that state-of-the-art system not long ago, and the late Alfred Findley had barely begun to explore its possibilities. He was the only one who had really understood the system, which he had quickly dubbed Cassandra, because she was always spitting out reports filled with doom and gloom. Still, we'd invested in it, and I was leery of starting over so soon, especially with someone I didn't know. "Does he expect to market this software? Because I wouldn't want him to use the Society as a stepping-stone and then leave us in the lurch after a year or two. I'd rather see someone who is willing to make a long-term commitment to this place."

Latoya nodded once. "Of course. I don't think this is about the money or selling his program. From what he's told me, it sounds as though it's pretty closely tailored to each individual institution and its needs. Can you at least give him an interview and let me know what you think?"

"Of course. His skills sound intriguing, even if he doesn't work out for the position here. Any other likely candidates?"

She shrugged. "A few, but nobody who impresses me as much as Nicholas, at least on paper. I've already met with him."

"When can he come in?"

"Tomorrow? As I said, he's currently employed, but he's in the city, so he could meet with you early in the morning before he goes to work. Does that work for you?"

I thought it might, but I needed to check with Eric first. I walked over to the door and stuck my head out. "Eric, do I have anything on my calendar for tomorrow early?"

He punched a couple of keys on his computer. "No, ma'am. It looks open. Do you want to add something?"

"Yes — pencil in an interview for the registrar position first thing in the morning. I'll confirm with you once it's set up." I turned back to Latoya. "Give this Nicholas a call and tell him coming in before he goes to work will be fine, then let me know if he can make it and what time."

Latoya stood up. "Thank you, Nell. I'll do that and get back to you. Oh, and I'll have that information on the Fireman's Museum collections later today." When she left, I went back to my desk, sat down, and thought.

I hadn't had any part in the hiring of our last registrar, and even if I had, the nature and demands of the position had changed substantially in the years Alfred had worked here. The Society was a collections-based institution, and those collections had been growing for well over a century. Unfortunately the tracking systems had failed to keep up, from the beginning. It was easy to imagine the very early days, when one curator/librarian could probably keep all the information in his head. Then had come the era of handwritten cards and the arrival of the first card catalog. Some order had been imposed, but as the collections expanded, classification systems had changed, and the physical distribution of the collections had changed even more often. By the later twentieth century the whole thing was all but out of our control. And then the digital age had arrived.

Alfred had bridged that gap. He had been good at his job — in part because he had no real life or love outside of the Society — and he had been instrumental in transferring significant portions of the catalogs to a computerized format, and even overseeing the digitization of a portion of those catalogs so that our members could access them online. He'd made great strides forward, but we'd been stymied since his untimely death. For all my lack of familiarity, I recognized that software cataloging systems were essential to contemporary collections management, and it sounded as though Latoya's candidate Nicholas might be a good fit. I looked forward to meeting with him and picking his brain.

The morning's confrontation with Marty had left me unsettled, and I needed to clear my head. I pulled on my coat and stopped to tell Eric, "I'm headed out to get some lunch. Tell anyone who calls that I may be a while."

"Right. You're in a very important meeting and can't be disturbed." Eric grinned at me.

"Exactly." I made my way downstairs and out of the building. On the front steps I paused, trying to figure out what I wanted. Mostly I wanted some space, and time to think. Maybe it was time to go back to the Reading Terminal Market — I hadn't been there since lunch with Arabella a few months ago, and I recalled that I had promised myself to visit more often. Certainly its bright colors and sounds — not to mention the wonderful smells — would distract me from the thorny problem of the missing fire engine. I set off toward Market Street at a brisk clip.

I had forgotten that the funeral for Allan Brigham would be taking place today, and that Market Street would be its route; it put a serious crimp in my plans. James had told me that firemen's funerals in the city were important events, but I was not prepared for the scale of the parade that was unfolding before me. Somehow I had timed my arrival to coincide with the head of the procession. I had to stand on tiptoe to see anything over the fairly thick crowd. First came a pair of drummers and a bagpiper, leading a modern fire truck draped in black bunting; the casket, covered with a flag, lay atop the truck. Two uniformed firemen rode on the truck's tailboard, flanking the casket. They were accompanied by a pair of Dalmatians, who sat still as statues, as though sensing the solemnity of the occasion. Additional firemen walked alongside the fire truck — probably some sort of honor guard. Following the truck were several groups of dignitaries — I saw the mayor and the city's fire chief among the ones in the front. They were followed by a slew of local firefighters — I recognized the uniforms — and then by what must be visiting firefighters in different uniforms. Toward the rear was a long string of fire vehicles, and finally cars. The whole of the procession stretched over many blocks, nearly to the waterfront, headed to the imposing mass of City Hall. I couldn't help but wonder whether this was a typical department funeral, or whether Allan Brigham had been particularly highly regarded in his community, even after retirement.

The sidewalks on both sides of Market Street were crowded with spectators, although it was hard to distinguish between mourners and gawkers. I wasn't sure which category I fit. Still, there was enough room that I could move to the front of the crowd without shoving, and when I arrived there I found Peter Ingersoll, looking pale. I tapped him on the shoulder, and he jumped and turned toward me.

"Hello, Peter. Quite an impressive event," I said.

"It is. Of course, our firefighters deserve it. You know Jennifer, right?"

I hadn't seen Jennifer, who was standing on the other side of Peter, looking equally unhappy. "Of course — hello, Jennifer."

"And this is my brother Scott." Peter gestured toward a man standing behind Jennifer. If Peter hadn't introduced me, I never would have pegged him as Peter's brother: Scott stood half a head taller and must have outweighed Peter by fifty pounds. "Scott works as a security guard part-time at the museum — well, when there's anything to protect. There hasn't been since the collections went into storage." Peter swallowed hard.

"Good to meet you, Scott," I said, extending a hand. Scott took it reluctantly and shook it, mumbling something, then turned his attention back to the procession. I noticed that he laid a hand on Jennifer's shoulder.

"And this is Gary O'Keefe, our curator," Peter added, and another, older man, moving clumsily, came forward to shake my hand.

"We appreciate your help, Ms. Pratt."

"No problem — that's what the Society is here for." I turned back to Peter. "I've collected at least part of the information you asked for. Can we get together so I can show you?"

"Of course. Let me call you after I get back to the office and we can set a time," Peter replied.

"That's fine. Are you going to the burial? Did you know the man?"

"Not personally, no. I just came to pay my respects. I feel so bad about what happened, like the museum is somehow responsible for his death."

Peter's mind seemed to be somewhere else, not surprisingly, so I decided to resume my search for lunch. "I'll talk to you later, then," I said, and turned away. It looked as though crossing Market Street would be out of the question for a while, so I headed back toward Chestnut Street, where I knew I'd find plenty of restaurants. After lunch, the afternoon passed quietly, until I was interrupted by another call from James.

"You sicced Marty on me," he began without preamble.

"I did not," I replied tartly. "She came to me after drawing the same conclusion that I did, based on the newspaper photo. I warned you she might. I just confirmed what she suspected. Was I really supposed to lie to her? She was mad at me because I had told you before I told her."

He sighed. "All right. Can you keep her out of this?"

"Marty? Not a chance."

"I was afraid of that. I suppose I should have known she'd end up in the middle of this. I assume you've told Marty that she has to be discreet about it?"

"I did, but if you see her, can you repeat that? You don't want her asking people the wrong questions, or maybe I mean asking the *wrong people* questions. If you know what I mean."

"Unfortunately, yes." I could hear the sound of a door closing on his end before he continued. "Listen, the autopsy showed that the guard was dead before the fire began."

I felt a chill. So it was arson *and* murder. Had the dead watchman been party to the arson, or an innocent bystander? "At least he had full honors for his burial. You were right — the procession was very impressive. What was the cause of death?"

"A blow to the head," James said, "but there's more than one way it could have happened. For the moment the police are treating it as suspicious rather than accidental. Please, keep that to yourself unless it's announced officially."

"Of course." The news saddened me. The fire was bad enough on its own, but this made it tragic — and complicated. "Have you shared the information about the fire engine with the police?"

"No. I'm not sure where that fits, and I'd rather they didn't know, unless they figure it out for themselves. At which time I'll be happy to cooperate with them — if they ask."

"You sound tired, James. Is everything all right?"

"Just busy. Look, Nell, try to stay out of this, will you? It's bad enough I have to manage Marty. I know you both mean well, but this is a criminal investigation."

"You were the one who invited me into the investigation, remember?"

"Yes, but in a limited capacity, based on your knowledge of the cultural community. Period. Please don't meddle with the criminal side of things."

Meddle? I didn't like his choice of words, but I grasped what he was asking. "Understood. I'll see if I can distract Marty — we've decided to do a thorough overhaul of the Terwilliger Collection here, so maybe that will do it. But if there's anything more I can do, just ask."

"I will. Thanks, Nell." He rang off.

I'd do what I could, but Marty didn't answer to me — more like the other way around. And she was strong willed. Handled right, she could be an asset in any investigation of this kind — but I wasn't sure either James or I could handle her.

CHAPTER 7

At precisely nine the next day, Latoya Anderson, looking smug, shepherded her handpicked candidate into my office. "Nell, this is Nicholas Naylor. Nicholas, this is the Society's president, Nell Pratt. I'll leave the two of you to talk." She turned and withdrew, closing my office door behind her.

Nicholas and I sized each other up. He was a tall, pale young man in his late twenties, with wavy dark hair, worn a bit long. Nicely dressed, as befit an interview, in tailored pants and a sports jacket over a collared shirt, no tie. He carried a leather folder, which I assumed contained a résumé. And he wasn't smiling. "Thank you for making the time to see me, Ms. Pratt. I appreciate the opportunity."

"My pleasure, Nicholas." He was definitely a *Nicholas,* not a *Nick.* Why was this self-possessed young man making me nervous? "Please, sit down." I gestured toward one of the chairs in front of my desk. He sat. Still no smile. "Do you have a résumé handy? I haven't had an opportunity to get it from Latoya yet." Which again put me at a disadvantage.

Wordlessly, Nicholas opened his folder and handed me a single sheet of paper. I glanced at it briefly and realized that half of the position descriptions on it were gobbledygook to me. "So, tell me about yourself. I understand you're currently working? Why would you want to give up a secure job at Penn to work here?" I knew it was hard to break into employment at the university, and I couldn't remember anyone I knew leaving it, except under dire personal circumstances or for a step up the professional pyramid. I didn't think the Society could compete with Penn in the latter regard. Certainly not in salary or prestige.

"I'd prefer a smaller milieu and greater flexibility. Did Ms. Anderson explain to you my area of expertise?"

"Briefly. Why don't you tell me how you define it, and how you see it helping us?"

"Certainly." He leaned forward, his expression earnest. "As I'm sure you know, the transition from traditional cataloging functions to the modern digital age has been erratic . . ."

I listened with half an ear, nodding at intervals. I'd spent enough time writing the grant proposals for our current cataloging system, and talking with Alfred, to understand the basic outlines of what Nicholas was describing. I had to admit that the program he had been developing sounded both innovative and potentially more user-friendly than what we had currently, which would be a big plus, since it might make it possible not only to integrate in-house tracking systems but also to permit a greater degree of member access, and even to allow transfer of higher-quality images for internal and external reproduction. A seamless and unified system certainly sounded appealing — but could Nicholas deliver, or was he just spinning me a nice story?

I noticed he was gazing at me expectantly — apparently he'd run through the set piece. "Sounds fascinating, Nicholas. I do have a few questions. For a start, is this a proprietary system? Does Penn have any claim to it?"

He shook his head. "No, this is mine. I've developed it on my own time. I've used some items from the Penn collections for a test run, but my supervisor has been aware of everything I've been doing and has had no objections. I've been aboveboard with him and with the department."

I found that emphasis curious. Was he protesting a wee bit too much? And if his software performed as well as he claimed it did, would his superiors be reluctant to see him go? "Does that mean that the Society would be your guinea pig, so to speak? Your first full test of a major collection?"

He had the grace to look slightly sheepish. "Well, yes. But I know it works on a smaller scale, and ramping it up shouldn't be a problem."

"You do know the scope of our collections? How would you prioritize your activities?"

He nodded. "I'm well aware of what collections the Society holds — I've always been interested in Philadelphia and Pennsylvania history. In my opinion, new and recent acquisitions here should take precedence, but as I understand it, those have slowed over the past few months?" I guessed that he had followed the news.

"Yes, that's true, and acquisitions may remain slow for a bit. I think that segment should be of a manageable size and would be a good place to start. But what approach would you use for converting earlier catalogs?"

"I'd start with . . ." Obviously I had

punched the right button, and he demonstrated that he had done his homework well. Nicholas knew our collections, their strengths (mainly in quality) and their weaknesses (in how we had tracked them — or hadn't — over the years).

When he stopped for a breath, I broke in. "I'm impressed. But I have another question: do we have the technology in place to implement all of this? The hardware or software or whatever? Because you have to know that money is tight, and we can't afford to replace a lot right now."

"I can minimize the computer storage required, and as long as you can upload . . ." And he went on. And on.

An extremely knowledgeable young man, clearly. But would he fit in here? "Nicholas, obviously you know the technical aspects of what you're working on, and it sounds as though you could do a lot for us. But this is a small place, and most of us are here because we love history, one way or another. Does that appeal to you? Are you a collector, in any sense of the word?" I guess I was asking if this would be just a job for him, or something more.

He seemed to get my drift. "As you can see from my résumé, I majored in history as an undergraduate. I've spent years trying to integrate methodical analysis with the vagaries of recorded history — you know, trying to correlate different contemporaneous reports of a battle, say, and see if I could arrive at some sort of consensus truth about what really happened. You might say I'm fascinated by historic minutiae, but at the same time, I'm skeptical of any individual report, absent corroboration. I suppose in layman's terms, what I think I'm trying to do is to computerize history."

I was beginning to feel overwhelmed. "Okay, one last question. You know our previous registrar had begun to update our records in our recently acquired software program. Can you integrate what he had accomplished into your own system? Because I'd hate to lose all that time and effort." Not to mention, I'd hate to erase Alfred's last contribution to a place that he had loved.

"No problem. I can write a transfer protocol that would . . ."

I'd heard enough. Nicholas was clearly qualified, and he appeared to want the job, for reasons I found more or less credible. He might be a stereotypical computer geek, although better dressed and more articulate than many I had encountered. I wondered how he would fit with our motley crew of librarians and administrators, but he did seem to have a genuine interest in history, and so didn't exactly fall outside the bounds of what passed for normal here. He was staring at me expectantly.

"Nicholas, you're definitely well suited for this position, and I'm flattered that you're interested. May I contact your references?"

"Of course."

"Do you have any questions for me?"

Nicholas appeared to reflect for about three seconds. "I think Latoya told me everything I need to know."

"Then let me get back to you, one way or another, early next week."

"That would be fine." He stood up and extended a hand. "Thank you for seeing me on such short notice. I look forward to hearing from you."

I stood as well and walked him to the outer office. "Eric, could you take Nicholas back downstairs?"

"Sure, Nell." Eric stood up. "Follow me, Nicholas."

As I watched them walk down the hall, I realized that not once during the interview had Nicholas smiled, tried to make any small talk, or said anything about his life apart from the software he had created. Nor had he appeared nervous. He was a serious young man. Maybe I didn't have a lot of experience with interviewing job applicants, but those I had interviewed had generally acted eager to please, nervous, or over-talkative. Nicholas fell at the opposite end of the spectrum: he was reserved almost to the point of stiffness, and while he had said all the correct things, I had learned very little about him, apart from his professional skills.

I decided I needed Latoya's input, so I walked down the hall to her office. She looked up from her superbly clean desk when I walked in. "Do you have a moment to talk about Nicholas?"

She closed the folder she was reading. "Of course. He's left already? What did you think of him?"

I dropped into the chair in front of her desk. "I guess I'd have to say I had mixed feelings about him. He seems very bright, and he has some interesting ideas. He said he could pick up where Alfred left off, so we wouldn't lose any ground. But personally? I guess he seems a little cold."

"And the Society is such a warm and fuzzy place?" Latoya arched one eyebrow.

I checked to see if she was being sarcastic, but she seemed sincere. "We have our share of odd ducks, I'll admit. But we do have to play well together, because nobody is working at the Society for the money or the glory. I know the registrar operates fairly independently, and certainly Alfred kept his interactions with staff to a minimum. So social skills are not a high priority." I wondered why I felt so defensive about a polite, intelligent young man's lack of warmth and humor — neither was a requirement for the position.

"Do you want me to keep looking?" Latoya asked neutrally, although it was clear that it took an effort. Did she expect me to reject Nicholas just because she was the one who had found him? I hoped I wasn't that petty.

I thought for a moment. "Give me the weekend to think about it, all right? I told Nicholas we'd get back to him next week. You've seen his résumé — have you called his references?"

Latoya relaxed slightly. "I'll get on that today. In his favor, let me say that his credentials seem solid, and I think he'd be a real asset. But it's your call."

Was it? Clearly he was Latoya's pick, and I didn't want to butt heads with her over something like this. "Then I'll let you know on Monday. On another note, have you heard from our friends at the FBI lately, about returning our collections?" And talk shifted to other topics.

When I turned to leave, Latoya said, "Oh, one moment — these are the records on the Fireman's Museum collection that you asked for. Not a particularly impressive group of artifacts." She handed me a slender file — far less substantial than the one Felicity had assembled for me.

"But people enjoyed the exhibits there," I reminded her. "Thank you, Latoya."

Back at my office, I stopped at Eric's desk and glanced around me: no one else in sight. "What did you think of the registrar candidate?" I asked Eric.

Eric looked up at me with a half smile. "Based on my two minutes of acquaintance, and the three sentences we exchanged? Kind of a cold fish, but smart. At least, he *thinks* he's smart."

I nodded. "That was about what I thought. I'll see what his references have to say about him — Latoya will be checking those. Thanks, Eric. Have I missed anything important?"

He handed me a few message slips. "I'd say the most important is from Peter Ingersoll."

"I saw him yesterday at the funeral — he said he was going to call. Thanks, Eric." I assumed Peter wanted to set a time to get the documentation we had found about the Fireman's Museum's collections, and I would be happy to turn over what we had assembled, but I was nervous about sharing anything regarding the destroyed fire engine. I didn't want to bring up the issue, but I was curious to see if he would say anything about it on his own. Back at my desk, I decided to first check with James.

"Did you need something, Nell?" he barked when I got through to him. He sounded harried, so I cut to the chase.

"Peter Ingersoll called while I was tied up, and I need to call him back. I ran into him yesterday at the funeral procession. I told him that I had collected the information about his lost collections. What do I do now?"

James sighed. "You can't stall him?"

"Would it make a difference? I've pulled together what we've got here, and I can get Eric to make copies. If I put him off, it makes me look sloppy or incompetent. I owe Peter a prompt response, as a peer and a colleague. Innocent until proven guilty, right?"

"I never said we suspected him of anything."

"You never said you didn't, either. I know

you and the police have to look at everybody."

"We do. Can you omit the details about the fire engine?"

"It would be kind of an obvious omission, since it's not only the centerpiece of their collection but also the one thing we'd be most likely to have information about, especially given the Terwilliger connection. Do you want me to give him the whole package and see how he reacts?"

"You can give him copies of what you have in your files, but do not — repeat, do not — bring up anything about what we suspect."

"You don't think he's come to the same conclusion himself?"

"If he has, he hasn't told the police, as far as I know."

Should I be concerned about that? Was Peter hiding something, or was he really clueless? Still, I could sympathize. If he had reason to suspect something suspicious was going on within his museum, he would be reluctant to bring any outside attention to it, at least until he was sure. I'd been in much the same position. Of course, if he was in on it, the result would be the same. I decided I should get to know Peter a bit better.

"Nell —" James began.

I cut him off. "I know, don't meddle. I'm just going to talk to a colleague in a difficult situation, one that I'm familiar with. Okay? No probing questions, no cross-examination."

"I'm not going to be able to stop you, am I?" James said.

"You're the one who asked me for insights into our community. And this is my business. Peter made an appropriate request for information he knows we have, and I'm honoring it. It's not like I'm stalking drug lords in dark alleys."

"All right. You'll tell me if you find out anything interesting, or if he turns green at the mention of the fire engine?"

"Of course. I'll talk to you later."

I had never aspired to be an undercover operative, and I was equal parts amused and annoyed at James's proprietary attitude. Peter had contacted me with a legitimate professional request, and I was responding in a likewise professional manner. Period. Before I could overthink the whole situation, I picked up the phone and called him.

Peter Ingersoll answered his own phone, and I could hear sounds of construction in the background. "Nell, thank you for returning my call," he shouted into the phone, and I winced and pulled the receiver away from my ear. "You said yesterday that you had something for me?"

"I've pulled together what we have here. How about we get together for lunch and I can give it to you?"

"What?"

I repeated my question, more loudly this time.

"That would be great! I can't hear myself think here. How about the Bourse?"

"Fine. Noon, at the café there?"

"Great. See you there."

After Peter had hung up, I called out to Eric. "I didn't have anything planned for lunch today, did I?"

"No, you're free. Are you meeting Mr. Ingersoll?"

"How did you guess? I'll need you to make copies of the documents we've gathered, to take with me."

"Of course."

I pulled out the folders and started to go through them, using sticky tabs to mark the pages I wanted Eric to copy — and I made a point of including the best and clearest pictures of the fire engine. Peter would have all the information we could offer. The question was, what was he going to do with it?

It was going to be an interesting lunch.

CHAPTER 8

Armed with the thick envelope Eric handed me, I left the building a few minutes early so I could enjoy the walk. The place Peter and I had agreed to meet at lay about halfway between our two institutions, so neither of us would waste any time. It wasn't upscale, but the food was decent, and it was busy enough that no one would pay us much attention. Along the way I took a moment to salute the odd frame structure that embodied the ghost of Ben Franklin's house on Chestnut Street — the house had been torn down nearly two hundred years earlier, and yet it lingered on. Maybe on the way back I would stop at his grave, in the cemetery not far from the Constitution Center.

I arrived first, and waited outside since the cool air felt good. I saw Peter before he saw me, and I watched him approach, accompanied by a man I recognized as the curator Gary O'Keefe — tall and broad, with a craggy open face and grizzled hair. Peter looked predictably frazzled; his rather nice suit showed traces of drywall dust. He smiled when he saw me.

"Nell, you remember Gary O'Keefe. I hope you don't mind that I brought him along."

Peter's companion extended a hand. "Nice to see you again, Nell."

I wondered briefly why Peter had included Gary in our meeting. Support? Or was Gary keeping an eye on Peter? "Good to see you, too," I said.

"Shall we?" he asked, opening the door to the building for me and Peter, and I led the way inside. At the café tucked in one corner a young waitress pointed us toward a table with a view of the busy core of the Bourse, a building that had once been part of Philadelphia's financial center but which now housed a delightful variety of shops and eateries.

We sat and ordered sandwiches and drinks. Up close, Peter looked even more tired. "I'm glad you suggested lunch, Nell," he said. "I really needed to get out of the museum."

"When I called you, it sounded as though construction was still going on," I began.

"It is. Don't take that as a good sign, but the contractors and the unions insisted that we go forward, in the event that we can reopen. We're going to have a lovely rebuilt shell with nothing to put in it."

"Peter, you exaggerate. People have already been very generous with in-kind contributions," Gary said.

Peter shrugged. "I guess," he said with little enthusiasm.

I realized I was going to have to pick my words carefully, to avoid looking like I was interrogating him. "Could you salvage anything from the warehouse?"

He shook his head. "Not a lot. They tried to keep materials from individual renters grouped together, and our area was the hardest hit. Seems odd to be wishing that they'd been a little more careless, doesn't it?"

"It must be devastating to lose so much, all at once. I can only imagine how I'd feel."

"But we look after our own," Gary said. "We'll have no trouble with the reopening."

I wondered briefly who he was trying to convince: me, Peter, or himself? "Peter, remind me how long you've been with the museum?"

"More than five years now. Before that . . ." We rambled on about our respec-

108

tive careers, which carried us through the sandwiches. When the table was finally cleared, I wiped it off with a clean napkin and laid the envelope I'd brought on the table, pulling out the thick stack of photocopies. Both men leaned forward. "Here's what my staff pulled together for you. It looks like you have — had — a very diverse collection. A mix of large and small items, including ephemera. I hadn't realized how competitive the early firefighters were — all these contests!" I waved at an array of copies of newspaper clippings and color lithographs depicting large groups of firefighters trying to outdo each other, and spreading a lot of water in the process. "The Society might be able to lend you some broadsides and posters, if you're going to try to recreate what you had."

"That's very kind of you," Peter replied. "You know, when we decided to renovate, we did review our display concepts. We have such limited space, and it's important to use it effectively. At the same time, we have to appeal to a broad audience. As you might imagine, school groups are an important part of our programming, and they tend to have different interests than visiting fire buffs, say. You don't have that problem, do you?"

"No, we're not really display oriented, although we've done some small exhibits highlighting one or another aspect of our collections. But most of what we have is paper-based, and that's usually neither eye-catching nor sturdy enough to be exhibited. But since we do have objects as well as documents, we still qualify as a museum, and you'd be surprised how many people walk in expecting to see things in cases somewhere.

"Did you have any particular interest in firefighting when you joined the museum, or was it primarily a professional move?"

"A bit of each. My father was a fireman in a small town, one of only a couple of full-time employees — the rest were volunteers. And of course most kids are fascinated by fire. A lot of adults, too."

"You didn't want to follow in his foot-steps?"

"I couldn't — I have asthma."

"Then the construction at the Fireman's Museum must be hard for you."

"It has been. That's why I really need to get out of the building every day. If I don't, my lungs just close up. I'll be glad when it's finished."

"I was a firefighter myself," Gary said, joining the conversation. "I had to retire after an accident on the job — that's where I got this gimpy leg — but I've been with the museum since it was incorporated as a nonprofit, back in the seventies. Going on forty years now, longer than I've been married."

Gary must be older than he looks, I thought. While Gary was talking, Peter picked up the sheaf of papers and leafed through it briefly, without stopping to examine any particular item — including the fire engine pictures — then returned it to the envelope. "I really appreciate your putting this together for me, Nell. We're going to be a lot more thorough with our documentation, going forward — and we'll back things up, off-site, from now on. Talk about putting all our proverbial eggs in one basket! I knew it was poor practice, but until now, it was hard to convince the rest of the staff to do it properly. No offense, Gary."

"None taken, Peter. I've never been good at the paperwork side of things, and I've never had formal training in museum management. I just picked it up along the way."

"Did I read somewhere that you still use active firefighters on your staff?" I asked Peter.

Peter nodded. "We do, to some extent. Mostly for school tours. The children love talking to a real fireman."

"They're municipal employees, aren't they? How does that work?"

"It's a little complicated. The city created a nonprofit organization to manage the museum, but its history goes back further than that. In some ways the city still feels it has some rights to the place. And a lot of our employees and members of the board have come to us through the city and the fire department."

Was it my imagination, or did Peter look less than happy with that situation? How much say did he have in who was hired? Was the museum a nice cushy niche for people who left the city employ? Or to put it another way, was I catching a whiff of political patronage? I didn't know Peter well enough to ask any more about this, but I could probably find out from other sources. Like Marty.

Peter checked his watch and started to stand. "I've got to go — I have to review the contractor's list of things that still need to be done." He held up the envelope. "Thank you again, Nell, especially for putting this together so quickly. I'll take care of the lunch tab. It's the least I can do."

"You're welcome, and thanks for the lunch. Let me know if I can be of any further help."

Gary had stood up as well, but he was hesitating, so I seized the opportunity. "Gary, do you have to leave, too? I'd love to hear more about your collections. There's a lot I don't know about Philadelphia fire-fighting history, but I was intrigued by what I found in our files."

He sat back down willingly. "And I'd be delighted to fill you in, Nell. Peter, I'll see you later?"

"You know where I'll be." Peter strode off toward the cashier.

Gary signaled to the waitress, then looked at me. "More coffee?"

"Sure." After the waitress had topped off our cups, I said, "Can you give me the nickel tour of Philadelphia firefighting?"

"Of course — I could do it in my sleep, after all these years. Let's start at the very beginning. When William Penn created the city in 1688, he planned his new home to be as fire resistant as possible. Of course, in those days that meant wide streets and open spaces. That's why he created the parks, you know — as firebreaks."

"Fascinating!" I was already impressed. "I did not know that! I knew it was Penn who laid out the city, but I hadn't realized that fire management was a major factor."

"Indeed it was. Then in 1696 the Provincial Legislature passed a bill about chimney cleaning and required that each household have two leather fire buckets. Plus people were fined if they were caught smoking on the street."

"I take it that's not enforced anymore." I laughed.

"Regrettably, no. Now, the city's first fire engine was purchased from England in 1718, but nobody tried to use it until 1726, at which point they discovered it wasn't in working order. They fixed it, but another fire in 1730 showed how poorly suited that machine was to the task, so they ordered three new ones, along with four hundred fire buckets."

"Where did Ben Franklin come in?" I asked.

"Ah, you know about that? Well, by the early 1700s the city owned equipment but had no organization to run it. So in 1736 Ben Franklin and twenty-nine other prominent citizens got together to form the Union Fire Company. This was intended at first to serve only its members, though they very quickly decided to expand to protect the entire city. But their charter limited the number of members, so other fire companies formed quickly. By 1771 almost every city official belonged to one or another of them."

I enjoyed watching Gary warm to his subject. I had to admit, much of the information was new to me. Listening to him, I was amazed that there hadn't been a fire museum much earlier, since Philadelphia had led the way, setting an example for urban firefighting. When I next looked at my watch, an hour had passed.

Gary noticed. "I'm sorry — I'm keeping you too long. People tell me I get carried away when I start talking about firefighting."

"Don't apologize! I've learned a lot. If there's any way the Society can help, please let me know." I stood up and pulled on my coat, with Gary's courteous help. "It was nice talking to you, Gary."

"I've enjoyed it, Nell," Gary said.

As I walked back to the Society, I tried to figure out what the dynamic was between the two men, while also trying to make up my mind what I'd tell James.

Peter had looked drained, but that wasn't surprising. My impression was that Gary had tagged along to support Peter. But I was troubled: it was hard to believe that these two men, who were intimately familiar with the museum's prized fire engine, had not seen the newspapers and were oblivious to the differences. Maybe they didn't want to call attention to the issue or discuss it with me, regarding it as an internal matter they didn't need to include me in.

Or maybe they were trying to hide something.

I decided to skip my visit to Ben Franklin's grave. After all, he wasn't going anywhere. Back at my desk, I was still debating about what to tell James when Eric told me that Agent Morrison was on the line.

I picked up a tad reluctantly. "Hi, James. I just got back from lunch."

"Oh, right, with Ingersoll."

As if that wasn't why he'd called. "Yes, and his curator, Gary O'Keefe. I thought that's what you wanted to hear about."

"Did either one mention the fire engine?"

"No, it didn't come up. I gave them the materials we'd collected, and they barely looked at them, although there were pictures of the engine in there."

"Anything else?"

"I don't think so. Peter seems to be on the up-and-up. The only hint of any discontent was the impression I got that the city might be packing his board with ex-municipal employees. If it wasn't about my lunch, though, why did you call?"

He was quiet a moment. "There's been another warehouse fire, early this morning. It looks like arson again. There were other, smaller fires over the past few weeks, so it could be there's an arsonist running around."

"What do you think? Are they all related?" From the way he was talking, I suspected he wasn't convinced.

He sighed quietly. "Nell . . . I think there's more to it."

I smiled, even though he couldn't see me. "Is that your gut talking?"

"Maybe. Anyway, the police department is telling us politely to stay in our corner and speak only when spoken to. In other words, we're consultants and that's it."

I bet that galled the FBI — and suggested a certain lack of tact on the part of the police department, which didn't surprise me. "And will you?"

He chuckled. "I've got to go, Nell. We'll talk later." And then he hung up.

I noticed that he hadn't answered my question.

CHAPTER 9

Over the weekend I wrestled with whether to hire Nicholas Naylor, while I kept my hands busy with gardening. Given that I lived in a converted carriage house, set behind the former "big house" — now the offices for a group of psychiatrists — my land consisted of a parking space, a patio big enough for two small chairs and a grill, and a three-foot strip of grass, which the tenants in the house kindly mowed. My garden was a few large pots that I usually planted with annuals and ignored for most of the growing season, with predictable results. I really respected plants that could look after themselves, since I tended to remember to water only when my petunias turned brown and lay down in defeat. As a result, my gardening efforts were limited to throwing away the very dead remains of the previous year's optimistic efforts, in preparation for repeating the cycle all over again.

Heck, in a good year the interval between "buy" and "die" might be as much as a month, and for that brief time I did enjoy a splash of color to welcome me when I walked home from the train station on long summer evenings.

I didn't even try to keep a pet.

Still, it was nice to dig my hands into the now-warm potting soil and tear out the old, dead roots. It made me feel virtuous, and I much preferred prepping my planters to doing the full spring-cleaning thing inside my house. Bad enough that the lengthening days made the cobwebs and dust bunnies more obvious. I opened the windows and hoped that they would all blow away to somewhere else.

So I had plenty of time to think about Nicholas. I knew that the salaries we offered were below the market average, even for chronically underfunded nonprofits. Of course, in some cases the recent economic woes might override that consideration, since these days any job was a good job — but Nicholas already had a job, and I'd be willing to bet that Penn paid more than we could. But the Society had no choice: the lousy economy meant that some percentage of our members might not renew this year, and we needed that income. Board contributions might also slip. Marty had ensured that the registrar's position would be adequately funded, but I hoped that the other staff members — who had been patiently waiting for even cost-of-living raises for the past five years or so — would understand that the registrar's position was important and would not begrudge its occupant a slightly higher pay scale. We didn't talk about salaries in-house, but somehow people always knew.

Of course, that made it doubly important that everyone get along. We had about forty employees, including part-timers, so everybody knew everybody else. We mingled — no artificial hierarchies, which always reminded me of playground cliques. As director of development I'd worked alongside many of them for years, shared lunch or dinner with most people at one time or another, and I didn't intend to stop just because I had a fancier title and a bigger office now. So, did I see Nicholas fitting in?

It was not an easy answer. I didn't have to do anything until Monday, when Latoya might have something to add from her contacts and Nicholas's references. We really, really needed to fill the position, which had been vacant now for several months. The right person could do a lot for us, and Nicholas had hit on some critical issues. He got points for his level of expertise. As for personality? I had found him hard to read, and I was reluctant to judge. Okay, to be honest I hadn't warmed to him immediately, but that wasn't a good basis for a decision. Maybe after a couple of months he'd loosen up. Maybe he'd even smile.

To distract myself I decided to turn to the Internet to bone up on the Fireman's Museum, which as Gary had explained in ample detail, was closely tied to the history of firefighting in Philadelphia. Old Ben Franklin had been one busy man. Not only had he had a hand in the formation of the city's first volunteer fire department, but he and his group had also suggested creating a fire insurance company, which came about in 1752: it was known as The Philadelphia Contributionship, which had survived to this day. And then, of course, there were all of Ben's other farsighted works — the founding of the country's first public hospital and the first public library, for example — and he managed all this between his writing and his scientific experiments. And his ambassadorial role during and after the Revolution. It made me tired just reading about him — when did he find the time or the energy?

It was clear that local firefighters had a long tradition of solidarity, which persisted to this day. Philadelphia has always been a strong union town, and the firefighters were in the thick of it. On the other hand, there were clearly strong loyalties to individual volunteer firefighter groups in the nineteenth century. They had proliferated rapidly and generated a lot of competitive spirit, that sometimes went beyond friendly and resulted in pitched battles on the streets, not to mention sabotage.

Did either deeply ingrained aspect of Philadelphia firefighting apply to the situation at the Fireman's Museum now? Could politics have played a role in the warehouse fire? Was that event intended to discredit the fire department in some way? Surely the museum must look foolish when their collection of fire-related memorabilia burned to a crisp. But who stood to benefit from their downfall?

Or was there a personal element? Had someone hated Allan Brigham? Was there some deep, dark secret about his exit from the fire department? That was a question James was better suited to answer. Or did someone have personal issues with Peter Ingersoll, strong enough to seek to destroy his museum to hurt him? Or was the museum itself the target? I had no way to answer any of those questions. Certainly I'd picked up no rumors of that kind of animus within our community. James was right: it would be better to let the police and the FBI deal with the whole thing.

Benjamin Franklin had coined the phrase *an ounce of prevention is worth a pound of cure* in urging greater attention to fire safety. I agreed in principle, but was there a way to apply it to my job? I amused myself on the train ride into the city on Monday with muddling metaphors: a lot of my job seemed to consist of putting out fires — figuratively, of course. No doubt there were some issues smoldering below the surface. Was I ready to take the heat for the decisions I made? The other passengers on the train must have wondered why I was smiling as I ran through increasingly silly analogies in my head, but at least I arrived at the Society in a good mood.

I greeted Eric when I walked in, and by the time I had hung up my coat he had appeared in my doorway bearing coffee — with Latoya hard on his heels. I would have liked a moment to absorb a little caffeine, but since Latoya had braved my den a second time, she must think this was important.

"Good morning, Latoya. Would you like some coffee?"

"No, I'm good." She sat down in front of my desk. "Listen, I made a few calls, as you asked, and everybody was uniformly enthusiastic about Nicholas. He's smart, he's meticulous, he's thorough. I think he'd be a wonderful addition to our staff."

I sat back and sipped coffee, reflecting that I had seldom seen Latoya so enthusiastic. "Thank you for following through, Latoya. I'm inclined to agree with you. If you feel comfortable with Nicholas, then I believe you should offer him the position. After all, you're going to be the one working most closely with him. And you'll have to bring him up to speed on our existing records and monitor his progress. All right?"

Latoya gave me a rare honest grin. "That's fine, Nell. I'm glad we can move forward. I'll get in touch with him today." She stood up, but before leaving she said simply, "Thank you."

I sat back in my chair, relieved. I'd actually made Latoya happy, and with Nicholas's hiring we would fill the last large remaining vacancy in our staffing, and we could finally begin to sort out our stalled cataloging issues. I'd have something positive to report at the next board meeting. Things were definitely looking up, and it was still only Monday. I had high hopes for this week.

I should have known it wouldn't last. A few minutes later I looked up to see Marty bustling into my office. She dropped casually into a chair and grinned at me. "I've got you a registrar!"

"You what?" I felt a sinking feeling in my stomach, and it wasn't from the coffee.

"A replacement for Alfred."

I sighed. I had, in the space of a morning, gone from no registrars to a surfeit of them. "Uh, Marty, I think Latoya's already made an offer to a candidate."

"Well, tell her to withdraw it."

I considered that idea briefly and shuddered. We'd look foolish and inconsistent to Nicholas, and Latoya probably would stop speaking to me. "Why? And I wish you'd consulted me about this. Who is this person?"

Marty's good humor had evaporated along with mine. "She's the niece of Edward Perkins — and he's agreed to make a nice contribution to the endowment for the collections management fund."

Ah, now Marty's enthusiasm made sense. "How did all this come about? Who is Edward Perkins? And do I assume the donation is contingent upon hiring his relative?"

"I was at a party over the weekend, and Eddie was there. If you don't know him, you should — we've been trying to lure him onto the board for years. Old money, but tight with it. I've known him forever, but not well. Anyway, we got to talking, and it turns out he's got a lovely niece who just graduated from college and has been having trouble finding a job, and he wondered if I knew of any openings. I should add, he doesn't have any kids of his own, so his nieces and nephews stand to inherit. So he tells me that she was a history major at Mount Holyoke and she just loves the city. I said we had a slot that might be a good fit."

I felt a small sense of relief. "Do you mean you haven't actually offered her the position?"

Marty cocked her head at me. "Nell, you know how this works. I made appropriately gushy noises about young Alice and then happened to mention that we were looking for funding, since it was such an important position. Eddie and I danced around that for a while, and I finally told him something in the low to mid five figures would be nice — and mentioned a few of his friends who were chipping in."

This was news to me. "I haven't heard

about any recent flood of contributions."

Marty waved a hand at me. "They'll come around. Anyway, Eddie was good with it but made it clear that Alice came with the package."

Oh, sh . . . oot. This put me in a real bind. Alice might be a lovely girl with a shiny new college degree, but she couldn't possibly match Nicholas's depth and specificity of experience. On the other hand, brushing Alice off could well mean saying good-bye to a nice contribution and alienating a potential donor and future board member, which was never a good strategic move. At the very least I owed it to Marty to go through the motions and interview this girl.

"Who's your pick?" Marty demanded.

"His name is Nicholas Naylor. Latoya found him, and I have to say, he's extremely well qualified. He's been working on his own version of software for managing collections for cultural institutions, which he would bring with him. He's got several years of experience, and his references check out. I told Latoya to make him an offer this morning."

"Well then, we have a problem here," Marty said.

We stared at each other. I owed my current position to Marty's behind-the-scenes machinations, and the longer I held it, the better I liked it. But there was no way I intended to be her puppet. I reserved the right to make my own decisions about administrative matters, including hiring. At the same time, I didn't want to alienate Marty, because while the Terwilliger fortune might have dwindled over the centuries, she knew everyone in the five-county area, she had a pretty good grasp of their current net worth, and she was happy to share her information and contacts with the institution she loved. So I couldn't just blow off her proposed candidate, no matter how unqualified she sounded. "We do," I said neutrally. "Why don't I talk with this Alice and see how the wind blows? Seriously, Marty, if she's an airhead, then it should be an easy decision. If she seems up to the job, we can consider our options."

"Fair enough. Want me to call her?" When I nodded, Marty continued. "You know, I'm not saying that you *have* to take her on. Sure, Eddie's money would be nice, but I care about the Society's collections, including my family's, and I don't want to see the cataloging screwed up. Can I sit in on the interview?"

"I don't suppose I can stop you. Do you know Alice? She's not a goddaughter or a fifth cousin, is she?"

"No, I don't really know her, and unlike Alfred, she's not related. Let me give her a call and see when she can come in." She pulled a cell phone out of her pocket and retreated to the hall to make the call. While she was gone, I tried to sort out what I felt. I'd defer any decision until after I'd met the girl, but I had a hard time believing that she'd hold a candle to Nicholas's qualifications. Well, decisions like this came with the territory.

Marty popped back in. "Three o'clock today. Eric says you're free."

That gave me time to come up with some sort of plan. Should I call Latoya and tell her to hold off? Maybe she hadn't reached Nicholas. Or maybe he'd turned us down. One way to find out. I picked up the phone and punched in Latoya's extension.

"Latoya? Have you talked with Nicholas yet?"

"I did. He seemed pleased to accept. He was going to check how much notice Penn wants him to give and figure out how much time it would take to finish up his current projects. He said he'd get back to us in a day or two with the details."

"Thanks, Latoya." I hung up and faced Marty again. "Okay, so we've made the offer, and you've got to know I'd hate to withdraw it now. In fact, I'm not even sure we can, without facing legal consequences — I'd have to check with Human Resources. In any case, I don't think it's fair to him. I think he's very qualified, but I'll talk to Alice and I'll try to keep an open mind."

Marty had a faraway expression on her face. "Nell, you may be worrying over nothing. You know, maybe we could set them both to working on the Terwilliger Collection, as kind of a trial, and see who does better."

On some level I was appalled. "Marty, that's not the best way to make decisions. And how would you measure that? Number of pieces cataloged? Quality or accuracy of entries?"

"Maybe not. But I'd love to see what they could accomplish in, say, two weeks? A little competition can't hurt. And then we can see how they like the work and the place, and they can decide if they like us."

I hated the idea. But I needed Marty's backing, both strategic and financial, so I said firmly, "We'll see."

CHAPTER 10

Marty must surely have realized I was not happy about the situation she'd created — not that she could have known about our offering Nicholas the position, but that she had overstepped by offering someone a position that wasn't hers to fill, without ever checking with me — because she vanished strategically back into the stacks. Sometimes I wondered just how much time she spent at the Society versus at home. Every time I turned around she seemed to pop up. I didn't want to discourage her, but it was disconcerting.

At three o'clock she appeared outside my door with young Alice in tow. I tried to read Marty's expression and failed: it seemed an equal mix of trepidation and glee.

"Nell, this is Alice Price, the girl, uh, woman I told you about. Alice, this is Nell Pratt, the president of the Society."

I wanted to appear welcoming, even

though I didn't hold out high hopes for this very young and slender blonde, so I extended my hand. "Alice, I'm glad to meet you. Please, sit down. Marty, you're joining us, right?"

"I am," she said cheerfully, and sat down on the settee against the wall. I hoped she'd at least have the good sense to keep quiet so I could get on with business. I was already on edge, at least in my own mind: I hadn't even told Latoya about this situation, mainly because I hoped the problem would just go away before it came to that. Part of me was hoping to find something about Alice that clearly disqualified her from the position of registrar. Dyslexia would do, or maybe a serious allergy to mold or dust, both of which the building and its contents were riddled with. Of course, neither of these would be obvious immediately. Alice on first glance appeared to be a very calm and self-possessed young woman. I didn't hold her age against her; we already had a few young hires on-site, like Eric and Rich, but Alice would qualify as the youngest. She looked almost comically conservative, dressed in a pale blue, light wool suit — with a skirt, no less — unscuffed leather shoes with low heels, and carrying a nice, real leather handbag. Her nails were neatly manicured but unpolished, and she wore minimal makeup. All she needed was a string of pearls and she could have stepped out of an ad from the 1950s. She studied me as I studied her, showing no signs of nervousness.

I cleared my throat. "You know, this all came about so quickly that I haven't even seen your résumé, so I know only what Marty has told me. Why don't you start at the beginning and tell me about your qualifications and why you'd like to work here?"

Alice retrieved a copy of her résumé from her bag and handed it to me before taking a seat. "As you can see, I graduated last June with a double major in contemporary history and computer science. I spent the summer traveling in South America — a gift from my family — and when I returned I started looking for a job. You probably know how tight the job market is these days, especially for liberal arts majors, even those with computer skills. I've found a few short-term data-entry jobs, but nothing with any long-term potential."

"How old are you?"

"Twenty-one. I skipped a year in high school and finished college in three years."

What a precocious young woman! "In a perfect world, what would you be looking for?" I asked.

She twisted her silky blonde hair over her shoulder. "Honestly? I'd love to do something to help foster struggling economies in disadvantaged countries, particularly where women's initiatives are involved. But I'm a pragmatist, and I know funding for such things has all but disappeared and isn't likely to come back anytime soon. My roots are in the Philadelphia area, and I'd like to stay here, at least for now. I've been looking at the nonprofit sector because I think my talents would be valued there. I have no interest in getting a law or business degree, although a number of my friends have chosen that path, mainly to defer the inevitable. What's this position all about?"

I was reeling from the directness of her approach, and her question caught me by surprise. Apparently Uncle Edward hadn't told her much. "The Society is a collecting institution, and we have over two million items in our various collections, all housed within this building. Since we've been doing this for over a hundred years, as you might imagine our cataloging systems are rather disjointed. We've begun digitizing the most recent catalogs, but the backlog is staggering. Until recently we had a registrar who knew the collections intimately and who was beginning to drag our systems into the twenty-first century, but unfortunately he . . . passed away. It's been difficult to find a replacement for him. And we want to make sure we find someone who will fit well and who has the skills we need."

Alice tilted her head like a bird. "Uncle Edward put you up to this, didn't he?"

Again I looked at Marty, and she shrugged. Well, if she wasn't going to help, I'd have to wing it. At least I hadn't made any promises. "Yes. Or kind of. He promised a nice contribution to the fund we've created to help support this position, if we hired you to fill it." I wondered how many rules — or laws — I was breaking, telling an applicant this kind of information.

Alice nodded, once. "That sounds like Uncle Edward. A bit of genteel blackmail. He's a sweet man, but sometimes I think he's living in the nineteenth century. I just wish he didn't think I was some helpless young creature who needed his help to find a job. But, let me get this right: if I walk away, he'll withdraw the offer of the money?"

"That's my general understanding," I said. Marty said nothing.

"And it's probably enough money that you can't just turn it down," Alice went on.

135

"Don't worry — Uncle Edward's got plenty. I'm sorry he put you in this position, especially since I obviously don't have the depth of experience I imagine you're looking for."

I let out a deep breath. "I'm very glad that you understand that this puts me in a difficult position, through no fault of yours. The truth is, Alice, we've already made an offer to a highly qualified candidate who suits our needs. Your skills are untested, and this is a position that's important to the Society, and we're looking for a long-term commitment."

Alice regarded me with steady blue eyes, and I could almost see the wheels turning in her head. "May I make a suggestion?" she asked.

"Certainly."

"Why not take me on as an intern? Pay me what you would normally pay for that type of position. I'd guess that Uncle Edward's contribution would cover at least my salary for a year. I'll work here and gain experience and build up my résumé, and you can go ahead and hire the person you've already chosen. It's win-win for everyone. Your position would get filled, I'd get a job, and you'd get to keep Uncle Edward's money. What do you think?"

What I was beginning to think was that this young woman scared me. What she was suggesting sounded vaguely unethical, especially as it applied to poor Uncle Edward, but I had a suspicion that Marty and Alice between them could handle him.

I was torn. She was offering us a sweetheart deal, one that involved only a little deception. She was certainly smart, and I didn't doubt she could learn anything she chose to. It said something about the state of the world that someone as talented as she obviously was would have trouble finding work. But would she be happy here, even if only for a year or two? She'd already leapfrogged her way through high school and college. "Alice, your offer is very tempting. But I'm concerned that this place isn't going to be able to keep up with you. You'll get bored, and that will make you unhappy. I'm guessing you don't handle boredom well? I don't want you walking out with a job half finished."

She dipped her head. "You'd be correct. But I do love learning new skills, and I'm sure I can find plenty to keep me busy here. And I promise I'll give you fair warning if I'm going to leave. What do you say?"

Rather than answering her directly I said, "Let me show you the collections." I had one more test to make before I committed to her creative if slightly skewed plan.

I stood up. Marty looked bewildered, but she stood as well and followed us into the hallway. A startled Eric watched our little procession pass by, but I didn't explain. I just kept going, to the door to the stacks. I pulled it open and let Alice and Marty enter before me, then stepped in after them.

It was, as always, dim, dusty, and quiet. Marty cocked her head at me; I nodded toward Alice, without speaking. Alice looked like a very alert cat, assessing the scene before deciding which way to jump. If she'd had whiskers, they'd be twitching right now, collecting information. She inhaled deeply and half smiled.

Come on, girl, take the hook, I said silently.

She looked at me. "May I browse?"

"Of course. I'd like you to get a sense of what we have here." And I let her roam.

At first she was efficient, noting the hand-scrawled numbers on the card at the end of each row, observing the precarious piles of large and unwieldy old books stacked on tables, windowsills, and wherever else there was space. She paced off the length of the aisle, no doubt calculating in her mind the total linear feet of materials. But then she disappeared into a side aisle toward the end of the room, and she came out with a book. She cradled it with her left hand and delicately turned a few pages, that curious half smile still on her face. I left her to the first flush of discovery, then finally approached. She held it up to me. "Look at this! Early eighteenth century, published in Boston. Original woodcuts. Gorgeous binding, probably later — right?" Her eyes met mine, and she grinned. I grinned back and nodded.

She was hooked.

Marty and I walked her out after another half an hour, during which Alice had become giddier and giddier, grazing through the stacks, collecting grime on her lovely interview suit without even noticing. It was funny, by the end she seemed both older and younger: older because she was being open about her excitement; younger because she looked like a child in a candy shop, with coins clutched in her increasingly grubby hands and all those treasures to choose from. She let her true enthusiasm shine. In the front vestibule she turned to me. "So, can I come back?"

I smiled at her. "Of course you can. Give me a few days to work out details. I'll call you at the end of the week."

"Thank you," she said simply. She stuck out her dirty hand, and I shook it proudly.

It was a pleasure to acknowledge a collections soul mate.

When she had left, I turned back to Marty, who had remained uncharacteristically silent during the interview. "Please don't do that to me again."

"What? Throw you a curveball?"

"No, undermine my authority. If she'd been the bimbo I half expected, nobody would have ended up happy — including Uncle Edward. You were lucky."

For a moment I thought Marty was going to get angry. After all, I had challenged her, and as a board member she had some sort of seniority. But in the end she nodded. "I may not like it, but you're right. You're the leader here, and I never intended to be a puppet master. For all of that, Alice may turn out to be an asset."

"Thank you. And I hope so. Now all I have to do is explain it all to Latoya. And find something for Alice to do. I'll let you handle Uncle Edward. And I expect to see that check by the end of the week."

"Done," Marty said.

CHAPTER 11

After Alice left and Marty disappeared back into the stacks, I felt as though I had been through a wringer. I should talk to Latoya, find out where we stood with Nicholas, and fill her in about Alice. I should figure out when either or both could start, and what I was going to ask them to do. No, that should be Latoya's decision, because they would both be reporting to her.

But I was beginning to hatch a plan, one I hoped I could sell to Latoya. It helped that she knew it was difficult to say no when Marty wanted something. I'd already asked Rich to shift the Terwilliger Collection to the third-floor workroom so we could finally get a handle on how much we had and how it was organized; one advantage of this was that it would be easier to reintegrate the stolen items that James kept promising the FBI would return any day now, and then decide where and how to store the whole thing, once the collection was all together again. We should probably plan on some grand opening down the line, to introduce the world to the Terwilliger Collection. Since it was largely uncataloged at the moment, the general public hadn't had much access to it. What we should do, I realized, was to create not only the fundamental cataloging but also a simpler finding aid that we could post on our website. And that might solve my problem of how best to make use of the odd couple of Nicholas and Alice, plus Rich. Rich was doing the basic description, Nicholas could begin inputting the entries into his software program, and Alice could craft a more user-friendly document.

Eric appeared in my doorway with a clutch of phone message slips. "Good interview?" he asked cautiously.

"I think so, unexpectedly. There are a few details to be worked out, but we may actually have two new employees shortly, and then we can get down to some real work. Any important messages?"

"Only one that won't wait until tomorrow — Agent Morrison."

Again? "Thanks, Eric. I'll give him a call." When Eric went back to his desk, I punched in James's office number.

"James Morrison," he answered automatically and then caught himself. "Hi, Nell — force of habit."

"Not a problem. You called me?"

"Yes. Do you have time for a quick drink around six? I've got a couple of things to discuss with you."

"Uh, sure." We picked a place near his office and close to my train stop, and agreed to meet at six.

Bolstered by something nice to look forward to at the end of the day, I braced myself to talk to Latoya and marched to her office, only to discover that she wasn't there. I checked my watch and realized it was after five — we must have spent more time in the stacks with Alice than I had realized. I was ashamed to feel relief that I wouldn't have to explain to Latoya right now. I went back to my office and resumed writing reports, one of my least favorite activities.

Shortly before six I collected my coat and bag and walked out of the building, nodding to the few people who were still around. The evening air felt good as I walked the couple of blocks toward City Hall — which, I recalled, sat squarely upon what had been one of William Penn's parks. He certainly had left his stamp on the city.

James was already waiting for me and

graciously helped me off with my coat. "Nice to see you again, Nell."

"Is this business, or can I have a glass of wine?" I asked, sitting down.

"A bit of business, but go right ahead. Hard day?"

"Yes and no. I think we've finally filled Alfred's old position, and then some."

A waiter approached, and James ordered for both of us before asking, "What do you mean?"

I filled him in on my unexpected employee surplus and my plans on how to utilize them both on the Terwilliger Collection.

"Speaking of the Terwilliger Collection," James said with a grin, "I've got good news. We're finally releasing the recovered goods to you, so all the collection will be together again."

"Oh, wonderful! And perfect timing, since we've now got the staff to deal with them. I was just thinking that once we get done with processing it, I'd like to plan a big media blitz and maybe a party. It's a classic collection with some wonderful material, and I think Marty — and the rest of her family — deserve the recognition. Do the documents all seem to still be in good condition?"

"I'd say so. What we recovered came from a private dwelling, but the — well, I can't say owner, but the person who was in possession of them took decent care of everything. Seems he was a real local history buff. That's why he kept quite a bit of the stuff he acquired — he was a genuine enthusiast. Prosecuting him may turn out to be a little tricky because he may well have purchased his collection items in good faith, though anyone who's into collecting and purchases materials of that caliber had to have known there was something fishy about it. Anyway, we've tried to treat the papers appropriately since."

"Like not shoving them into a leaky warehouse?"

"Exactly."

"Do you know if much is missing?" I asked, not sure if I wanted an answer, or if he could give one. I knew the thief had tried to sell some of the choicer items on the black market.

"You'd know better than I would. We still aren't sure how long the pilfering was going on, after all. Still, you may get lucky."

"Well, I guess that's the upside of all this. I for one will be glad to put the whole episode behind us and move on."

"There was something else . . ." James began, seeming at a bit of a loss.

"What?"

"It's about the fire and the Fireman's Museum."

I took a sip of my wine before responding. "Is there something new? Are you actually on the case now?"

"Yes and no. That's the problem, you see. You've told me, in confidence, that you think the fire engines were switched, and I'm inclined to believe you. Marty came to the same conclusion, and she's got a pretty good eye." He stopped.

"But?"

"It's been several days, and nobody from the Fireman's Museum has come forward about it. They're all busy mourning their lost treasure, as far as I know. And I don't know a lot, since the police don't know, and I won't be involved unless there's a clear case of fraud here, or the police ask us for help with the death, assuming it's murder, which isn't proved, either. I told you that the autopsy was inconclusive about who or what caused the blow that killed the watchman, so that doesn't help."

"Huh," I said intelligently. I needed a moment to think this through. "You don't want to take your suspicions directly to them?"

"I could, but if I'm wrong there are quite a few people who wouldn't be very happy with me — my boss, the city of Philadelphia,

146

the entire fireman's union, the museum . . . The FBI is on a pretty tight leash these days, along with everyone else, so I can't indulge in an investigation just because I have suspicions. But it's difficult, because without revealing my doubts, it's less likely that I'll be asked in to investigate that aspect."

I nodded. "I see your problem."

He sighed. "I hate to say this, but I may need your help on this again."

This was interesting. I sat up straighter in my chair. "Seriously? I thought I'd done all I could." Or all that he would let me.

He was shaking his head, more to himself than to me. "I really hate doing this. Involving civilians is never a good idea." He took a swallow of his own drink, then looked at me. "As I see it, we've got a limited number of possibilities. One, it's simple arson with an accidental death, and we're wrong about the charred skeleton of a fire truck — maybe the fire warped it or something. Two, someone switched the machines, then torched the building to cover it up, and the death was an accident — the watchman heard something, ran to investigate, and tripped and hit his head and died. Three, same as two except somebody killed the night watchman with a blow to the head because he knew something or he'd seen something, or he was even in on it and someone wanted to cut him out, which adds murder to the mix."

"That sounds like it about covers it. So, who are you looking at?"

"That's the kicker — I don't know. An anonymous arsonist or someone connected to the museum? Or another one of your rabid collectors who really wanted an antique fire engine?"

"I'm sorry — I still don't see what you want me to do, now that I've handed the materials over to Peter."

He looked away, barely stopping short of rolling his eyes. "Do you think he really doesn't see the difference? Is he hiding something? Or covering for someone else?"

"James, I've spent maybe two hours total with the man. How am I supposed to tell you what's going through his mind? And whether he's involved in a major theft and cover-up, and maybe a murder?"

"The FBI can look into Ingersoll's background and the rest of the board members for the nonprofit — or I should say, I can do that much on my own time without alerting anyone that I'm investigating. But you are part of the museum community, and you can ask different questions, come at the problem from a different angle, right?"

"I suppose. Although how I'm supposed to determine who at the museum is capable of committing or initiating a major crime isn't exactly clear to me."

"I know. Just nose around and see if there's any talk about the place. I mean, you know how boards are put together. Are there any people who stand out as inappropriate at that museum?"

"What — you think a board member might have engineered this? With or without Peter's participation?" I wasn't quite sure what an inappropriate board member would look like. I knew that the Society's board was pretty homogeneous — that is, older white men with money — but there were some oddballs in the mix. I gathered there were plenty of people involved in firefighting one way or another on the Fireman's Museum board, but not knowing much about that profession, either, I couldn't guess who didn't fit in. "I don't know. I do know that it's kind of a cushy position for some city employees, current or former, but that's not all that unusual."

"Does any money change hands?"

"You mean, do the board members get paid? Generally not, but I'd have to check the details. Certainly not at the Society. We'd rather they give *us* money."

"Well, maybe that's part of the problem at the Fireman's Museum. Maybe somebody's expectations were not being met and he saw a quick way to make some money."

"What an awful idea! I mean, to kill a man and destroy a city collection for a quick payoff?" It occurred to me that I had no idea what the fire engine might be worth.

"I know it's not something you would do, Nell, but someone might."

I sighed. "So what do you want me to do? Tell Peter Ingersoll what I suspect?"

"No! At least, not yet. We don't want to tip anyone off. If he comes to you with a question about the fire engine, since you were the one who gave him the documents, that's a different story. You play dumb and let me know ASAP."

"I'm so flattered that you think I can appear stupid," I said.

"Nell," he began to protest, and I held up a hand.

"Yes, I know this is serious. Just give me some time to think about it, all right? I want to help, but I don't want to go blundering in and make things worse."

"Understood. But you know as well as I do, the longer this drags on, the less likely it will be solved."

"What, now I have a deadline? Tell me, can your art theft guys trace where that fire engine might have gone? I mean, it's not like you can stick it in a tidy box and put it in the mail. It's big, but at the same time, it's fragile. Somebody would have to have had a really large truck of some sort, to get it away from the warehouse. Don't the police have spy cameras on every corner? I thought I remembered reading about the city installing those, a few years ago."

"Some. Not everywhere. This isn't one of those television shows where you can follow a single car for miles through the city."

I grimaced. "I know — this is Philadelphia. So you don't know how the piece might have left the building?" If it really was gone.

"Not yet — we're still collecting information. And again, we don't even know when it might've happened, either. The night before the fire? Six months? We don't even have footage going back more than a couple of weeks."

"You're certainly making it easy." I laid my hands firmly on the table. "Let me see what I can come up with. What would I get out of the FBI?"

James's mouth twitched. "Only our deepest respect and gratitude — off the record, of course."

"Is that like a get-out–of-jail-free card the next time I have a problem?"

He shrugged, which was not helpful.

"All right," I pressed, "let's talk about something more solid. When will you be delivering the wandering Terwilliger documents?"

"Is tomorrow soon enough?"

"Perfect. I'll tell Rich to get ready for them. And Marty. Thank you." I checked my watch: I could just make the next train. "I'll talk to you tomorrow," I said as I stood up and started to pull on my coat.

James appeared startled. "You're leaving already?"

I smiled. "Hey, if you wanted a date, you should have said so. Call me tomorrow and we can make plans. Good night, James."

My departure may have seemed a bit abrupt, but I wanted time to think about what James had asked me to do. Regardless of whatever tenuous personal relationship we were nursing along, this was business, and I needed a clear head to consider what he had suggested. On the brisk walk to Suburban Station and during the ride home, I had plenty of time to go over what James had said. I'll admit I didn't have a very clear grasp of how the FBI worked, but I knew enough that it wasn't like in the movies — they couldn't just swoop in anytime they wanted. I'd already learned that, at least in some cases, they had to be invited by the local authorities before they could act. In this case, people were still questioning whether there was a crime at all, let alone one that fell under FBI jurisdiction, or at least they hadn't said so publicly. So James couldn't do much more than he was already doing, sniffing around the edges. If we could prove there was an art theft and/or fraud involved, that would be different.

Could anyone autopsy a dead fire engine?

CHAPTER 12

I awoke with the word *fire* running through my head. Fires were fascinating, primitive. Why else did so many people gather to watch a fire in progress? I'd been guilty of that myself, when years earlier a house in my neighborhood had been struck by lightning and the attic caught fire. I'd felt a mix of fear and fascination. From what little I'd read about the subject, firemen had always been kind of macho types. I mean, really — they used to hold competitions to see how far they could squirt their hoses?

I spent my days amidst literally tons of dry, old paper, which anyone could ignite with a single match and which could quickly burn out of control, and if I allowed myself to think about it, that made me very uncomfortable. Note to self: *Look up the status of the Society's fire control systems.* Second note to self: *Make sure my home fire extinguisher is in working order and figure out how to use it.* Once a fire had started, it would be a little late to stop and read the instructions.

As I ate breakfast, I continued to puzzle over James's request. The FBI strongly discouraged its agents from involving civilians in investigations, with good reason — and James himself had told me so on more than one occasion. On the other hand, I had insights into a particular community that most agents lacked, so I could make a contribution. On the third hand, someone had died, which made this situation more critical. On the fourth hand — or was I up to feet now? — I didn't want to betray any confidences that a colleague might share with me, because I had to keep working with these people in the long run. I didn't know Peter Ingersoll well, so I was unlikely to receive any particularly personal revelations. All I had to do was listen and ask a few innocent and appropriately professional questions. Right?

When I arrived at my office at the Society, Eric was already waiting with a few message slips and a cup of coffee for me. "Do you have spy cameras on the corner outside, so you know when I'll be here?" I joked.

Eric smiled shyly. "Nope, but I looked up the train schedule, and I know you generally take the same train every day. I can even check to see if the train is on time."

Ah, the wonders of modern technology — which took the mystery out of a lot of things. I reached for the coffee cup and said, "Anything important this early?"

"Agent Morrison left a message. And Latoya's called twice — she seems upset about something."

That didn't sound good. Did she know about Alice already? I had been planning to tell her, really — this morning. Of course, as president I had every right to hire whomever I chose, but maybe I ought to have at least left Latoya a message. Had Marty said something?

"Thank you, Eric." I decided to finish my coffee before I confronted Latoya. Which was a nice theory, but it didn't work, because three minutes later she came charging into my office.

"When were you planning to tell me about this little *intern* you hired?" She made it sound as though I'd brought in a hooker or something.

I was not going to apologize. "Latoya, this only came about late yesterday. When I went to tell you, you'd already left for the day. Shut the door, will you?" When she grudgingly complied, I went on. "This is more

156

complicated than it appears — she comes with dollars attached, and hiring her is a favor to Marty Terwilliger and a donor. I'm sure you can find something for her to do. In fact, I've got an idea." I proceeded to outline my grand if vague scheme for focusing on the Terwilliger Collection.

Eventually she nodded. "I can see that makes sense."

"How did you even find out about her?"

Latoya smiled, not without malice. "She's waiting downstairs in the reading room."

"Oh," I said lamely. Well, the girl was certainly eager. "I said I'd get back to her by the end of the week. I thought we ought to get Nicholas settled before we saddled him with help. Has he given you a firm date yet?"

She gave me a long look and then started laughing. "Apparently he and his employer agreed that there was no point in waiting. He'll actually be here later this morning, too."

I had to join in her laughter. "Well, there you go. Fully staffed, and more."

"I'll let you know when Nicholas arrives. I think we should talk to him and Rich and the intern together. You can explain your vision to them, and I'll walk them through the details. Finish your coffee now," she said sweetly, and she stood and went out the door.

I seized the free moment to return James's call.

"There's been another fire," he said without preamble when he picked up the phone. "Warehouse. Different neighborhood. I'm still not sure the museum's fire is part of this series, but I thought it might be helpful if you and I talked with a specialist."

How had he known I was going to agree to help? "What kind of specialist?" I asked.

"An arson profiler."

"I didn't even know there was such a thing."

"There is — and there's a good one in the Philadelphia area. Could you meet tomorrow at nine?"

"That should work," I said, looking at my calendar.

"Actually, her office is close to your neighborhood — West Chester. You want to meet at the university there?"

I did some mental calculations. West Chester was definitely the suburbs, like my neighborhood of Bryn Mawr, but it was actually west and south of me. Why was it that people who lived in the city had no clue where anything outside of the city was? "Why don't you pick me up at my place on your way? Then we can ride together back to the city."

"All right. I'll be there tomorrow by nine." He hung up.

By the time I'd replaced my phone, Latoya was back with Nicholas in tow. "Here he is, Nell. Where do you want to start?" I could see she was enjoying my confusion — things were moving a little too fast for me.

And then the pace picked up. I was trying to think up a response to Nicholas and Latoya when the phone rang and Eric called out, "It's Bob at the front desk. Something about a delivery from the FBI?"

Oh, shoot — the missing documents! James had said he'd release the recovered papers today, but he hadn't said they would show up this fast. I picked up my phone. "Bob? Can you please send the delivery people around to the back entrance? I'll meet them there."

"Will do."

I turned to Latoya. "We've got to find Rich. The Terwilliger papers are here." When she looked confused, I realized I hadn't had a chance to tell her about my conversation with James, either, and I hurried to explain. "The FBI has finally returned our stolen documents, and apparently they're here, right now."

Latoya sniffed. "A little notice might have been helpful." She considered for a moment. "Where do you want to put them? In the vault? Or with the rest of the collection upstairs?"

I was surprised she had even asked. "I don't know — what do you think? They're probably not organized, since the FBI has been sitting on them for a while. I know Rich has moved most of the Terwilliger Collection to the third floor, and we can't just put the other stuff into a public space."

"Then I recommend we bring them up here to the third floor for processing," Latoya said.

"Fine by me," I replied promptly. "Why don't you go down and accept delivery, and I'll see if I can find Rich and let him know."

With that problem solved, sort of, I still had to deal with Nicholas, slouching against the door and looking vaguely disapproving, and with Alice waiting in the reading room. "Nicholas, come with me. I don't know how much you've heard, but we had some theft issues, and the FBI was involved. We've recovered a portion of what was taken from us, and now it's come back to roost. We can use your help in going through it. Oh, and welcome to the Society. We can deal with the formalities later, but right now we have

160

to get this sorted out."

"Good idea," Nicholas said, pushing himself off the door frame.

I led the way to the workroom at the back of the third floor, praying I'd find Rich there. He was, and I thanked the gods. "Rich, I'm so glad you're here!" I looked around the room: there were file boxes scattered everywhere, although I could see they were carefully labeled. "We've got a . . . situation. The good news is that the FBI has released the missing Terwilliger documents. The bad news is that they were just delivered."

"What, now?" Rich looked around the room. "You're telling me you want to put them here?"

"We need to go through them and figure out what's what. At least you'll have help — this is Nicholas Naylor, our new registrar." The two young men exchanged cautious handshakes and kind of mumbled at each other, but I wasn't going to worry about the social niceties. "We just hired him, and I haven't had time to make an announcement to the staff. And there's more help on the way." Rich looked confused, but I didn't have time to explain Alice's presence right now. I turned back to Nicholas. "I have a list of what we know was missing from our collections, and there should be information on the registrar's computer — I know, you haven't even seen it yet, but I'm sure you can figure it out — I'll get you the password. I'll give you a hard copy, which will at least get you started. Rich, Latoya is downstairs at the back door. I asked her to accept delivery, but she'll need help getting things moved upstairs. Can you go down?"

"Uh, sure," Rich said, still looking a bit startled. Whatever he had planned for the day clearly wasn't going to happen. He headed out the door.

"Nicholas, do you think you can set up some sort of method to inventory what's coming in?"

He nodded, unruffled. "Sure. How much stuff are we talking about?"

I realized I wasn't exactly sure. Items had vanished from our collections over a long period, but I didn't know how much had been recovered. "I really don't know. Maybe we should go down, too, and take a look? Follow me."

I led him down the back stairs to the loading dock at the back of the building. Latoya met me as I opened the door from the hall. "Nell, you've got to see this," she said, her eyes gleaming. She led me out the back door onto the loading dock, where a truck was backed up, its doors open.

"What?" I said, looking at her, then at the truck.

"How many boxes did you expect?" Latoya asked.

"I don't know. A dozen?" And then I realized what she was saying. "Wait — there's no way we lost this much stuff. Is there?"

She shook her head. "No. I've gone over our records, such as they are, with a fine-tooth comb. I've been in regular contact with the FBI. This far exceeds my estimates."

"Is there an inventory list? Are you sure this is all for us? They want us to sign something."

Mutely she handed me a clipboard with a multipart form attached. I scanned it quickly, but it didn't help much. All I could make out was a line item: *Documents (167 boxes)*. Ours was the only name on the "Deliver To" line. I gulped. "This can't be right," I whispered, mostly to myself.

And then the light dawned: oh my God, James must have sent us *everything* the FBI had recovered, not just ours. Which made sense, because how could the FBI have known which pieces were ours? But 167 boxes? I glanced at Rich, and he looked as panicked as I felt.

"Uh, ma'am, I need a signature so I can start unloading," the delivery driver said.

I looked at Latoya. "Do I sign?"

She shrugged. "I'd rather we had the documents under our stewardship than bouncing around the city."

She had a point. I had no idea how the FBI had handled them, but further wear and tear jostling around in the back of a delivery truck, not to mention repeated loading and unloading, couldn't be good for fragile documents and artifacts — assuming that's what they all were. I took the pen clipped to the board and signed. "Start unloading. Rich, can you coordinate? We'll need a couple of rolling carts or dollies, at the very least."

Rich snapped out of his apparent shell shock. "Okay. And let me go up and segregate the T-Collection, so we don't get even more muddled."

"What do you want me to do?" Nicholas asked.

"I guess go with Rich and help him prepare upstairs. We can't start processing everything until we've got all this unloaded." One hundred and sixty-seven boxes, and not a label on any one of them. I felt faint. And if they weren't all the Society's materials, what the heck was in those boxes?

He and Rich exchanged nods, and Nicholas followed Rich back to the hallway, leaving Latoya and me to cope with the unloading. "What's going on here?" she said.

"I didn't know anything about this until late yesterday. From what I understand, the FBI located our missing items in the home of a local collector. My guess is that they've decided to dump everything they retrieved from him in our laps, and leave it for us to sort out. Good God, who knows how long this guy has been collecting, and from how many sources — and how much is his, acquired legally? This is one royal headache."

It was only when I'd reached the front elevator that I remembered poor Alice. I continued past the elevator to where she waited in the reading room. "Alice," I said. She jumped to her feet. "I thought you were going to wait to hear from me, but I'm glad you're here. Follow me."

She did. In the elevator she said, "I didn't mean to barge in, but I talked to Uncle Edward last night, and —"

"We can talk about it later. Right now we have a crisis, and you can help."

"Okay," she said, looking bewildered.

I led her to the workroom, currently Rich's domain. "Rich, Nicholas, this is Alice Price. She's our new intern. I'll explain later. Right now we've got to deal with this delivery, so put her to work. Rich, do you have a lab coat or something she can wear? This may be a bit grubby."

Rich rallied quickly — it probably didn't hurt that Alice was young and pretty, although I knew that he'd been seeing Carrie, the membership coordinator, for a while now. "Uh, sure. Come with me. And then you can start moving the boxes on the table here to that corner" — he pointed — "to make room for the new stuff."

When Rich had herded Alice away, Nicholas turned to me. "Is it always like this?"

I shook my head. "Almost never, I swear. Look, you all work out how to unload everything, and then we can reconvene. Okay?" I figured that would keep them busy while I called James with a few questions.

He nodded again and turned to follow Rich. I stormed back to my office, startling poor Eric. I did manage to refrain from slamming the door behind me. I sat, took a couple of deep breaths, and called James.

When I finally got through, I said, "What the hell is going on?"

"Problem?" he asked.

"Quite a few, thanks to you. When you said you'd release the documents, I thought

166

there would be a nice orderly process and a little advance warning. You know, you'd call, we'd set up a delivery time, deal with all the paperwork — that kind of thing. But no, you have to dump all this stuff on me at once, and I don't even know what most of it is, except I'm pretty sure it's not ours. And you know how crammed our building is — where did you think we'd find space to shove all one hundred and sixty-seven boxes on short notice?"

He did sound a bit taken aback by that. "Oh. I didn't know there were that many. I haven't seen them."

How convenient. "Uh-huh. Well, you're lucky we'd cleared out the upstairs processing room so Rich could spread out the Terwilliger Collection. Otherwise I'd be chewing your head off."

"You aren't doing that now?"

Oh, I was just getting warmed up. "And what about all that other material? I mean, really, we can't be missing more than, oh, a dozen boxes of documents, some small artifacts. What's the story on the other one hundred and whatever? You just delivered a *truckload* of stuff. We didn't *lose* a truckload of stuff!"

"I'm sorry — I didn't get a chance to discuss it with you when you left so quickly.

167

I sent you everything that we found at that guy's house. We don't have the expertise to pull out the bits and pieces you've lost."

"Don't you have an inventory? Or some sort of super database for stolen art?"

"Of course we have an inventory, but since it was written by some field agents, it reads kind of like, *old document, dated 1783.* And we've got a couple of stolen-artifact databases, in fact. But the records are incomplete or inconclusive. If they are stolen, a lot of places may not know they've lost anything, or they chose not to report it. You should know all about that, Nell."

I did, only too well, based on our own experience, and I'd talked to several of my colleagues at similar institutions. Sometimes admitting your security wasn't up to par was worse PR than losing the items themselves.

He went on. "And as you have pointed out before, written descriptions of historic documents aren't worth a whole lot. Scanned images or photographs, now, we could work with —"

"Yet that's precisely what most places like the Society don't have, for the bulk of their collections," I cut in, finishing his statement for him. "I know that, you know that. So, what — all these boxes are orphaned documents?" I leaned back in my chair.

"For the moment. Look, I'm out of my depth here, and that's why I turned to you and your team of experts. If you can identify any of these documents — and there's other stuff mixed in, in case you haven't looked yet — then we will return them to their legal owners."

"Did this guy come by *any* of it legally?"

"He could produce purchase records for some of it, but we're still checking to see if they're legitimate. We just impounded all of it."

I swallowed, feeling overwhelmed. "Please tell me, in words of one syllable, what the ownership status of all those documents is?"

"Murky. Sorry, that's two syllables. But it's true. The Society kept decent records, particularly for the important stuff, which describes mostly what went missing, and you and Marty can identify those pieces that came from the Society. As for the rest . . ." He trailed off. "I thought you'd be pleased."

Immediately I felt contrite: he thought he was doing something nice for me, and here I was yelling at him. "With all the other boxes of who-knows-what?" I sighed. "Maybe I will be, once we figure out what's what here. What do you want me to do now?"

"As I said, catalog it."

"James! I don't have the kind of staffing or time to do that. Certainly not pro bono." But a thought was creeping into my head. "Unless, of course, you plan to pay us for this?"

He was quick to answer — and I thought he sounded relieved. "Of course. The Society would receive an appropriate consulting fee for its services." He named a figure that stunned me into momentary silence. We could do a lot with that kind of money . . . if we ever actually saw it. I didn't quite trust government agencies. And we'd have to staff up, just a bit. Maybe. We did have two new hires . . .

"What about items that you can't identify as either legitimate or stolen? What happens to them?" I suspected there could be quite a few.

"I'd have to look into that. But you'd rather you had custody, don't you?"

I sighed again. "Yes. At least we know how to take care of the items, so they won't deteriorate. The problem is, at least one of my so-called experts is untested, at least by me. If he's good at what he does, we're in pretty good shape, but I really don't know yet what he's capable of. What can you tell me about the guy who collected the stuff?

When you said *house,* I was picturing something like a two-story modern colonial with a cozy den lined with shelves, but to house all of this stuff — not to mention keep it hidden from people — he must have had quite a large space."

James chuckled. "Actually, you're not far off about the house, but he stored everything in an old bomb shelter. It was under the house, and he did modify the heating and cooling to protect his precious collections."

"Was it damp?" Which could mean all sorts of bad things for the documents.

"He kept a permanent dehumidifier going."

That sounded promising. "What on earth did his wife think?"

"She hated the shelter and never went down there. She did, however, wonder where all their money was going. I gather collecting is not a cheap hobby, even if you get a lot of your pieces under the table, so to speak."

James believed he had done me a favor, and reluctantly I had to admit that he was probably right. The Society was reasonably well equipped to assess the mass of purloined papers, or whatever they were; certainly far better than FBI field agents, and I

171

doubted they had a lot of specialists on staff. And since he was willing to pay for our expertise, it was a win-win situation. Kind of. I just wished he had warned me. Now I'd have to figure out who to assign to what, when I didn't even know the capabilities of my new staffers. Plus I'd have to figure out what of our own work could wait while we sorted through the FBI materials.

"You'd better work out how you want to handle ownership before I ask my staff to take this on."

"Would the Society be interested in keeping the orphaned materials?" Now he sounded mildly amused, and I suspected he was manipulating me.

"Not until I see what's in the boxes. Let me get back to you on that." After all, maybe it was all dreck and we wouldn't want any of it.

"I'll see you tomorrow morning, at nine."

My head was spinning. In the space of a day, we had added two new employees — and a mass of material for them to work on, that would occupy far more than the time they had. But there could be a financial reward, and some good PR (if the FBI would let us talk about helping them out), and maybe even some new acquisitions (if we could work out the sticky ownership questions). It was a lot to take in.

Before I ascended to the giddy heights of the presidency, I would have been in the cataloging room digging into the boxes with both hands. Now I couldn't even consider that: this was a collections problem, which meant Latoya was responsible for it, with the help of her fledgling employees. I decided to compromise: I'd restrain myself and go back to my desk and do presidential things, but I'd visit the cataloging room periodically, just to keep an eye on things. That way I'd get to know our new hires and see how they worked with each other and with Rich, and I'd get to snoop through all those boxes and see what was really in them. It could be dreck — but it could be wonderful, and I was itching to find out.

And then James and I would have a serious talk. "I think you owe me a dinner. Or the FBI does," I said.

He surprised me by saying, "Tonight?"

"Uh, okay." At least by then I'd have a better idea of what he had dumped in our laps. "You want to meet me here?"

"Sevenish?"

"Sounds good. See you then." I ended the call and sat back in my chair. This day was not turning out the way I had expected.

■ ■ ■ ■

I divided the rest of the day between trying to get my regular work done and visiting the processing room to see what progress the crew was making with the FBI documents. All right, I'll admit I sneaked a few peeks into some of the boxes while I was there, because I was curious to see what we'd reaped. I liked what I saw, but as a whole the project seemed daunting.

Since most people had cleared out of the building by seven, I went downstairs to wait for James — after taking one last look at the boxes stacked all over the processing room. Rich, Nicholas, and Alice were still hard at work but looked a bit frazzled now.

"Rich, if you're going to stay much longer, can you see that Alice and Nicholas get out of the building safely and make sure the alarm is activated? Oh, and I've got an appointment out of the office in the morning, so please check in with Latoya first thing about getting your employment paperwork started. So, what do you think?"

"We've got everything up here now, so by tomorrow we should be able to start sorting out what's what," Rich volunteered.

"I'll bring my laptop in the morning,"

Nicholas said. "My software's already installed on it, and I can set up an entry protocol."

"Sounds good. Remind me tomorrow to set you up with the former registrar's system — you'll need a password. Alice, how do you think it went?"

"Wow," she said. "There's some great stuff here. I can't believe I get to lay hands on it all. With gloves, of course," she added quickly.

"Of course," I said. "Then I'll see you three tomorrow. Good work, all of you!"

Downstairs I let myself out the front door and stood in the lee of the massive bluestone columns in front of the building, watching for James. I knew he'd probably be on foot, since his office was only a few blocks away. Maybe that was how he stayed in such good shape. Did the local FBI offices have a gym on the premises? If so, were agents required to use it?

He still managed to sneak up on me. "You seem to have survived the day," he said, arriving at the bottom of the steps.

"No thanks to you," I said, joining him on the sidewalk. "As I've already said, a little warning might have been helpful."

He shrugged. "It wasn't my call. The materials were cleared, and the powers that be wanted them out of our storage facilities ASAP. I figured you could handle it. You still mad?"

"Not really. You were just darned lucky that we're adequately staffed to handle your little gift. And I'll hold you to that offer of a consulting fee."

"I expect nothing less," he said. I suspected he was quashing a smile. "Where do you want to eat?"

"I haven't got the energy to enjoy anything fancy. Why don't we stroll over to Spruce Street and see what looks good?"

"Fine. You said you've added staff?"

I filled him in on the circumstances surrounding Nicholas's and Alice's precipitous arrival this morning, which took us the short distance to Spruce Street, tree lined and pleasant in the spring dusk. I couldn't remember if I'd eaten lunch, or if I had, what it was. We picked a small bistro that looked quiet but smelled wonderful, and were escorted by a waiter to a fairly private corner table.

"So, tell me more about your daring rescue of the purloined documents," I began after we ordered drinks.

James stopped me quickly. "Nell, can we save the business talk for some other time? Tomorrow morning, maybe?"

It took me a moment to realize that he was referring to our appointment with the arson profiler. "Well, all right, if you want. Was there something else you wanted to talk about?"

He smiled. "You said something about a *date?*"

"What, this is a date?"

He looked at me then. "It is if we manage to talk about something other than business."

"Oh." He'd caught me by surprise. Sure, we had been seeing each other, sort of, for a few months now, but our time together usually involved FBI or Society activities rather than anything personal. I realized I wasn't sure I knew where to start. "You know, I probably know more about you than you know about me."

"From cousin Marty, I assume?" he asked.

"Yes. She still thinks of you as one of the gang, not as an FBI agent. You know, serious and scary."

"Am I scary?"

"Well, you do carry a gun."

"There is that. Look, Nell, if this is making you uncomfortable, we can go back to talking about art theft or whatever."

Was it? I wasn't sure — and I wasn't sure if I'd respect myself if it was. "Okay, cards on the table? I've got a new job at a place that's struggling to survive, and it keeps me very busy and eats up most of my energy. I'll be the first to admit that I have next to no life outside of the job. The only reason I met you was because of Alfred's death and the thefts he uncovered. I have no idea what would have happened between us if we'd connected through a computer dating service or at a party somewhere. I probably would have written you off as a stuffy bureaucrat."

"You're saying it's strictly business between us?"

I could swear he looked disappointed. Interesting. "No. Or, I mean, maybe that's what it's been so far, but that doesn't mean that's what I want going forward."

Of course the waiter chose that moment to appear with our drinks and ask for our orders, and I hadn't even managed to read the menu. At least that gave me a little breathing room, although I picked a dish at random. Regardless, it was not enough time to decide what I really did want from James.

"And what is that?" he said gravely.

"What?" It took me a moment to realize what he was referring to. "You mean, what do I want? I . . . don't know. Look, I like you. A lot. You're a good guy, all around.

And because we keep getting thrown together for reasons that have nothing to do with us, I guess I haven't had to make any decisions about how to move onward."

"Would this be easier if I was an accountant?"

"Maybe. Then it would be my choice. Can I ask you a question?"

"Of course."

"Have you ever been married?"

"No. Came close a time or two, but the job — and that gun — kind of scares a lot of women off."

Some women, maybe. "I was, once — but of course, you know that. It was nice, but it ended — we just weren't a good match. I have no regrets. I like my life — at least, most of the time. I like not having to answer to anyone. Can you understand that?"

"I think so. But is it enough for you?"

"It has been, until now." I paused to take a sip of wine. "What about you? Are you content to play the lone wolf? I mean, you know about me and Charles. Hasn't there been anyone in your life?"

"Now and then. It never lasted."

I sat back in my chair and stared at him. "So what are we doing here?"

He sat back as well and returned my look. "I do want something more. I think you're

179

an extraordinary woman — smart, capable, sympathetic, hardworking, dedicated to what you believe in. I want to know you better. I want you to know *me* better. I want us to find the time to make that happen."

"Who gets the chicken?" the waiter said, hovering with hot plates.

CHAPTER 13

Somehow the waiter's intrusion had broken the mood, and by the time he had distributed our food and departed, James and I had backed away from whatever brink we'd been teetering on. But the question was now out there and hanging between us: what did we want? What I had said was true: I thought he was a great guy. I was definitely attracted to him, and since he kept showing up, I guessed that he was attracted to me. But finding a way to take the next step was tricky. Maybe after we'd sorted out whatever had happened to the fire engine and who was behind it, we could take some time for ourselves. Right now we needed to focus on that, rather than on the chemistry between us. If we could.

Always the gentleman, James had walked me back to the nearest station after dinner so I could catch my train home. I was used to walking the dark streets of Center City, but it was comforting to have his solid presence next to me. Suburban Station did not lend itself to intimacy, even late in the evening, so our good-byes had been anything but steamy.

In the morning I was waiting for him when he knocked on my door. He seemed startled that I opened it so quickly. "Good morning," I said brightly.

"I see you got home safely," he replied.

"I did. Thank you for dinner, and for the escort."

"My pleasure."

Jane Austen would have been proud of us. Could we get any stuffier?

"May I come in?" he asked.

"Of course. Would you like some coffee, or are we in a hurry?" I stepped back to let him into the house.

"Coffee sounds good. Professor Evans said any time this morning would be fine — she doesn't have any classes until this afternoon."

"Coffee it is, then." I went to the kitchen to boil water.

I could hear James roaming around my living room, even though as I knew he had seen it before. But then, there wasn't room for two people in my tiny kitchenette. When the kettle whistled, he drifted over to the entrance to the kitchen and leaned against the door frame.

"How will you plan to explain my presence to Professor Evans?" I asked as I poured boiling water over coffee grounds.

"By telling the truth: you're assisting the FBI in their inquiries."

"That's pretty vague. Are you — or the FBI — officially involved in the case now?" I handed him a mug of coffee.

"Yes, finally. There have been five arson fires in the last month, and the police are officially stumped. They've asked us to help, formally, but only for the arson aspect."

I wasn't sure if that made me feel better or worse. Clearly the police knew they were out of their depth and had done the right thing, but that also meant that this case would be getting a lot of public attention, which sometimes made it harder to find who was behind it. After all, this guy had already successfully set five fires — if in fact they were all related — and gotten away with it. "What about the dead guard? Is it officially a murder now?"

"We're downplaying that for the moment."

A nonanswer. Well, that wasn't my department anyway. "Do we have time to sit for a few minutes and drink our coffee?" I asked.

"Of course." So we sat at my small dining table and talked about nothing of importance for a few minutes. I could tell he was getting impatient, so once I'd emptied my cup, I said, "Are you ready to go?"

He drained his mug. "I am. How far is it to West Chester?"

"About half an hour, depending on which route you take — and how fast you drive. Are you in a hurry?"

"I'd like to be back in the city by noon."

"Then we'll take the nonscenic route."

In fact, it took almost precisely half an hour to reach West Chester — and another ten minutes to find parking at the university. It was a midsize member of the state's public education system, with maybe fifteen thousand students, most of whom appeared to own cars and park them on campus. I knew from experience — I had visited the town's nice, small historical society on more than one occasion — that searching for parking in the surrounding town wouldn't be any more fruitful. I wondered if FBI agents could get parking tickets fixed.

We arrived at the Department of Criminal Justice a few minutes past ten. James apparently knew where he was going, and after a few turns he stopped in front of a door with a frosted glass panel, knocked, then went in ahead of me. Professor Celia Evans turned out to be a woman maybe ten years older than me, with a short, no-nonsense haircut and intelligent eyes. She came around the desk to greet him — with a hug. "James, it's good to see you again! It's been too long. And this must be . . . ?" She turned to me.

I extended a hand. "I'm Nell Pratt, from the Pennsylvania Antiquarian Society."

"Of course. James mentioned you when he called, said you were helping him on an FBI problem."

"I'm happy to help if I can."

"Please, sit down. Coffee?" We both declined the coffee, and Celia resumed her seat behind the desk. "So, where do you want to start? Nell, do you know anything about what I do?"

I shook my head. "James hasn't really had time to fill me in. Can you give me the short form?"

"Sure. As you can see, I teach, but I also founded the Arson Study Forum, oh, twenty-five years ago now. We study the people who set fires, and that extends to domestic terrorists. That's where I intersect with the FBI, which keeps a database of arson events nationwide — they've been kind enough to share their statistics with me. I've written and lectured extensively on

185

the subject. So, what've you got for me, James?"

"Five warehouse fires in the past month, within Philadelphia city limits."

Celia nodded. "Of course. I've been reading about those." She leaned back in her swivel chair and laced her fingers together. "Now, why do I think there's more to it than a possible arsonist?" Her eyes darted briefly to me.

As did James's. "As you've probably read in the papers," he began, "one of the fires destroyed a local museum collection that had been put in storage during a renovation campaign. What you haven't read — and this is off the record, Celia — is that there's an outside possibility that the fire was deliberately set for just that purpose, in order to claim the insurance."

"The museum needed the money more than it needed its collections?" Celia arched an eyebrow.

"One piece in particular was worth a nice chunk of change. If it actually burned," James said. When Celia looked confused, James nodded toward me for an explanation.

I looked back at him. "James, how much am I at liberty to say?"

"You mean, can we trust Celia? Of

course."

"All right, then. The collection that burned belonged to the Fireman's Museum."

Celia laughed briefly. "Oh my! I'm sorry, but you have to admit that it's rather ironic."

James nodded. "We didn't broadcast that to the public. It *would* be funny, if the night watchman hadn't died in the fire. Or at least, his body was found there afterward."

Celia sobered immediately. "Oh dear. That is a tragedy. But you two believe it was something more than arson? Was it aimed at the watchman, do you think?"

"He was dead before the fire began — a blow to the head — but it's not clear whether that was an accident or not. The watchman was a former firefighter named Allan Brigham, and there's nothing in his record that suggests he was a target."

Celia looked critically at him. "What aren't you telling me?"

"If — and it's still a big if — the collection was the target, then Brigham's death may have been collateral damage. Or he may have been a participant at some point and then was eliminated. We still have a lot of questions."

"And how does Nell here come to be involved?" Celia asked.

My cue. "The president of the museum

187

came to me shortly after the fire to ask for whatever records we had of the collection, to file the insurance claim. We didn't have a lot of material, but I gave him copies of what we had, including pictures of the antique fire engine that was the centerpiece of the collection. To make a long story short, when I compared those photos to the photos of the charred hulk that appeared in the *Inquirer,* I thought they weren't the same piece of equipment. And I told James."

"James, did you agree?" When he nodded, Celia went on. "So you suspect that this fire was set deliberately not only for the insurance but also to conceal a theft?"

James jumped back in. "I was skeptical at first, but I thought the pictures that Nell showed me were convincing enough to warrant further investigation. I haven't seen all the reports, but I think there's something funny going on here."

"Have you talked to anyone at the fire department?" Celia said.

"Not yet. This is tricky, you know. The museum in question has close ties with the city and the fire department. I don't have any friends on the inside there, and I don't want to go barging into a city department and start flinging accusations around."

"What about the museum side? I take it

that's where you come in, Nell?"

I nodded. "As I said, I'm acquainted with the president of the museum, but we're not even close to friends. But since he asked me to help, James thinks I can nose around from my side and see if I can learn anything — for example, if the museum is in serious financial trouble, which could explain a motive. Or if there's some disgruntled employee or ex-employee who wants to do harm to it. But as James pointed out, you've also got to remember that this is kind of a quasi-municipal institution. They're officially a nonprofit organization, but their ties to the fire department are pretty tight. It's hard to separate them. Do *you* know anyone there?"

"At the museum? I may have met a few people on the board, but my interests are primarily academic, and the talks I give are not well suited to the museum's interests. Nor, as I recall, do they have any public space for lectures. I've had more contact with the fire department, as you might guess." She thought for a few long moments. "What are you asking of me?"

James and I exchanged a look, then answered. "There are only a few people who knew the museum collection was in the warehouse that burned, and who would also

189

know how to sell the fire engine. This wasn't just a smash-and-grab — this took planning. And the same thing would apply to the fire. Whoever did this had to make arrangements to get into the building and remove the fire engine and then replace it with another, less valuable one, and only then could they set the fire to cover up the theft. And apparently they were careful in how they set it, because it took awhile to really catch."

"So clearly it was not a spontaneous act," Celia said. "And they were trying to delay anyone noticing? Does that mean they knew the watchman was . . . out of commission and unlikely to report it?"

I hadn't even considered that. Whether or not the watchman had been in on the theft, he had been taken out of the equation before the fire was set.

James nodded. "Exactly. And as I said, only a few people had knowledge of where the collection was. Unfortunately most of them would also know of how to dispose of it, and would have plenty of knowledge about fires and how to set them."

"I see your problem. But again, what are you asking of me?"

"If the fire that destroyed the museum collection was a fire-for-hire, so to speak, how likely is it that the others are related? Is it possible that the multiple fires were intended to cover up the museum one and make it look less obvious? Or did whoever stole the fire engine take advantage of what was already going on, and apparently still is? And where do you go to recruit an arsonist?"

Celia laughed. "Well, that's quite a few questions, isn't it? How much do you know about arsonists, James? Or you, Nell?"

"Only what I've seen on television," I said, "and I don't assume that's accurate."

"I've worked on a couple of arson cases, but I can't claim to be an expert," James added.

Celia nodded her approval. "All right. You have to ask, does this person, whoever he is, now or as a child, have any behavioral problems? ADHD? Difficulties in school or with personal relationships? Is he aggressive and confrontational? Is he a bully or known to be cruel to others?"

"Are you sure it's a man rather than a woman?" I asked.

"That's generally true — among arsonists men heavily outweigh women, particularly at a younger age. Are your suspects young or old?"

Exactly who were we considering suspects? I asked myself. If it was a museum insider, that meant a pretty short list of Peter and Scott Ingersoll, Jennifer Phillips, and Gary O'Keefe. Maybe a board member? How was I supposed to answer Celia's question? "I'd say adult, not young, but I have no information about their earlier history. Tell me, would it be unusual for someone to suddenly turn to setting fires later in life, or would there be a pattern leading up to it?"

"To some extent, yes, it would be unusual, and yes, there usually is a pattern. But you also have to remember that the person who planned this and the person who carried out the fire may not be the same person."

I hadn't wanted to consider that, since it would only complicate things, but now it was on the table. "So, either there's an arsonist setting the warehouse fires and someone else took advantage of that to start a fire for his own ends, or maybe whoever organized the theft commissioned the fire. That sounds odd, doesn't it? Are there arsonists for hire? I mean, people who don't set fires until and unless someone pays them?"

Celia sighed. "Nell, none of these are simple questions. Yes, it's possible, although I would say that most arsonists act for personal reasons, not for monetary gain, but it has been known to happen. And let me add, just because someone sets a fire doesn't mean that he is an arsonist, in the broadest sense of the word."

I digested that for a moment before asking, "What's the relationship between firefighters and arsonists?"

"Another complicated question. Very broadly, a true arsonist acts to satisfy some internal compulsion, even if he can't explain it, while a firefighter acts to protect the public. At least, we hope so."

"You're implying there are exceptions?"

"On occasion. But that's not to say that firefighters are closet arsonists, in general."

"But would firemen know any arsonists? Even at arm's length? I mean, are there people who have a reputation as fire starters, even if they've never been caught?"

Celia laughed. "It's a very reasonable question, but it's hard to answer. I'd guess firefighters become aware of specific individuals, based on the details of the crime — timing, what devices or accelerants they use, and so on. But that's still a long way from knowing their names or how to find them. I won't say it's impossible, but it seems unlikely. Are you asking if a member of the fire department, or someone who knew a member, could locate an arsonist for hire? It seems rather far-fetched." Celia was silent for several long moments. "You know, putting all these facts together, it sounds as though someone harbors a lot of hostility toward firefighters in general."

"Why do you say that?" James asked.

"If this was a planned crime, as you're suggesting, someone had to have known about the collection and where it was stored. That same someone would have known of the presence of a watchman, and yet, if what you're implying is correct, that fact didn't deter him. Maybe this Brigham wasn't meant to die, but the possibility was there. Psychologically, the arsonist would have taken some perverse satisfaction in simultaneously ripping off the museum devoted to firefighting, stealing their most precious item, and making them look foolish by actually burning the rest of the collection. Sort of a triple whammy. Which doesn't mean he intended to murder anyone."

James nodded. "I hadn't looked at it that way, but you're right. So all we have to do is look for someone associated with the museum who hates firefighters? When most of our suspects have public ties to firefighting?" he asked.

"Don't take this lightly, James," Celia said. "We may be looking at a rapid escalation in behavior following a long history of minor incidents that may never have been reported, and who knows what he might do next? I know that doesn't provide you with much guidance, but it's the best I can do absent any more concrete data."

"I understand, Celia. So let me get this straight: we're probably looking for a man, and he may have had a long but unreported history of setting fires, which may have been prompted by any number of reasons, but which involve some sort of anger toward the fire department or firefighters in general."

"I know it's not much to go on," Celia said. "I'm sorry." She looked at her watch. "I've got a class in an hour, and I need to prepare for it. I can send you some published papers to look over that might be of help to you. Of course, there's my book." She dimpled briefly, and she reached for a bookshelf behind her to pull out a trade-size paper-bound volume. "Nell, let me give you a copy. I think it covers what you need. Then let me know if you think you need more?"

James stood up, and I followed suit. "Thanks, Celia. I appreciate your time." He handed her a large envelope. "These are the reports of all the recent fires. I'd appreciate it if you take a look and see if anything jumps out at you. And keep them under your hat."

Celia took the envelope. "Of course."

"And you know where to find me if anything else occurs to you," James added. "This is an odd one."

"I agree. Nell, nice to meet you. Let me know if you have any further questions." She handed me a business card, and I tucked it in my bag.

"I'll do that. Can I ask, whatever made you go into this line of work?"

She smiled at my question. "I wanted to be an FBI agent, but all they asked was if I could type. I figured this was a good end run." Then the smile left her face. "And I think what I do is important."

"It is, Celia," James said quietly. "We'll get out of your hair now, but thanks again."

"Thank you!" I called over my shoulder as I trailed after James.

As we hiked back the mile or so to the car, I asked, "What did we learn?"

James looked down at me. "Did you want a simple answer? Celia's one of the best researchers in the field, but she'll be the first to admit that people set fires for a wide variety of reasons, logical or not, and it's not easy to pigeonhole them. She was being cautious, but I'd guess that she sees it as unlikely that a fireman would hire an arsonist to do his dirty work, even if he could find one. If — and I mean that seriously — a fireman felt the need to set a fire, either out of compulsion or for illegal purposes, I'd bet he would do it himself."

"Makes sense to me." I was pleased that I had no trouble keeping up with James's long strides — all that walking to and from the station seemed to be paying off. "So that limits the field to people who would know how to set fires — which includes almost everyone involved with the Fireman's Museum. Great."

"You didn't think this would be simple, did you?"

"It never is."

CHAPTER 14

As we drove back to the city, I realized that I was pleased that James had included me, but I was still confused by what I had heard. "James, you said you handled arson cases before?"

"Now and then. That's why I know Celia. She's kind of a unique resource. Read her book," James said, his eyes on the road. "She does provide some broad profiles for the different types of arsonist."

I nudged his shoulder. "You have to turn here to get to the Schuylkill."

"Got it." He moved onto the on-ramp and sped up.

"I guess my problem is, I have trouble seeing any of the people I've met from the Fireman's Museum as arsonists." And, I reminded myself, killers. That was even harder.

"Are you talking about Peter Ingersoll?"

"In part, I guess. He's an administrator,

and he said he has asthma, although I suppose he could have lied about that. But I don't see him hauling heavy equipment around or torching a warehouse. And I was in the room with him when he learned about the warehouse fire. I saw how he reacted. When was it set, do you know?"

"Early morning, according to the fire department, but it spread slowly. It took the department awhile to put it out, and then they found the body. And then they had to figure out who the place belonged to, and only then did they get a handle on who had stuff there. Ingersoll would have had plenty of time to set a fire, go home, shower, shave, and make it to your luncheon."

"So it's not an alibi. I wonder where he lives."

"Rittenhouse Square."

"Do you have a file on him?" I turned in my seat to look at James.

"The police and the FBI have looked at all the principal players."

"Don't tell me you have a file on me!"

"No comment." James's mouth twitched.

I took that as a yes. At least I had nothing to hide, but I wasn't sure how I felt about the FBI snooping into my life. Not that anybody could hide much in this Internet age. Sometimes I yearned for the simpler days when people wrote letters to each other, which often took days or weeks to arrive. Was that why I oversaw collections full of them? Since they were far fewer in number than modern communications, they were more precious, at least to those who cared about such things. And somehow I doubted we would be collecting emails of the rich and famous any time soon.

I pulled my mind back to the arson. "Did you find anything important about anyone?"

"Nothing about setting fires, but they all have some connection with the city fire department or another department."

"Not just Gary? Even Jennifer?"

He nodded, keeping his attention focused on navigating the notorious Schuylkill Expressway. "Jennifer was married to a firefighter and still collects a pension from the department. Peter and Scott's father was a fireman."

"What about criminal records?"

"Only Scott Ingersoll — he seems to be a hothead and has gotten into a few fights, but there's nothing arson related."

I wasn't sure if that was good or bad news. "Well, for the moment I reserve the right to believe that it is possible for anyone to hire a thug to do their dirty work. Have you had any luck identifying a trucker?"

James sighed. "I should have known what I was letting myself into when I asked you to help. I don't suppose I can ask that you limit your questions to your areas of expertise?"

"Look, I understand about confidentiality and FBI rules and all that stuff, but I'll be much more useful to you if I have a better picture of what's going on. What you're looking for. What you've already covered and dismissed. That kind of thing. And you're right — you should know me well enough by now to know that I'm not going to sit quietly in my corner. You may have your own law enforcement turf to protect, but the Philadelphia cultural community is *my* turf. And you know I can keep my mouth shut."

"You are the perfect Girl Scout, Nell. It's not that I don't trust you, but as you point out, I have protocols to follow. Plus, much as I hate to say it, we're just getting up to speed on this whole investigation now, and I don't have a lot to share with you."

"The blind leading the blind. Great. Tell me this — do you think there will be more fires?"

"I don't know. I still don't have enough evidence to say whether the ones we've had are related, or whether there's more than one arsonist running around. It's a big city. And there's another angle we haven't even talked about: it wouldn't surprise me if someone had commissioned these fires to make the fire department look more essential — you know the city is looking to cut the department's budget."

"What, fires as a public relations tool? That's an awful idea."

"Well, if you exclude the one fire that interests us, the others have been relatively benign — no significant loss of property, and they were put out quickly."

"And that looks suspicious?" I asked. "You really think it's just more than the fire department doing a good job?"

He shrugged. "Maybe. Look, I don't want to throw stones at anyone. I respect the fire department and the job they do. But you'll have to admit it's a good cover for the fire engine switch, especially if someone knew there were going to be other fires."

"James!" I said, appalled. "You're really thinking there are two conspiracies here? One to boost the public perception of the fire department, and another to rip off the museum? I'm glad I'm not you, seeing nefarious plots under every rock."

He glanced briefly my way. "Nell, it happens more often than you'd like to think.

But you go right on thinking the best of people. It's part of your charm."

Great. Nell Pratt, aka Pollyanna. Still, I'd rather look for the best in people than assume everyone had an ulterior and malicious motive. Of course, I spent most of my time living with the past, while James was on the front lines of the present. Maybe that made a difference.

We arrived in front of the Society building. James pulled into the bus stop space and stopped the car. "Will you be seeing Ingersoll again, or anyone else associated with the Fireman's Museum?"

"Not that I have scheduled. Do you want me to try to plan something?"

"Only if it looks natural. And I'll trust you not to ask stupid questions."

"You mean, like, *Have you met any arsonists lately?*"

"Exactly." He grinned at me, and I swatted his arm.

"I think you've given me enough work to keep me out of trouble for a while. Let me know if anything else comes up — or burns down." I climbed out of the passenger seat and waved as he pulled away, before marching up the stone steps.

I managed to make it all the way to my office without being interrupted, but when I arrived there Eric looked ready to burst. "Oh, there you are, Nell. It seems like half the staff is looking for you. Rich has called a couple of times, and then Latoya — something about processing the new materials? And Marty's waiting in your office."

Great. If I'd been hoping for a little time for myself, I was out of luck. "Thanks, Eric. I guess I'll deal with Marty first."

I marched into my office and hung up my coat. "Hello, Marty. To what do I owe the pleasure of this visit?"

Marty had been sitting on the settee against the wall, leafing through an issue of *Antiques,* but she jumped up and moved to a chair in front of my desk. "What the hell is going on in processing? I thought your people were working on the Terwilliger Collection?"

I sat down behind my desk. "So no one told you?"

"Told me what?"

I sighed. "The FBI finally released the documents they had seized."

Marty nodded impatiently. "Well, we figured they'd be coming, didn't we? Why is everybody running around like a bunch of headless chickens?"

"Because your cousin James decided to release *all* the documents they'd seized. One hundred and sixty-seven boxes' worth, to be precise. And he sent 'em all here."

It was interesting watching Marty's expressions change, and I sat back and enjoyed the show. First anger, that James had interfered with the processing of her family's beloved collection. Then speculation, as she began to wonder just what else might be in there. Then a kind of glee, when she realized that there might be some really good stuff mixed in and she had first crack at all of it. I waited.

Finally she said, "I don't know whether to kick or kiss that boy. Have you looked through the stuff?"

"Not yet, beyond peeking in a few boxes. It all came in yesterday and what time we had we spent hauling them upstairs. And both Nicholas and Alice showed up early, and I barely had time to introduce them to Rich before the avalanche. And this morning James and I paid a call on an arson expert."

"Why?" Marty relaxed back into her chair, apparently over her snit.

"Because there's been a whole series of fires recently, and he's trying to figure out where the Fireman's Museum fire fits. If it does."

"That's not our problem," she said, brushing aside the issue of the fires. "What're you going to do with the mess here?"

"Most of the materials will be things that we know didn't come from the Society's collections. Nicholas has made some impressive claims about his software package. I figure I'll let him loose on the new materials and see what he can do. And before you ask, the ownership of this stuff is kind of up in the air, so it makes sense if Nicholas keeps it independent of the Society's data, at least for now. He can give his results to the FBI, which should win us some points."

"Any chance the Society'll get to keep any of it?"

I shrugged. "I really don't know. According to James, it depends on whether any of it can be identified as belonging to another institution." Marty snorted. "I know, it's unlikely that we'll be able to trace its ownership. But I also don't know what the FBI can or will do with it. Right now James has asked us to sort through it and identify what we could, period."

"You know anything about the guy who collected all of it?"

"Not much. I think James told me when they arrested the guy that he was into the Civil War, but that's about all I know."

"You gonna let me get my hands on any

of this?" Marty said with an evil gleam in her eye.

I was surprised that she actually asked permission. "Within limits. You can identify the Terwilliger stuff, which demonstrably belongs to the Society, so we need you there. That means you're going to have to be involved in sorting through it all, at least the first pass. Will that make you happy?"

"It's a start." Marty stood up. "Want to get going?"

"Marty, I need to get some lunch, and I need to go smooth some ruffled feathers and make sure everyone is working together. Not necessarily in that order. Why don't we go over to the workroom now and make sure nobody has come to blows yet?"

"Excellent," Marty said, and led the way.

I had to rush to keep up with her. She pushed through the doorway with me on her heels, and we were confronted by a scene of controlled chaos. At least I hope it was controlled; the chaos part was a steady state. It was a large single room with windows along the outside wall. Large tables were distributed throughout the room, and various supplies and works in progress were scattered around the perimeter, on shelves, under the tables, and anywhere else there was room. Now there were 167 boxes shoehorned between the tables — and three people at opposite corners, looking none too happy.

I sneaked a look at Marty, who appeared to be enjoying herself. But then, she wasn't the one who had to clear up the mess, literal and figurative. It was time for me to step up to the plate. "Rich, Nicholas, Alice — I'm glad to see you all here." That much was true. "And I'm sorry I wasn't here earlier this morning to explain and to get you pointed in the right direction, although I'm sure Latoya and Rich can do a much better job with that last part. Grab a stool, why don't you? This may take a little time."

They sat, without moving any closer together, and I reviewed for them what I understood about the situation, based on what James had told me. I wouldn't swear that I had the whole story yet, but it was the best I had to work with. I finished up by saying, "I think this is a great way to get you started — you can jump into sorting and cataloging with both feet, and we have no idea what you'll find. Pretend it's a treasure hunt. Plus you'll be garnering the gratitude of the FBI, which can't hurt — especially if you're planning anything il-legal." When nobody even smiled, I hurried to add, "That was a joke. We take honesty, and the integrity of our reputation, very seriously here. All I'm saying is that this is a good opportunity for you to learn to work together, and you could find some interesting material here. Nicholas, you'll be using your software for this? You won't be hampered by having to compare it to our current records, in the event that your software isn't compatible with ours. Rich and Marty between them can cull out the Terwilliger papers, and you can handle the rest."

He nodded, his expression still serious. "That makes sense. I don't have to hand my software over to the FBI, do I?"

"Just the output, not the program."

"What do you want me to do?" Alice said.

"Whatever Rich asks you to do. Plus I'm hoping that you can take what Nicholas comes up with and create an overview report that we can send to the FBI. You know, more qualitative than numerical, describing the scope of the collected materials, their quality, and so on. You all can work together on this, can't you?" I scanned the group and was relieved to see that they were beginning to look a little happier. "How about you three come up with a preliminary assessment by, say, the end of the week? And include how much time you estimate it will take to get through all this. Then we can sit down together and work out a plan. Sound good?"

Three heads nodded.

"Great! I'll go talk to Latoya about it. You three — get to work!"

I turned on my heel and went out the door, with Marty close behind. "That was fun!" she said.

"Maybe for you. Do you agree with my plan?"

"I do, overall. And I'll hang around and make sure they don't miss anything from the Terwilligers."

"Why am I not surprised?"

CHAPTER 15

Now I had to go explain the whole situation to Latoya. How was it that I kept having to defend myself to that woman? Yes, collections was her domain, and she was entitled to make decisions that pertained to collections — acquisition, cataloging, physical maintenance. I subscribed to the idea that one should hire good people and let them do their job, without hovering over their shoulder and second-guessing all their decisions. Not that I'd been the one to hire Latoya, although I had no argument with her qualifications. Still, I know I'd resent that kind of treatment, and yet here I was, stepping all over Latoya's toes. But I was in an unusual and awkward position, since it was my *special relationship* with the FBI that had created this problem. There was no way I was going to give Latoya the option of saying no to the FBI.

I squared my shoulders and marched

down the hall. When I reached Latoya's door, it was closed, so I knocked and waited politely for her to invite me in. She took her own sweet time about it. When I finally walked in, she looked up in surprise. "Oh, Nell — I didn't know it was you. What can I do for you?"

I sat without waiting for her to ask. "I wanted to give you an update about what's going on with that material we received yesterday."

Latoya sat back in her chair. "Ah, yes, the FBI dump. I did check in on the young ones this morning and encouraged them to cooperate with each other. I take it you've talked to your, uh, contact at the FBI?"

"I have. He says the agency wants us to go through it and see what we can identify. Our missing items, of course, but we should at least give him enough written detail on the rest that he can compare the other pieces to any of the available databases of stolen items."

"I see. Did you tell him we have no space, no staff, and no time to undertake something like this, particularly without warning?"

"I did, but I also told him that we would find a way to make time. We stand to gain much more than we lose by doing this, starting with the goodwill of the FBI. Not to mention, they'll pay us, enough to support the new staff for the time it takes. Plus there's some possibility that we might get to keep the confiscated materials, if legalities permit."

"Ah," she said. "I wish you had done me the courtesy of discussing this with me first. But all right. What do you want me to do?"

"Supervise the team. I've asked them to do a first pass and create an action plan and a timetable. You need to make sure they're on track."

"What about the Terwilliger Collection?"

"I've already talked to Marty, and she's okay with this. You can bet that she's going to be involved all along the way, because she's the best person to sniff out her family's documents from the piles. In fact, she's already in the workroom."

"Very well," she said at last. "I'll keep an eye on them. All of them."

"I already put them to work, so sooner would be better than later. Have you contacted human resources?"

"Of course." This time it looked as though Latoya was swallowing a reply. "Was there anything else?"

"No." Apparently I'd been dismissed — again. When was she going to acknowledge me as her boss? And when was I going to stop feeling like a guilty schoolgirl every time I walked into her office? I stood up. "Let me know if you have any other ideas." I walked out with what I hoped was a dignified demeanor.

Instead of stopping at my office, I kept on going down the hall to Shelby's office. My old office. Sometimes I wished I was still there, and all I had to do was produce pages of numbers and concise reports and the occasional request for funding. Alas, no more. "You had lunch yet, Shelby?" I inquired from the doorway.

She looked up from the papers on her desk and smiled. "No, ma'am, I haven't, but you must be a mind reader — I was just thinking about it. You want to go somewhere?"

I lowered my voice. "Anywhere that isn't in the building. I seem to keep stirring up hornet's nests."

"How about that Indian place a couple of blocks over? I love their lamb korma."

"Terrific. Let me tell Eric and get my bag, and I'll meet you in the lobby."

Back outside my office, I updated Eric. "And if the FBI calls," I ended, collecting my bag, "tell them we're working on it."

"On what?"

"Everything. Anything. Don't worry about it. See you later!"

Shelby was waiting downstairs, and together we emerged out the front door. "Hard morning?" she asked as we started walking toward the corner.

"Interesting," I hedged. It took the whole walk for me to bring her up to date on the materials the FBI had unloaded on us. We reached the restaurant and walked in. Everything smelled wonderful, and I found myself smiling at the idea of a nice hearty curry.

When we were settled and had ordered, Shelby leaned closer. "So how are things going with Mr. Special Agent?"

"Slowly. By choice. We're both crazy busy, and we're not in a hurry. Besides, our dealings have been mainly business related." All true, more or less, but for how long? At least I didn't mind Shelby asking me.

"You think this little present of his is a way of showing you that he likes you?"

I had to giggle at that idea. "You know, if he wanted to give me a token of his affection, something smaller than a bread box would've been nicer. Seriously, as long as James says it's okay for us to talk about the recovered collections, you're going to have to think about some good ways to spin this, for the next newsletter and the website."

"Do we need to raise money for any of this?" she asked.

I was happy to see that she was thinking like a development professional. "Not yet. The FBI says they'll pay us for our services, and it's not clear what will happen to the material in the end, so we can worry about that later."

The food arrived, and I spooned a good-size serving over white rice. I ate several bites before going on to what had really been bugging me. "When do you think Latoya is going to see me as her boss? She treats me like an annoyance."

"I think that's just her way," Shelby replied. "She doesn't warm up fast, does she?"

"You, too?" I looked at her, and she nodded. "I keep working on it. The Society needs her. She's smart, and she knows her stuff. But I don't think we'll ever be friends."

"You don't need friends, Nell — you need people who work for you and who will do a good job for the Society. Liking them — or them liking you — is just icing on the cake."

"I know." I sighed. "Remind me again why I thought I could run the place?"

"Because you're smart *and* most people like you. Killer combination."

"If you say so. Anyway, I put the little ones to work on sorting, and Marty's helping out. Or snooping. I couldn't stop her if I wanted to, but at least she'll work hard, and she's got a good eye."

"Listen to you — *little ones.*" Shelby made air quotes.

"What, they don't seem awfully young to you?"

"Of course they do. Remember, I've got a daughter their age. But are we supposed to mother them?"

"I hope not! Speaking of offspring, how is Melissa doing?" And talk drifted to non-business matters for the rest of lunch. After we had stuffed ourselves, we strolled back. A lot of other people had had the same idea, and the sidewalks were surprisingly crowded. I found when we arrived back at the Society that I really wasn't ready to face . . . anybody. Luckily I realized there was something I needed to do anyway, and now was as good a time as any. "Shelby, can I rifle through your files?"

"Of course you can! What's mine is yours," she said grandly. "What do you need?"

We boarded the elevator. "I want to check the status of our fire suppression systems. I know I wrote a grant proposal for an up-grade a couple of years ago, but I want to

217

refresh my memory."

"Need help?"

"Maybe. You can ask me the obvious questions, and I'll see if I can answer them." I went out to the bank of four-drawer filing cabinets and leafed through the tight-packed files. Where had I stored that information? "Boilerplate"? "Building Description"? Not the dreaded "Miscellaneous"! Finally I located a thick and battered file for one of the national granting agencies — one that had consistently ignored our carefully crafted pleas. I took it with me back into Shelby's office and dropped into a chair, conveniently out of sight from the hall so no one would see me. I opened the file and started reading. Once I could have spouted all of the information it contained from memory, but it had been a few years since I'd had occasion to review it.

"Nell? You still there?" I looked up and realized that at least fifteen minutes had passed as I read. Bless Shelby for leaving me in peace for that long.

I closed the folder. "I had forgotten just how depressing this material is."

"That doesn't sound good. What makes you say that?"

"In case you haven't studied it yet, I'll give you the short history of the building. The site when it was purchased by the Society included a nice country manor house — hard to believe this was considered country, isn't it? When the time came to expand, early in the twentieth century, they found that there was too much rot in the foundation to support a larger building, so they razed it and started from scratch. And, logically, they wanted to make the new building as fireproof as possible, according to the standards of the day."

"Of course." Shelby nodded her encouragement.

"Hence all the stone and steel and concrete. It was kind of interesting — there were sliding metal doors that would shut automatically in the event of a fire, and all the bookcases and tables are also steel, painted to look like wood — believe me, they're a pain in the derriere to move for events. And all the floors are concrete. And if that wasn't enough, there was the holiest of holies, where the cream of the collections was stored: the fireproof vault. You know, that room off the reference room? That's where we've been keeping the Terwilliger Collection. There've been a lot of changes over the years, and the fireproof vault is really the only room that retains those original sliding doors, which are now artifacts in their own right."

"Cool," Shelby said. "So tell me what we've got now?"

"Original sprinklers, but as you can imagine, soaking documents would be a disaster, only slightly less awful than letting them burn. Although I suppose you can argue that you can restore a wet document, but not a pile of ashes. Anyway, there are new and improved water based systems coming along, that are more localized or use less water, but we don't have them."

"Do go on," Shelby drawled. "I'm fascinated."

In a truly dignified manner I stuck out my tongue at her. "A decade or so ago the Society actually had some money for remodeling and installed a new halon fire suppression system in some parts of the building." When Shelby looked blank I continued. "Halon is a gas, or a mix of gasses — basically it deprives a fire of oxygen. Much less destructive to the collections than water."

"So that's good, isn't it?" Shelby asked.

"Yes and no. It won't do great harm to documents, but recently it has been phased out because of environmental issues. You can still get a halon gas system for a museum, but it's very expensive. Plus you can't just keep using it. Once you've zapped a fire, you have to replace the gas, which is also expensive."

Shelby thought for a couple of moments. "So, we're more or less safe at the moment with a mix of sprinklers and halon, and it would cost a lot to change anything. How well do the systems work?"

"Actually, there's never been a fire here, so I have no idea. I'd hate to be the first president to find out."

"Amen," Shelby said fervently. "Is this typical of local museums and libraries?"

"It is. There's one other important fact: most fires in museums are caused by electrical problems. We've already had our electrical systems checked out and they're adequate, not that we should be complacent. But it's different for libraries. Want to guess what the single largest cause of library fires is?"

Shelby again looked at me blankly.

"Arson," I said. "Nearly forty percent of library fires are deliberately set."

CHAPTER 16

Talk of arson naturally led us to discussing what might have happened to the Fireman's Museum collection.

"Look, anything I say here has got to be in strictest confidence, because this really isn't my secret to share. But I can use your help," I said.

"I won't tell a soul, cross my heart," Shelby declared. "What do you need?"

"Okay, how much do you know about the management structure of the Fireman's Museum?"

"Not a whole lot," she admitted. "I'm not even sure where it is."

"I've only been there once myself, for an event. I don't think it's far from your neighborhood. But what's interesting is that it's kind of a homegrown organization. It was originally created from within the fire department, but after a while they figured they should get serious, so they set up a nonprofit corporation, created a board, and so on. But the ties to the department are still real tight."

"Based on what I've seen here at the Society, board members aren't always real involved in what's going on day to day. Is that true there, too?"

I smiled at her. "That's where you come in."

"Me? You want to drag me into this mess?" Shelby didn't look too worried about the idea, if her smile was any indication.

"I sure do."

"What's in it for me?"

"Well, aside from the undying gratitude of the local FBI, which might dispose them to be more willing to let us have first crack at that collection we're sorting, you can have a lot of fun playing investigator."

"Deal. What do you need?"

"Let's pull together background material on the Fireman's Museum board and staff. I'll bet we already have profiles in the files for the board members, but information access has probably improved a lot since those files were put together, so see if you can flesh them out now. For the staff, we may have to start from scratch. Certainly take a hard look at Peter Ingersoll."

"You think he's in on whatever's going on?"

I considered. "I really don't know. But maybe we can find out if he has a motive."

Shelby nodded, then said slowly, "You know, you might end up treading on some political toes if you aren't careful."

Maybe she hadn't been in Philadelphia long, but she'd figured out how things worked. "What do you mean?"

"The firefighter's union, for a start. They've got some clout — and if you start looking at them cross-eyed, they might find themselves taking their own sweet time when and if we ever need them here. Heaven forbid!"

"Good point. Anything else?"

"Let me dig around a little and see what I can find. Thank you for trusting me, Nell."

I felt better as I headed back toward my office. It helped to share the problem with someone. I expected Shelby to be circumspect, but I needed her help because she could lay hands on a lot of information without alerting anyone, since it was part of her job. The more she knew about the who was who in administration and management of Philadelphia cultural institutions, the better she could present the Society to funders, individual donors, and the outside world.

Eric perked up when I appeared. "Nell, I thought you'd disappeared. Must have been some lunch!"

"I came back a little while ago, but I had to talk to Shelby about some research. Did you need me?"

"I wanted to remind you about the Bench Foundation reception tonight. I just got a follow-up reminder in my email."

Shoot, I had entirely forgotten. The foundation was announcing their new and improved funding strategy for the next couple of years, and since it would attract a good crowd, no doubt some members of the Fireman's Museum would be there: when the Bench Foundation made pronouncements, people jumped. They were a major force in the local funding community. And this would be the first of their events that I'd attended since becoming the Society's president. Eric had made a good catch, and I was glad he had reminded me. "Thank you, Eric — that had completely slipped my mind. Details?"

"It's from five thirty to seven, at the Bellevue. Should be well attended."

"You're right. Eric, how did you get so smart, so fast?"

"I pay attention, and I've been reading through the files when I have time."

"Well, keep it up. You're doing great. Anything else?"

He handed me the usual sheaf of call slips. "Nothing urgent."

Just past five o'clock I dashed into the bathroom to run a comb through my hair and take the shine off my nose. At least I'd worn something decently professional this morning, and I'd blend into the crowd. Conveniently the Bellevue was right around the corner. It was always a treat to enter the grand old hotel, even though I could barely afford to breathe the air in the much-gilded lobby. The reception was being held in a function room on the twelfth floor, so I boarded the ornate elevator along with several other suit-clad people who looked vaguely familiar. Upstairs I surveyed the crowd, looking for familiar faces. I wouldn't have called it a glittering throng exactly, since most people had come straight from their offices and ran more to grey flannel than to sequins. But the room was filled with the movers and shakers of our little cultural community. Of course, the fact that the foundation provided an open bar and excellent hors d'oeuvres didn't hurt, either.

I spied Arabella Heffernan of Let's Play barreling toward me. "Nell, how nice to see you — again!"

"We must stop meeting like this, Arabella," I said, hugging her. "It looks like the sharks are circling." I gestured toward the crowd, then snared a glass of wine from one passing waiter and something in puff pastry from another.

"We can all use the money, and the Bench people sit on a lot of it." She leaned in closer. "Awful thing about the Fireman's Museum collection, isn't it?"

"I know — it makes me shudder. And of course, it forces us to check out how well protected the Society's collections are." I swallowed the delightful hors d'oeuvre, then snagged another one from the next waiter. After all, this was my dinner, and I figured I'd earned a few smoked-salmon-on-crème-fraiche-topped-with-a-sprig-of-dill goodies.

"Of course — all that paper! However do you sleep at night?"

"I cling to a firm belief in the goodness of humanity."

"As do I, my dear. It's just easier to see it among children."

I did another quick scan of the room before asking, "Do you know the director of the Fireman's Museum, Peter Ingersoll?"

"Not personally, apart from events like this. You?"

"I met him only after the fire happened.

227

Is he here?"

Arabella turned to search the crowd. "I don't . . . oh, there he is." She pointed across the large room.

I followed her gaze. Yes, there was Peter, and even from this far away I could tell he didn't look any better than he had the last time I'd seen him. I was surprised to see Jennifer Phillips clinging to his arm — or holding him up. I had seen her at the fundraisers' luncheon — was that event really only ten days ago? — but her presence here was unexpected, since usually only the highest levels of management were invited to Bench events. Maybe Peter wouldn't have made it here without her support.

"Who's that with him?" Arabella asked.

"His assistant, Jennifer. She was at that luncheon, and we shared a table. I think I'll go over and say hello to Peter. Can I catch up with you later, Arabella?"

"Of course, dear. Poor Peter looks as though he needs all the friends he can get."

I wiped my fingers on a tiny napkin and began to wade through the crowd that was growing rapidly. It took me a couple of minutes to make my way to where Peter was standing, since I had to greet several people along the way.

Finally reaching him, I said, "Hello, Peter.

How're you doing?"

"Oh, Nell, hello," he said in a distracted tone. "As well as can be expected, all things considered. You've met Jennifer Phillips?"

He really didn't remember? "Yes, we met at that luncheon at the Marriott." *Not to mention at the funeral procession.* I extended a hand. "Nice to see you again, Jennifer." I leaned in closer. "You must find yourself in a difficult position at the moment."

"You mean, trying to raise money? Thank you for saying so, Nell. You know how hard it is when your institution is under a cloud. But I must say our supporters have been very generous — they want to see us rebuild our collection, and I think that's a real tribute to Peter's leadership. Our exhibits may be small, but they've always been popular, particularly among school groups."

"More so than ours, I'd guess. Our demographic is a bit older — by a few decades."

Jennifer laughed politely. I noticed she was keeping a watchful eye on Peter, who indeed looked like he needed support. His complexion was greyish, his hair was greasy, and there was a reddish blotch — ketchup? — on his silk tie. As I had suspected, under normal circumstances Jennifer would not have been included in an august gathering such as this, but either Peter had dragged her along for companionship, or she was there to make sure he didn't do anything unforgivable in front of a major philanthropic organization as well as his peers.

As I watched, Peter pulled an inhaler from his pocket and breathed in a puff. He noticed me watching and said apologetically, "The stress has been awful. And I hate events like this, but I have to be here."

Jennifer laid a hand on his arm. "Gary could have handled it, Peter."

He shook her off. "I know, but it's important that I show my face here, Jennifer. You understand, don't you, Nell?"

"All too well."

At the dais at the far end of the room, it appeared that the Bench people were preparing to launch into their spiel. Time for me to work the crowd. "Peter, let me know if there's anything else I can do. Jennifer, nice to see you again. Call me if I can help with anything."

"Thank you, Nell. I may take you up on that," Jennifer replied.

"Bye, Nell," Peter said, his tone dismal.

I dove back into the crowd. I waved at a couple of Society board members, wondering which of their institutions they were there to represent. The Old Guard of Philadelphia tended to sit on multiple boards, and I hoped they didn't have to wrestle with conflicts of interest too often. Still, sometimes their names on our letterhead were enough to spur giving, and I wasn't going to complain.

I recognized quite a few other faces, not that I could put names to them all. For all that Philadelphia had a population of one and a half million, we moved in small circles within it. This was my tribe gathered here. Was one of them capable of murder, arson, and fraud?

Probably. I knew full well how invested people became in their collections, both the getting and the keeping. I looked at the near-empty wineglass in my hand: better stop with one, if I wanted to keep a clear head.

I listened with one ear to the doughty representative of the mighty foundation, who outlined what sounded like a fairly reasonable plan for allocating scarce resources among so many worthy candidates. I noticed that one fiftyish man stopped to talk to Peter, while Jennifer stepped back and watched them, looking anxious. I didn't recognize the man, but as the speaker wound down, I edged in his direction, at the same time that Peter and Jennifer made their farewells and drifted toward the door.

The man stayed behind, giving perfunctory attention to the speaker, and more attention to the highball glass in his hand. It took him a moment to focus on me, even when I stood in his line of sight. I stuck out my hand. "I'm Nell Pratt, president of the Antiquarian Society. You know Peter Ingersoll? Terrible thing about the collection." My words came out in a rush, because I didn't want to give the man an opening to brush me off.

Finally he focused, noticed my hand, and gave me a brief handshake. "Walter Barnes. Yes, it's an awful thing. I'm on the board."

Score! I knew him by reputation: he managed a major real estate development company in the area. "I understand from Peter that people have been providing a lot of support in rebuilding the collections?"

He looked at me more sharply, and I wondered if he wondered how I knew, so I enlightened him. "Peter asked me to see what records the Society had about your collection. I was happy to help him out."

Walter seemed to relax just a bit. "We appreciate it. Yes, people have been very helpful."

"So you'll be able to reopen on schedule?"

Walter's eyes were roaming the crowd. "What? Oh, yes, I think so."

"Are you associated with the fire department?" I thought I'd get in one last shot, before he found an excuse to move on.

He turned his full attention back to me. "Why do you ask that?"

I smiled innocently. "I'm kind of intrigued by the museum's corporate structure. Unusual, isn't it? But it seems to have worked well for the Fireman's Museum. I wish we had that kind of enthusiastic involvement."

"Yes. Thank you. Excuse me — there's someone I need to talk to. Nice to meet you." He moved away quickly. If I'd been the sensitive type, I might have been offended at being dismissed so summarily. As it was, I wondered why I made him uncomfortable. I made a mental note to tell Shelby to check him out thoroughly in the morning.

CHAPTER 17

The next day I had hoped once again for a peaceful morning, but as usual, that didn't happen. I arrived at my office and stopped at Eric's desk to say hello.

"How'd the event go?" he asked.

"Good. Make sure you get a copy of the foundation's new guidelines — they should be posted on the Bench website today."

"Anything for us from the foundation?"

I was tickled that he used the term *us.* He hadn't been at the Society very long, but apparently he'd taken it to heart. "I'll have to read through the details, but it's possible. Oh, and give Shelby a copy, too, will you?"

I had barely settled myself behind my desk with my coffee when Marty appeared and threw herself into a chair. "Good morning to you, too, Marty," I said. "Please, make yourself at home. What can I do for you?"

"What you can do for me is tell me what you and James are doing about the Fireman's Museum."

I should have known she wouldn't stay out of it. "What makes you think we're doing anything?" I asked innocently.

Marty saw right through me. "The FBI's been invited to the party. The museum community is involved. I just put two and two together."

"What has James said?"

"He's trying not to say anything, and he wants me to mind my own business. I reminded him that this *is* my business. You willing to share?"

Was there no way to keep a secret here? I contemplated my options: bring Marty up to speed and risk annoying James and the FBI, or shut Marty out and tick her off. Definitely a lose-lose proposition. But James had assigned me to the museum side of this investigation, and he couldn't deny that Marty was in the thick of that, so I'd have to go with Marty.

"Marty, let me remind you that James considers you" — I searched for a term that wouldn't offend her — "somewhat unpredictable," I began. Marty's mouth twitched. "He asked me to see if I could pick up any talk among my colleagues, but I really haven't had a chance to do that yet. I asked Shelby to check our files and see what she

235

could find out about the museum's staff and board members."

"You could have asked me," Marty muttered.

"I know." I thought about trying to defend my choice and gave up. Marty was a straight shooter and knew everybody, but she had no patience for tact. "But if you want to help, do you know anybody associated with the museum? Or the board?"

"My cousin Selden Pepper."

Why was I not surprised? "Who's he?" I didn't recognize the name.

"Well, he's more like a second cousin, and before you ask, I'm not sure James remembers that he exists, and you know he doesn't socialize much with the family. Or maybe they don't socialize with him. Anyway. Selden's the token starving artist in the family — he paints. The museum asked him to do a painting of the place a few years ago, for some fundraiser. It was a raffle prize. That meant he had to spend some time there, inside and out."

"Okay," I said cautiously. "Have you talked to him?"

"Of course. And don't worry — he has nothing to do with them these days, so he can't tip anybody off. Besides, I'm one of his biggest patrons, so he'll be careful."

"I get it, Marty. Did he have anything useful to say?"

"He got kind of chummy with Jennifer, because he was in and out at all sorts of odd times — he likes to work from life, rather than from photos, but he doesn't like to work when there's a crowd around. So he'd check with her to see what the foot traffic looked like or if there was a school group scheduled — in other words, when the coast was clear. Naturally they got to talking. Anyway, you wouldn't believe how incestuous that place is — everybody's involved with firefighting somehow. Even Jennifer — she used to be married to a Philadelphia fireman, but he died on the job. The pension kind of sucked, so she was offered the job at the museum to make up the difference."

"Interesting. But isn't it hard for her to be there, and to be reminded about her husband's death?"

"Her choice. I'd guess she needs the money."

"I've met her, and seen her with Peter. Are they close?"

"You mean, like, involved close?" Marty thought for a second. "Huh. Selden didn't say anything about that, but it was a couple of years ago. Or maybe he never saw them together. Besides, so what? They're both unattached."

"I don't know. I'm just collecting facts at the moment. Do you know Gary O'Keefe?"

"Everybody in Philadelphia knows Gary. Maybe Peter's name is on the letterhead, but Gary's the face for the museum. Nice guy."

"Is he hurting for money?"

Marty shook her head. "Personally? Not that I've ever heard. He had to leave the department because of a work-related injury, but that was in the old days, and I think they looked after their own better back then. But like Jennifer, the city found a place for him at the museum, and he's been there ever since. You haven't met him?"

"I did, first at Allan Brigham's funeral procession and then when I gave Peter the copies of the information from our files, right after the fire. I had the impression that he invited himself along because Peter really needed someone to keep an eye on him. Of course, if Gary's curator he should be concerned about the collections. He seemed like a really nice guy. Is there something more I should know about him?"

"If you say one bad word to him about the fire department or anyone in it, he'll bite your head off. So he hasn't said anything about the fire engine?"

"Not to me. You'd think the curator would notice the discrepancies, wouldn't you? James said nobody from the museum had mentioned it to the police or the FBI. So that's all Selden gave you?"

"Just about. Like I said, he was involved there for a short time maybe three or four years ago, and he hasn't been back. Is Shelby in the know about what's going on?"

"Yes, she is. I'm only one person, and I can't talk to everyone and do research for the FBI and run this place single-handed. I'm not worried about Shelby spreading this around."

"I believe you. But James is going to have a fit."

"Listen, he asked me to look into things from our side. He didn't say how. He's going to have to trust me."

"Hey, I'm just saying. I know he thinks I'm the world's biggest blabbermouth, but I can keep my mouth shut when it matters. Well, I told Selden, but that was because I knew he could help. Besides, he's family."

"Okay, you told Selden and I told Shelby. Let's hope it ends there. And let's hope we learn something useful soon!"

"Amen." She sprang out of her chair.

"Well, I'll leave you to . . . whatever you're doing."

No sooner had Marty left than Shelby walked in, clutching a stack of papers and looking very pleased with herself. "Don't tell me you've finished already?" I said, nodding at her to close the door as she came in.

"Not finished, no, but I've got the basic outlines, and I want to run this stuff by you before I dig any deeper."

"Sit and speak."

Shelby sat. "How much do you know about the Fireman's Museum? Just so I don't end up repeating myself."

"It's small. The nonprofit was created back in the seventies, I think, to manage it. Generally well regarded. That's about it. You want to pick up from there?"

"Sure will. You're right about small, or at least partly. I pulled up their 990."

I interrupted. "Good job!" All nonprofits were required to file 990 tax forms with the federal government, and the submitted forms were accessible to the public online. They provided a good snapshot of each nonprofit institution: management, finances, funders, et cetera. I was happy to hear that Shelby knew how useful they were.

"Hey, I may not have your wealth of

experience, Madame President, but I've been doing this for a while."

"Points for you. Go on. What did you learn?"

"Management: tiny. I make it six or seven employees — the president, who you've met. A secretary, who I'd guess doubles as development person, public relations director, and about anything else that comes along."

"You've met her, remember? At the event at the Marriott? And she was at the Bench Foundation event last night — Jennifer Phillips. She and Peter Ingersoll seem tight."

"Well, despite her multiple titles, the job pays diddly-squat. Then there's a couple of vice presidents, the curator, and one or two other employees — the 990 doesn't explain what they do. The pay is uniformly pathetic."

"Interesting. I've heard that the fire department provides a lot of the staffing on a volunteer basis, but the actual employees must be making money somewhere, if what you say is true."

"Or not — which might give somebody a good motive to make off with a fire truck."

"Maybe," I agreed. "You have anything else?"

"The board listing. Funny — the board is

huge. The fire commissioner is a member of the board, no surprise. But there are like thirty people total."

That really was quite a lot for a small institution. "Any names you recognize? People who overlap with our board?"

"Nope, but you'd probably recognize some."

"I met one of the board members last night, Walter Barnes. Do you have anything on him?"

"Just the name. Nothing much in our files. Want me to find out more?"

"Please. He didn't seem to want to talk to me and ducked out as fast as he could."

"And you of course assumed he had a dark and dirty reason. Sure, I'll see what I can find."

"How do the museum's overall financials look?"

"Okay, I guess. They haven't had any outside grants lately. They sell a couple of publications, and the gift shop makes a little money. Nothing jumps out at me, except that I'm not really sure how they stay in business. Or why anyone works for them, unless they've got other sources of income."

"I'm not sure how the museum's relationship with the city works, but I hear what you're saying." I sat back and thought for a moment. "So basically what we're seeing is a nice, simple nonprofit organization that plenty of people like. I don't think it's appropriate that we do in-depth profiles of all the board members, aside from the twitchy Mr. Barnes, apart from what you can pull from our own files. Besides, if the FBI really cares, they're better equipped to do that. And thanks for checking. Anything else?"

"Oh yeah. I checked what we had in our files on their current employees."

"Shelby, how late did you stay last night?"

"Late enough that my hubby actually made dinner for himself. Don't worry about it — I was having fun. Besides, I like looking through the files here. People have collected such weird information, like what kind of dog someone has."

"Hey, it's a good way to get a conversation started at an event. Don't knock it — you never know what might be useful. It's all about making a connection with people before you hit them up for a contribution."

"Hey, I'm from Virginia, remember? I learned all that at my mama's knee."

"Well, you're way ahead of where I was when I started. Okay, what've you got on Peter?"

"Forty-three. Undergrad degree from Kenyon, and a master's in public administration from Yale. Grew up in New Jersey, lives in Center City now. He's been involved with the Fireman's Museum for about six years, and had a couple of museum jobs before that, in New Jersey and Delaware. Divorced, no kids. A couple of minor publications. That help?"

"Not really. Anything on the curator, Gary O'Keefe?"

"Oh yeah, there's plenty of information on him, because he gets lots of press. Everybody loves him — if you want to set up a tour of the museum or check out the archives, or if you want information about anything relating to firefighting from Ben Franklin on, Gary's the go-to guy in Philadelphia."

"I know — I've met him. He seems to be one of those people who truly loves what he's doing. Oh, and you might add a note that he retired from the fire department several years ago because of a work-related injury. I wonder if Latoya knows him? She told me she once dated a firefighter."

"Speaking of Latoya, does she know what you're — *we're* doing?"

"No, and let's keep it that way. I think she'd disapprove. She's very by-the-book, even though the FBI did ask for our help, so we have a legitimate reason to be asking questions. Sort of. And you're just doing your job — donor research — at my request." I had a feeling James hadn't expected me to be doing this kind of digging. He'd probably assumed I'd have some nice lunches and network with my peers, trying to work in a discreet question here and there. But that wouldn't necessarily be easy, because (a) it was hard to know who knew what about the extent of the Fireman's Museum losses, (b) I hate to gossip, and (c) at the moment I had no time to make the rounds having lunch with the spectrum of Philadelphia administrators. I figured the Society's prospective donor files, some of which dated back decades, were a pretty good proxy. Couple those with what was available online these days, and we could find out a whole lot about people, without anybody even noticing. "Anything else interesting in his background?"

"Firefighter through and through. Joined the department straight out of high school. You're right — he got sidelined by an injury about the time the museum administration was being formalized. He signed on, and he's been there ever since. I couldn't find one bad word about him in the press, and he'll give an interview to anyone who asks, from high school newspapers on up."

"I'd assume he got some sort of pension or disability payment from the city, so I guess he can afford to work at the museum."

"That sounds about right. So now what?"

"I . . . don't know." I really didn't. I trusted that Shelby had plumbed the depths of our records. I didn't want to pull Marty in any further. Maybe I really had to do what James had suggested and talk to live people.

"I'll see if I can find a reason to talk to Gary again. Oh, and since I didn't know that Peter was from New Jersey, can you do a quick computer check and see if anything comes up there?"

"I'm on it, Chief."

CHAPTER 18

Eric popped in as Shelby bustled out. "Agent Morrison's on the phone for you, Nell."

It was already eleven — where was the morning going? I took a breath to steady myself before I picked up the phone. "James, what can I do for you?"

"You have time to meet for lunch? The Market Street Deli at noon?"

"Sure, sounds fine."

"Good. See you then."

No frills, that was James. I paused briefly to count exactly how many words we had exchanged: twenty. I hoped he'd be more forthcoming in person.

At quarter to twelve I left the Society and headed toward Market Street. James was waiting for me when I arrived. "Hello, Nell," he said, rising and pulling out the plastic molded chair for me.

"Hello, James. Love the decor here." I sat

and shrugged out of my jacket.

"This is business. You want something upscale, wait until this case is over. The mayor's breathing down my neck. He wants this solved like yesterday, so we don't tarnish the reputation of the fire department."

"I'll hold you to that. What's up?"

We were interrupted by a harried waitress and ordered sandwiches and coffee. When she had left, he said, "We've found video footage of a truck appearing at the loading dock at the warehouse the night before the fire was discovered."

"That's good news, isn't it? Whose camera was it?"

"The warehouse's. The only one, and a cheap one at that so it's crappy quality, but better than nothing. We can make out someone unloading something large, and someone loading something else large. Well, a couple of someones. They needed to use a ramp for the truck, and I'm guessing they had a winch inside to help move the machinery. You have any idea how heavy an antique fire engine is?"

"No, sir, I do not. Why on earth would I?"

Unperturbed, James went on. "It's heavy. No sign of the guard in the pictures."

"Does that mean he . . . wasn't involved?"
I'd have to think about that — the guard
was dead, or at least unconscious, before
the truck was moved? Did that clear him or
implicate him? "The fire was discovered,
what, in the morning of the next day? Let
me guess: there were no markings on the
truck, right?"

"Morning, predawn. It was set up to burn
slowly — it wasn't just someone splashing
gasoline around and tossing a match. The
truck was plain, light colored. The recording quality was so lousy we couldn't even
read the license plates — don't believe all
that trash you see on television about
enhancing the images. But we know there
was a plate on the front."

"And that was important why?"

"Assuming it was local, that rules out
Pennsylvania and Delaware, both of which
do not require a front plate. Of course, it
could have come from any of the other
thirty-eight states that do require one. But
I'm betting on local, maybe New Jersey. I
can't see anyone driving halfway across the
country to steal a fire engine. Or knowing
where to find it."

"It's probably happened, for the right
artifact, but in this case I agree. So you're
still looking at people at or connected to the

museum?"

"Of course. Aren't you?"

"That's what you asked me to do. That's what I've been doing."

"And?"

I contemplated how to answer that. "James, this might work better if you told me if you had any suspects and I told you what I've found out about them. In case you haven't noticed, we're looking at a pool of about forty people here."

"Staff and board, right?"

"Yes, but I think we can focus on only a few of those — the ones who are most closely connected to or are most active at the Fireman's Museum. We've been through our files, and what I do have is more or less limited to the staff there, and more anecdotal."

"Wait a minute — *we?*"

"Yes, *we.* I asked Shelby to help."

James's expression darkened. "I asked you to keep this confidential."

I hated being put on the defensive. "And that's what I told Shelby. I trust her. Besides, Marty already knows what's going on." I decided not to mention that Eric knew. And Selden Pepper. "Do you trust *her?*"

His shoulders slumped. "I try to forget

that Philadelphia still thinks like a small town. Okay, what do you mean by *anecdotal*? Gossip?"

"Sort of," I admitted. "For example, say we host an event like the gala, the one you attended? Afterward, all the staff who were there sit down and we pool information, anything we heard that might be relevant to the Society. Like who's getting a divorce, which means we might not get as big a contribution this year, or none at all. Or who's had a death in the family and stands to inherit a nice sum. Or who's had a bad experience with another institution and might want to switch their favorite nonprofit. A lot of this never makes it to public records, but we look at the whole picture from a different angle. We use this kind of information to plan our solicitation strategies. Sometimes we have records that go back for years, when we're keeping an eye on a particular individual, waiting for the right time to make an approach for a contribution or a board position."

"I never thought about all that," James said with something like admiration in his voice. "It's almost like what we do, although we place more emphasis on criminal activities. You don't run across that much, do you?"

"Rarely." I smiled. "Although I will say that we've been known to look the other way if a prospective board member is introduced and we know he has a somewhat shady past . . ."

"As long as he writes a big enough check?" James finished the statement for me.

"Exactly. I can't defend it, but we're just trying to survive, and there's a lot of competition. And we have procedures in place to ensure that we do not accept stolen property, but it's not always easy to prove what's legitimate and what isn't, if someone claims that it's been in the family for a century. Plenty of institutions larger than we are have been burned that way."

"Interesting problem." Our lunch arrived, and we were silent as the waitress deposited our sandwiches. "So, what've you got for me?" James resumed when she'd left.

"Remember, I've only been working on this for a couple of days. So far I haven't found anything negative about Peter Ingersoll. His assistant, Jennifer, was with him at an event last night, and it looked to me like she was holding him up."

"Was he drunk?"

"No, or at least I didn't see him drinking. More like he's falling apart — we already know he has health issues. Still, he has to

252

go through the motions and stay in the public eye — I heard him say so."

"Are they an item?"

"Not that I've heard, although there's no reason why they shouldn't be, or why anyone would tell me, for that matter."

"You mean you don't record the juicy stuff like that?"

"Only if it will help us ask for money." Before he could say anything, I held up a hand. "No, I don't mean blackmail! Just who knows who, and how well." I decided it was time to cut to the chase. "I assume you've been looking at all the staff?"

"Of course. They knew where the fire engine was."

"True. And their salaries are pathetic."

"You know this how?"

"Nonprofits have to post public records with the IRS, and they include salaries. I'm sure you know that. And fundraisers access that information all the time. We look at who's on their boards, or what grants they've received recently."

"Duly noted." He took a bite of his sandwich and chewed. When he had swallowed he went on. "Do you know the curator, Gary O'Keefe?"

"Not well. I met him briefly at the funeral procession, and then he tagged along when

I had lunch with Peter and gave him the collection information. From all I've heard, he's an honest guy. Do you know anything different?"

"No, just checking. What you've told me about the salaries there matches what I've found. Nobody's made any unexplained large deposits lately, and nobody's suddenly living way beyond their means."

"Maybe they're being careful. After all, everyone knows law enforcement can access financial records easily these days, and I don't think the people I've met are the kind to have connections to offshore banks." Another thought struck me. "Do you think this could mean that whoever stole the fire engine hasn't sold it yet? That it's stashed somewhere while they wait for the right moment, or until things quiet down?"

"Could be."

"I've been wondering about the timing of the theft," I said slowly. "The collection has been in storage for months now, but since the construction is almost done, they would probably be moving it back fairly soon. Do you think that's why they decided to act now? I mean, someone could have made the switch when the collection was first moved, and probably no one would have noticed for months — no one would have any reason to visit the warehouse. Why now?"

James gave that due consideration. "Do you know what the estimated completion date was?"

"I think they were hoping to be open again before June, maybe? In case you don't know it, teachers get pretty desperate to fill time at the end of the school year, and they love field trips. Assuming, of course, that there's any money left in the school budget for buses and that kind of stuff by then. Anyway, assume they were planning to reopen in June, both for the schools and to catch the tourist season, and of course the collections would have gone back to the building sooner than that for installation."

"So their window was going to close shortly."

"Yes. What about this: they saw this rash of arsons happening and they thought they would be a good cover?"

"Seizing the opportunity? Maybe. Obviously the police are talking with the fire department's arson investigators, but there's nothing particularly unusual about the fires, except their timing."

"Did you find anything pertinent about Allan Brigham?"

"No criminal record, except for an arrest for public intoxication a while ago, never repeated. No unusual financial activity. He was a —"

This time I finished his sentence. "A retired fireman. I know."

"Sure is one tight-knit community, isn't it?"

"I think that's been true since the first fire department was founded, according to the reading I've been doing. Which means they aren't going to want to rat on each other, right? Not that I'm implying that there's anything to tell."

"Exactly. Certainly not to me, as an outsider and a federal agent. In a way, the local police could have better luck. At least they're kind of a brother organization."

"Nobody at the museum has a history of arson? Obviously I don't have access to criminal records."

"Nope, although Celia'll tell you that a lot of arson cases never get reported. There are even holes in the FBI database, because if a fire event doesn't go to prosecution, we don't hear about it."

I could see the frustration in his face. "James, how do you manage all this? I mean, are you just looking at background, or do you actively interview people you think might be involved? Are you at the point where you're checking alibis?"

"The police are taking the lead on that side of things, and we're providing background. As long as we don't get in their way, they're pretty good at sharing what they've got."

He hadn't answered my question. "So, do you know if the staff members have alibis for the times in question?"

"The usual: *I was home alone watching television or reading a book. No, nobody called me,* and *I wasn't on the Internet.* So there's no real way to verify the alibis. None of them were together."

"Have you looked at the board members?"

"Briefly. I can't see any motive for any of them. Can you?"

"Not really. They don't benefit financially, and the institution they're serving suffers. Of course, if any of them had lost a lot of money lately" — as had many of our donors — "they might have jumped at the chance to steal the fire engine. Although that wouldn't explain the murder. I assume you've looked at all their financial records?"

"We have. Nothing out of the ordinary."

"How about one of the volunteer firefighters who's pissed off at something?" I wondered if I should mention Walter Barnes's brush-off, but I couldn't be sure whether he'd been rude because I asked about the

Fireman's Museum or because he'd thought I was boring and not worth his time.

James groaned. "That's another fifty or so people to look at, and believe me, the fire department is touchy about sharing their records if they think we're looking for dirt."

Funny how many ex-firefighters or their kin ended up needing money, I thought. Was money behind this? Or something else? We both fell silent, and I was suddenly aware of the noise and bustle around us. Life went on for most people in the city, and here we were trying to untangle a knotted mess involving multiple crimes while trying to avoid antagonizing anyone in the city. Not a simple task.

Finally James asked, "Nothing fishy about the museum's financials, from your perspective?"

I shook my head. "In their official reports they claimed to have assets and a positive cash flow. If the city's supporting them somehow, it doesn't show up on their books, or at least on the report. But I hardly think city administration or the city council would destroy the collections and kill someone for a paltry five- or six-figure line item in the city's multibillion-dollar budget. That would hardly solve the city's financial problems, and there are more quiet ways of dissolving an organization."

"I'll take your word for that." Suddenly he was all business. "I'll get the tab — it'll go on my expense report, since you're an informant."

I smiled. "You know, that sounds really odd. I don't think I'll put *FBI informant* on my résumé. I wish I could have given you more." Somehow I wasn't sure I had told him anything he didn't already know.

"I appreciate your insights, Nell. Let me know if you come up with anything else, will you?"

"Of course." I watched as he stopped at the cashier's desk, then left. I dawdled with the last of my coffee, thinking. The odds that an outsider had pulled this off were small, but if it was an insider, that left a pretty small pool: Peter, Jennifer, or maybe Gary O'Keefe — that nice-guy facade might hide a bitter and twisted person. Maybe I should seek him out and talk to him. Maybe I should talk to Peter again — I would probably offer a more sympathetic ear than the police or the FBI. And wasn't that why James had involved me?

CHAPTER 19

Sometimes I wished there was a way for me to sneak back into my office, sight unseen, so I could actually get some work done without everyone showing up and demanding things from me. The building did have a side door and the back stairs, but if I took that route, I'd have to go past Latoya's office to get to mine. Was I avoiding Latoya? I hadn't admitted it to myself. In the end I decided to go that way, because it would mean passing only one person, even if that person was one I would prefer not to talk to, rather than going through the public entrance and running the gauntlet of half the staff.

As my luck would have it, Latoya was actually standing in front of the collections filing cabinets looking up something, so there was no way to avoid her. "Oh, Nell, there you are. A moment?"

"Of course," I replied, following her into

her office. She gestured gracefully toward a chair; I sat. "What do you need?" I asked.

"While I might have asked that the whole situation with the new hires and the FBI materials be handled somewhat differently, I think things are turning out far better than we might have expected."

Whoa! Was she actually saying something nice to me? I was momentarily stunned. "I'm very glad to hear that. I think the Society will benefit in the long run."

Latoya seemed to recognize my effort. "I agree. I can understand that the FBI's actions put you in a difficult position. I'm sure things will go smoothly from here on out. And the new staff does seem to be capable, despite their youth," she admitted.

"Thank *you,* Latoya. I hope so." I stood up and fled before I could say something to shatter our fragile accord.

Of course, I couldn't resist the urge to keep going and take one more look at the kids' progress in the processing room. I was curious to see just what was in the collection — and what parts the Society should fight to keep, if it came to that. I poked my head in the door of the processing room. Everybody was still busy, but the stacks of boxes had been moved around, and most bore sticky notes with cryptic markings.

"Hey, looks like it's really coming along!" I said as I walked in.

Rich looked up from the list he was checking. "Oh, hi, Nell. Yeah, once we worked out a system it went really fast. We've got the boxes grouped by period and material now, and I was wondering whether we should start on the box-level inventory?"

I quickly surveyed the room before answering. "Do me a favor, will you? Make sure you ask Latoya? After all, she's the one in charge here."

Rich gave me a quizzical look, then nodded. "Got it."

"Anything interesting turn up?" I needed a quick boost, and news of an unusual discovery might work.

To my surprise, Alice was the first to answer. "I found one thing — it's really sad. There's a folder here with a series of letters from the Civil War period." I walked over to where she was standing, and she opened the folder carefully on the tabletop. "This woman, she lived in Kentucky, and she had two sons — and they fought for different sides. See, there are photos and everything."

I peered at the contents of the folder. There was a lot of correspondence: both sons were apparently diligent letter writers, and their mother had kept every scrap.

There were only two photographs, small studio portraits of each son, each in his uniform. I looked up at Alice. "Do you know if they survived the war?"

She shook her head. "No. Those letters are in the file, too." For a brief moment we silently mourned the long-dead brothers.

Then I shook myself. "You know, this might make a nice short write-up for our quarterly magazine. There's a real human interest element here. You could do a little more research on the family and see what you can find. When you have time."

Alice dimpled. "I'd like that — as long as they don't mind." She nodded toward Rich and Nicholas.

"It's your find, so you have first dibs. I'm sure they'll come up with some treasures of their own, along the way. Maybe we could make this part of an ongoing series." Assuming we got to hang on to some or all of the collection. But I was pleased that the kids were actually getting along, things were getting done. Should I tackle something else now, while my luck held, or quit while I was ahead?

Back in my office I sat at my desk for a while, staring at nothing and thinking about my lunchtime conversation with James. For once no one interrupted me, and the phone didn't ring. I was flattered that James thought I could help; I was more flattered that he had actually *asked* me to help, despite his stated reservations about involving outsiders in FBI investigations. I wished that I had something to offer him in the way of brilliant analysis or observation, but so far I was coming up with only a few crumbs. Until recently I had never fully appreciated how much crime went on behind the scenes among local museums, and I didn't think it was unique to Philadelphia. The public thought we were staid and stuffy, sheltering our dusty artifacts and providing adults and children a way to pass a quiet few hours out of the rain. I didn't think they'd be happy to know about the murder and mayhem that lay beneath the peaceful surface.

One ongoing problem I faced in looking at the Fireman's Museum problem was that it still wasn't clear to me whether there was an arsonist at work, or whether the theft was the primary event and the fire was set merely to conceal the theft. Or whether it was an insurance scam, although I was pretty sure that James or the police would have checked that out quickly, and Marty would have her brother Elwyn on the lookout for anything like that. Or, as I had suggested to James, whether there was in fact an arsonist and the thieves had taken advantage of that for their own purposes. What defined an arsonist? Someone who happened to like to set fires? Or someone who couldn't help himself from setting fires? Everything I knew came from snippets I had read in the popular press and, as I had told Celia, what I had seen on television and in the movies, and I wasn't about to put a lot of faith in those.

It wasn't as though I expected an arsonist to have a blazing scarlet *A for Arsonist* on his forehead, but how was I supposed to look at any of these potential suspects and reach any conclusions? Heck, for all I knew it was the night watchman who had set up the theft *and* the cover-up fire. He could have had some long-standing grudge against the fire department for letting him go, and he thought this would be a good way to get back at them, and firefighters in general. His death could have been no more than the result of tripping over something in the dark and hitting his head as he tried to get out of the building after setting the fire. But of course, that wouldn't explain everything about the theft: according to the surveillance recording, there were other people involved. Could all these events be unrelated? The theft, the fire, the death? Or only two out of three? But which two?

My peaceful — if frustrating — contemplation ended when Marty barged in, towing someone I didn't recognize, a rather weedy thirty-something man whose limp hair was already thinning. I was just as glad for an interruption, since all my thinking was getting me nowhere. "Hi, Marty. Who's this?"

"My cousin Selden. The artist. I mentioned him this morning?"

The one who had done the painting for the Fireman's Museum. What pretext had Marty concocted to bring him here?

Marty plowed ahead, answering my question before I could ask it. "He was in town, and I thought you might want to talk to him. Don't worry, he won't blab. He doesn't talk to many people anyway."

I looked to see how Selden was taking Marty's description of him. He appeared resigned to her characterization. He stuck out his hand. "Nice to meet you, Nell. I'm Selden Pepper. Marty's filled me in about the fire and all. Awful thing, wasn't it?"

"Yes, it was, and we're trying to help the authorities get to the bottom of it. Please, sit down. Marty, can you shut the door, please?"

Selden perched on the edge of the chair.

"Don't worry, I know when to keep my mouth shut. I'm not sure what Marty thinks I can tell you, though."

"I'm embarrassed to say that before all this happened, I didn't know much of anything about the museum. Marty said that you spent some time there working on a painting?"

"That's right. I've got some modest local renown, and they asked me if I could do a piece for them. They wanted a prize for an event they were planning, and they held a raffle for the picture. Since then they've used the image for some items that they sell in the gift shop, like note cards, calendars, that kind of thing."

"Were you there long?"

He shrugged. "Not really. It was a water-color, so it didn't take long. I spent a couple of days doing preliminary sketches, getting the feel for the place and the neighborhood. Maybe a week, total."

"Did you work with anyone in particular?"

"Mainly Jennifer — she gave me access to whatever I needed, and handled all the arrangements. At least I did get paid."

"Did you meet Peter Ingersoll?"

"Sure, once or twice. Seemed like a nice enough guy. Pity about that fire engine — it was beautiful. I'm not qualified to judge the engineering of it, but the decoration was elegant. You know, garlands and goddesses and gilt."

I wasn't sure what Selden was adding to what little I already knew. "Did you talk to Jennifer much?"

"Not really, apart from scheduling. Jennifer and I did have lunch one day, though."

"Do you remember what you talked about?"

Selden shook his head. "Hey, it's been a few years. It wasn't exactly a memorable conversation. I think we talked about New Jersey, since I live there and she's got family there. Art, maybe. She was the one who suggested the note-card tie-in, and I appreciated that. It meant a little more money, and it got my name out there. I'm sorry, but I don't see that this is going to be of much help."

"You never know. Did you see much of the curator, Gary O'Keefe?"

"Blustery older guy? Sure. It was impossible not to see him. He was there all the time, and he loved to talk. I prefer to work alone, and I had to ask Jennifer to let me know when Gary wasn't around, just so I could have a little peace. Not that he wasn't a nice guy, but nosy, into everything."

Maybe that was the dark side of Gary: he

couldn't let go.

"Did you meet Peter's brother Scott?"

"I . . . don't remember. Does he work there?"

"I understand he's worked security for the museum, although not since the collections have been in storage."

Light dawned on Selden's face. "That kind of burly guy? I never would have guessed he was Peter's brother — they don't look at all alike. Sure, he let me in a time or two, but we never exchanged more than a couple of words."

I really couldn't think of anything else to ask. "Selden, I appreciate your coming in. And you never know what might turn out to be important."

"No problem. Is that all you needed, Marty?"

"Yes, Selden, we're good," Marty said. "And thanks. I'll call you next week."

"Sure thing. Nell, nice to meet you. Let me know if you ever need my artistic services here."

I stood up to say good-bye. "I'll keep you in mind. And thanks again."

"I'll take him downstairs," Marty offered. "Be right back."

When they'd left, I sat back down. Selden was right: he hadn't added much to my stew of facts, aside from the fact that Jennifer had ties to New Jersey, as did Peter, at least in the past. But a lot of people lived in New Jersey and worked in Philadelphia. It was an easy commute by any of the bridges over the Delaware River or public transportation.

There was a knocking at the door, and Shelby stuck her head in. "You're looking frazzled. I can come back later."

Marty appeared behind her, having sent Selden on his way. "Is this about the Fireman's Museum research? Because I know what you know."

I sighed. "Okay, come in, both of you, and shut the door again." Shelby came in and sat down, and Marty took the second chair. I looked at the two women in front of me. "I hope one of you has something new, because otherwise we just keep going in circles. I had lunch with James today, and he's frustrated — the police and the FBI are working together, but they don't have anything solid yet. I've been trying to help, but I haven't come up with much. Shelby, what've you got?" I said.

"I found something I think you should see." She looked down at the papers in her hand. "After we talked earlier, I started thinking more about Peter Ingersoll. His file says he grew up in New Jersey, so I looked there, as you asked. When I searched on *Ingersoll* and *firefighter* together, I got a lot of references to Peter's father, mainly from local newspapers. Seems he was a real hero type, so he got lots of press coverage — the major papers even picked up the articles now and then. He was a big guy, kind of John Wayne-ish, and he looked really good in all the fireman's gear, so he got his picture in the paper a lot."

I wasn't sure where she was going with this. "That's nice, but Peter already told me about him. Peter wanted to follow in his father's footsteps, but he couldn't join the department because of his asthma, so he figured running the Fireman's Museum was his best substitute. Is that all?"

"No, ma'am, it's not. I found Peter Senior's obituary, which lists all his achievements and awards and so on. It also lists his surviving family, which includes Peter's brother Scott." She pushed what I saw were photocopied newspaper articles across my desk.

"I know — I've met him. Why is this relevant?"

"I did a little checking on him, too. From what I did find, Scott is kind of the anti-Peter — never went to college, has held a

271

string of dead-end jobs, none of them for too long. And he's got a criminal record, mostly for minor offenses."

"Shelby, how do you find out all this stuff?" Marty asked, clearly impressed.

"There's all sorts of good info on the Internet, if you know where to look."

James had already told me about Scott's less than pristine background, but he hadn't seemed to think it was relevant. "Any mention of arson?" I asked.

"No, but there aren't a lot of details about his criminal activities. So maybe it's possible?"

I had to wonder: was it possible that the son of a much-decorated firefighter would become an arsonist? I had no idea, and I wondered what Celia would have to say. Could Scott have been doing it all along, acting out against his hero dad? But Dad was dead now. Scott didn't stand to benefit . . . or did he? How did he feel about his brother Peter? Would he want to trash his brother's professional reputation by making him look like a fool when his precious collection burned up?

"James told me he had run background checks on the people involved," I said slowly. "He mentioned that Scott had a record, so I suppose he could find out more about Scott's criminal background — and who he knows."

"If he's any good, he should have found this already. If the police are looking . . ." Marty had little patience with city government.

"He may not know about Scott's father, though." I smiled, thinking of what Celia had told us. Was Scott acting out against hero Dad? "Thank you, Shelby — good work. Is that all?"

Shelby gave me a fake pout. "Well, there's no handy signed confession in the file, if that's what you're looking for."

"Ha, ha. Now shoo, both of you. I'll pass this tidbit on to James."

Marty and Shelby exchanged looks, then stood up in unison. "Yes, ma'am. We're out of here, ma'am!" Marty said crisply.

Then they linked arms and marched out of the office together. I smiled at their retreating backs before picking up the phone to call James.

"Morrison," he barked.

"Pratt," I responded in kind.

"Hi, Nell," he replied with a laugh. "You have something?"

"Maybe. You mentioned that Peter's brother Scott had a record?"

"Yes. We've looked at him. He's got an arrest record, mostly for things like bar fights or public drunkenness. No arson, if that's what you're asking. At the moment we can't tie him to this. Of course, we can't rule him out yet, either."

"Did you know that Peter and Scott's father was a firefighter?"

"Yes, I did, Nell. Why does it matter?"

"Did you know that dear old Dad was a media grabber who liked to pose with rescued kittens? And collected a fair bit of news coverage?"

"Ah . . . no, I guess not. Where are you going with this, Nell?"

"Think about it. Peter wanted to be a firefighter but his asthma prevented him. But what about Scott? There must be a story there. You could ask Celia if any of his background or criminal record fits one of her profiles. Does he have an alibi?"

"No, not that I know of — the police are checking that. But having no alibi doesn't prove anything. Do you have an alibi for the right time period?"

"Uh, no. But why would I have set the fire, assuming I could even figure out how? Because I hated Peter Ingersoll? Because I'm planning to eliminate all the museum competition of Philadelphia so I can be queen of whatever?"

I could hear a stifled chuckle. "You have anything else for me?"

Nothing that Selden had told me was worth passing along to James, and I was pretty sure that James did not want to hear that yet another civilian was now privy to details about this case. "Not yet. You'll be the first to know. Thanks for lunch."

"Right. Talk to you later." He hung up.

What had I learned today? Not much. James was doing whatever James did, and I had Shelby and Marty on the hunt on my end.

The only key player I hadn't talked to lately was Gary O'Keefe. I picked up the phone again.

CHAPTER 20

I met Gary O'Keefe in a dim bar not far from Independence Hall. I'd debated for a few minutes about how to approach him, but my creativity had failed me — it had already been a long day — and in the end I came straight out and told him that I was helping the FBI with the investigation of the fire and could I talk to him? He'd agreed instantly and suggested the bar. He was waiting in a booth when I walked in, and stood up when I approached the table.

"Good to see you again, Nell, although I might wish the circumstances were happier. I have to thank you for helping us with the collection information, and so promptly. If nothing else, this awful event has taught us to keep our records backed up."

I sat down and ordered a Guinness, one of my occasional guilty pleasures when I could get it on tap. "Did you lose much of them?"

"More than we should have. Normally the archives and the administrative records are kept on the third floor, which the public doesn't see, or only by appointment. But there were a lot of unexpected structural issues with the renovation, and we had to clear out most of the working space. It's a wonder we still had offices, even if they had no more than plastic sheeting for walls. Your material helped to fill in a lot of the holes."

"Were you able to use the information to file an insurance claim?" I asked.

"We did, but as I think I told you, most of the collection was of limited financial value. And we hadn't upgraded the coverage for the fire engine, for reasons of cost yet again, so we won't get much on that. Certainly not enough to replace it. Ah, she was a beauty . . ." He stared over my head at nothing.

I wasn't surprised: insurance on collections usually bore little relation to the market value of the collection. I had to keep reminding myself that I wasn't supposed to come out and talk about the theft of the *real* fire engine. Why was it that Gary, with the nominal title of curator, hadn't made the same observation that Marty and I had, that the two pictures didn't match up? Or had he, and chosen not to say anything? I could understand his not bringing it up with me — that would be disloyal to his own institution, and I'm sure he'd prefer to keep it quiet. But ethically and legally, surely he should have told the authorities? Was he involved somehow? I felt like I was walking a tightrope, choosing my words carefully. If Gary knew anything about the swap of the fire engines, now would be the perfect opportunity for him to bring it up, and I paused to give him a chance.

He leaned in, and I held my breath, but when he spoke, it wasn't about fire engines. "Poor Peter — he's having a hard time of it. To have such an awful thing happen on his watch."

I had to agree. "I saw him at the Bench Foundation event last night. He doesn't look well, does he? I can only imagine how I'd feel if such a thing happened at the Society. I'd be tempted to throw myself on the fire, too. Oh, sorry — is that in bad taste?"

Gary shook his head. "I'll take that in the spirit in which it was intended. We do tend to become rather attached to our collections, don't we? A terrible thing," he repeated.

We observed a moment of silence, during which time our drinks appeared. Then I said tentatively, "I saw Jennifer there with him. He seems to be depending on her a lot these days."

"He's been lucky to have her. He's not a well man, as I'm sure you've noticed, and this dreadful event has hit him hard." After Gary had taken a healthy swallow of his ale, he said, "So, what is it you want from me?"

I took a deep breath. How far did I dare trust Gary O'Keefe? I didn't know, but I was getting nowhere being tactful and oblique with my questions. "Cards on the table? As I said on the phone, since the last time we met the FBI has asked me to take a look at the fire and the destruction of your collection, from my perspective — inside the museum community. They still haven't decided whether this fire was simply one of a string of arsons or it was a deliberate attempt to destroy what you had stored there, and of course the death of Allan Brigham makes it all the more critical to follow all avenues. I'll admit that I don't know your museum or your staff very well, so I was hoping you could give me some insights into the personalities and the interactions there?" That sounded sufficiently neutral, I hoped. We were closing in on two weeks since the fire and the death had occurred, and there was no solution in sight. "You of all people know exactly how many others knew where the collection was." *And knew how to start a fire,* but I didn't add that out loud.

"I hope you're not suggesting that I had a hand in it?" Gary said, his expression sober.

I responded quickly. "Good heavens, no! Gary, most of us wish we had your kind of public profile. You're one of the most visibly helpful people in the city. In fact, you'd probably have a good shot at winning an election for mayor."

He laughed and threw up his hands. "Heaven forbid! I can't imagine trying to manage this city. I'm happy right where I am."

"You told me you were a firefighter, right?"

"Once a firefighter, always a firefighter. I left the job because of an injury, but as you can see, I just couldn't stay away, so I found myself a way to stay involved."

"From what I've read and heard from other people, the local firefighters are a very close-knit group."

He nodded. "That's more than true. When you lay your life on the line to save people, it brings you together. The same could be said for the police, but at least in our case few people shoot at us. I don't know if you're old enough to remember the MOVE fiasco? That was, what, the mid-eighties?"

I shook my head. "I've heard the name, but I don't know any details." I would have been in grade school — how old did he think I was?

"Not the city's finest moment. The police moved in on a row house that was home to a militant liberation group, and they dropped a bomb on the roof. Then they wouldn't allow the fire department to fight the fire that resulted, and eleven members from the house died. Worse, the fire spread and destroyed an entire city block. That was one time when the police and the fire department failed to work together. But in general our relations have been good."

"I can see that it must be a very intense experience. What can you tell me about arson and people who deliberately set fires?" I said carefully.

Gary got a faraway look in his eye. "A fair question. Tell me, Nell, do you have a fireplace?"

"I do."

"Do you use it?"

"Now and then. Why?"

He didn't answer the question but asked, "When you do use it, why is that?"

I had to think for a minute. I had in fact made a point of adding a working fireplace to my former carriage house, which hadn't had one when I bought it. It had been an indulgence, but for some reason I hadn't ever examined too closely, it had seemed like an essential part of any house. It spoke of home, as in hearth and home. "When I want to feel safe, I guess. Or during romantic moments." I briefly thought of cuddling with someone in front of a cheerful blaze — something that hadn't happened very often.

"Ah, you've hit on something there. Fire has its fascination. When there's a building burning, people are drawn to it. Maybe starting a fire gives the guy a feeling of power, or control. You have to admit it makes a very big statement, to destroy a building. In a way, the safety of the people who might be inside the building is a very minor part of the equation — well, save for us firefighters. Maybe that's the difference: we put the lives first, and an arsonist doesn't care. It's all a mass of contradictions, isn't it? The arsonist cares about the fire, not the people, but for the firefighters it's the other way around."

"It is." I hesitated before asking my next question, although Gary showed no reluctance to talk. "I've heard that there are cases in which a firefighter will set fires in order to make himself appear to be a hero. Are you familiar with that?"

Gary straightened up in his seat. "I have no personal experience with that, but I can tell you that if he were discovered, his colleagues wouldn't stand for it. Goodness knows there are plenty of opportunities to act the hero without manufacturing them."

"Is heroism part of it?"

He looked down at his glass, swirling the liquid around. "I think we go into the job to do good, not to be heroes, but it seems to come with the territory." He sat back and took a long pull of his drink. "I'm probably not explaining myself well, even though I've given this plenty of thought over the years. Let me put it this way: fire is an elemental force, for both good and bad. We firemen are charged with keeping it under control, but we respect it, its power. We don't take kindly to those people who misuse it. Can you understand that?"

"I think I do. Tell me, is there a profile of people who choose to join the fire department? Any particular personality type?"

"I can tell you the obvious: we're mostly big, strong, healthy guys who value good judgment and teamwork — you can't fight a fire alone. Is that what you mean?"

Although he might not know it, Gary's passion came through loud and clear. "You mentioned health — I recall Peter saying at our lunch last week that his father was a firefighter but that he couldn't follow in his footsteps because his medical problems wouldn't allow it."

"I was surprised that he brought it up with you — he doesn't talk about it much. I know it still eats him up. Of course he looked up to his father, and he's never shaken the feeling that he disappointed him."

"You know, Gary, you're quite the psychologist."

"I like people, and I pay attention to them. I love to talk about firefighting. That's why I'm still at the museum, guiding tours, helping out anyone who wants to do research. It's not for the money. I don't know how I'd fill my days if it weren't for this job. I'm not into playing golf or woodworking."

From all I'd seen and heard, I'd have to say that Gary was exactly what he appeared to be: a decent and open man who loved firefighting. Of course, he could be a skilled actor, and I wasn't about to tip my hand, just in case. I'd give him one last chance to mention the fire engine, and I had to ask, "Tell me, Gary, what do you think happened?"

"With the fire?" He shook his head sadly.

"I'd hate to guess. The string of arsons in the city? It's an awful thing, but it happens, now and then. It's spring, right? That brings out something in people — a restlessness, an itch. The fires could be related. Or not. I'd really prefer to think it's only one sick individual who's behind them all."

I sensed some misgivings on his part. "And if they weren't related, was the museum's collection the target?"

Gary shook his head. "I can't for the life of me see why. What harm do we do?"

"The watchman had been a firefighter. Could he have had a grudge?"

"I knew him slightly. He was an angry man, felt he'd been given a raw deal in life."

"By the fire department?" I asked. "Was he let go?"

Gary hesitated before answering. Finally he said, "Yes. He had problems dealing with the stress, and he took to drinking too much. After awhile he couldn't be trusted, so the department eased him out. I know what he was offered when he left the department, and it was fair. He was the only one who thought he deserved more. But I can't see him doing something like this."

"Given his problems, would he have panicked when the fire started? And in his rush to escape, stumbled and hit his head?"

Gary shrugged. "I'm not one to say. It's been a long time since I've seen him."

Another question occurred to me. "You know, I'm not sure I know the extent of the fire. Was the warehouse completely destroyed?"

"No, our men reached it before it went too far."

I noted that once again he had identified himself with the current firefighters, despite the fact he hadn't been part of the department for years. "Do you know where the fire began?"

"The back end of the building, where it would be least likely to be observed. That was logical."

And careful, I added to myself. It showed planning. "And that just happened to be where the museum's materials were stored?"

Gary tilted his head at me, surprised. "You really think that the collections were the target?"

Instead of answering, I asked, "You haven't considered that?"

"But why? I mean, it's not as though there was much of value there, except to us. Sure, some old stuff, but there's more of it around — we've already managed to replace a lot of it through donations. There was the fire

286

engine, of course. That was a real loss to us."

Finally he'd brought it up. *Tread carefully, Nell.* "It was insured."

He nodded. "Surely you aren't suggesting that someone destroyed it just so the museum could claim the insurance? It's not enough to make it worthwhile. We get by financially. The renovations are mostly paid for, from outside sources, so it's not like we needed the cash for that. There's no good reason to destroy the collection . . . unless it was anger at the place."

He didn't seem to know that the real fire engine hadn't perished in the fire — or he wasn't about to admit it to me. Interesting. "Why would anybody be angry at your museum? Disgruntled ex-employees?"

"You've met us all, and we're all still here. What do you think?"

"I can't see any of you doing this, but I don't know you well. What about your board?"

Gary sat back again and blew out a long breath. I waited. Finally he said, "I will not accuse any member of our board of a crime. After all, most of them are firefighters, or have been."

"But?"

He avoided my eyes. "This is just between

287

the two of us, but there are those on the board who think we've outlived our usefulness, that we're just a drain on city funds."

Several reactions buzzed through my head, not very coherently. "But didn't they just help out with the renovation?"

Gary nodded. "They did — but of course the renovation was set in motion a couple of years ago. Things are different now, and pennies count."

"But surely what it costs them to support the Fireman's Museum isn't enough to make a difference to the city budget?"

"It's a matter of perception. You do recall that members of city government run for office? And there are candidates who want to be seen as proactive in slashing costs, especially these days. We're an easy target. Of course, they could just cut our funds and tell us that we'd have to find our own way to replace them. Frankly, we wouldn't last long."

Once again I was glad that the Society didn't depend on the city's support. But what Gary had said raised another issue: if someone within the museum feared a withdrawal of city funding, that might have been enough to make the insurance money look tempting. The museum's operating expenses were low, and a check like that could sustain it for a year or two, long enough to let the economy recover, or the political climate at City Hall change, or to identify new funding sources. Great, now I had a whole set of motives — random, personal, and institutional. But it kept coming back to: who could have set the fire, or found someone who would do it?

"Gary, I know this is hard, especially when you know so many of the people involved. And I don't want to put anyone in a bad light, but we have to eliminate the possibility that someone wanted the collection destroyed. I know Peter has been very torn up about this. What about Jennifer?"

"Jennifer? She's a good woman. Her late husband was a firefighter, you know."

"I'd heard that he didn't leave enough for her to get by."

He looked pained. Still, he answered, "Yes, and that's one reason she's working at the museum."

"How long ago did she start?"

"Oh, five, six years now? Her husband had died a year or so earlier." He smiled. "She's indispensable at the museum — does just about everything."

And doesn't get paid nearly enough for it, I added to myself. I wondered why Jennifer had put up with the lousy pay for five years now — couldn't she have found a better job? I had to regretfully acknowledge that I had learned little from Gary, who had gone out of his way not to implicate anybody. I was out of questions, and it was getting late: time to wrap things up.

"Gary, thank you for meeting with me, and for being so honest. I want you to know that everyone is working hard to lay this to rest. Will the museum be able to open on schedule?"

"Most likely. The fire departments in the city and beyond have been scouring their back rooms and attics for old equipment and such — they've been extraordinarily generous. That lovely engine, now — she'll be harder to replace."

"Where would you find one? Are there auctions for such things?" I asked. I honestly didn't know.

"Now and then they go on sale. But we couldn't afford one at auction at any rate. This last one was donated, years ago. Still, we'll manage. I hope I've been able to help you, Nell."

"You have, Gary. I appreciate it. And you let me know if there's anything else I can do. There may be more information in our collections that would be useful to you."

"I'll keep that in mind. Are you all right

for getting home?"

"I can pick up my train just down the block. Good night, Gary."

Once I'd found myself a seat on the train, I had time to reflect on what Gary had said — or not said. All I had heard so far was how wonderful and noble and honest everybody even remotely involved was. Gary had even managed to avoid overly bad-mouthing Allan Brigham, even though he clearly knew of his flaws. Nobody closely associated with the museum had voluntarily brought up the question of theft; either they were brilliant at covering things up, or they were suspiciously ignorant. Or they were all working together. Or nobody was involved.

And I was getting exactly nowhere.

CHAPTER 21

I did not relish going to work the next day. I felt a bit dirty, digging into the personal lives of my peers, even though it was for a good cause. Worse, I wasn't coming up with anything useful. James had asked for my help, and I'd done my best to follow through, but I had discovered little that he couldn't have found himself more quickly and efficiently. I wasn't even sure this was a collections issue — or even a deliberate crime, beyond the unknown fire setter's urge to destroy something.

I was getting conflicting impressions from various people about why anyone became a firefighter, and why anyone would try to do their modest museum harm, directly or indirectly, individually or collectively. Certainly firefighting was an honorable profession and always had been throughout its long history — which had begun right here in Philadelphia. The tragic events of 9/11 had burned that image into the public's vision. Firefighters were the good guys, committed to protecting and helping people, and nobody wanted to hear anything bad about them — which made this investigation all the more difficult. There was always the chance that a few of them were danger junkies or were looking for some public adoration to boost their own self-esteem, but it was a long jump from that to burning down buildings and killing people.

I had to wonder how many arsonists were eventually caught. Hadn't Celia said that many arson crimes weren't even reported? That meant that someone could have been building up toward a major event like this without leaving any sort of trail. I wanted to believe that if all these recent fire events were the work of one person, then he would at some point slip up or leave some crucial evidence and then be identified and caught. Five fires in less than a month. All set by the same person? Or had someone taken advantage of the flurry of destructive activity to conceal one very different fire?

Gary had put his finger on some interesting aspects of the problem. There was no question that fire fascinated people, but obviously they responded in a variety of ways. Why, when I had always lived a modern suburban life, did I react on some primitive level to sitting in front of a fire in my own home? Why did it still have this almost magical appeal in this modern era, when we no longer depended on fire for heat and light?

And how was I supposed to make sense of all this?

In my office — before Eric, for once — I called James, who was also already in his own office, no surprise.

"You have something?" he asked after we had exchanged basic hellos.

"Not really. I talked to Gary O'Keefe last night."

"The curator? And?"

"He seemed surprised that anyone could have wanted to target the museum's collection. He couldn't think of anyone who might have a grudge against the museum. He didn't want to think that the night watchman had anything to do with it, although he said he thought the guy was a malcontent and had a beef against the fire department. He did hint that there was a rift in the board, between the ones who wanted to keep things going and the ones who wanted to see the museum quietly go away. He didn't say a word about the possible swap of the fire engines. Have I added anything new to what you've got? One blessed, bleeping thing?"

"You sound frustrated."

"Shouldn't I? Look, James, I want to help, really. But I like these people, and everybody likes firemen. Nobody's admitted to being strapped for cash, at least any more than usual. Everybody is good buddies with everybody else, and there's no skullduggery going on anywhere. And that's all I can tell you. Tell me you have something better. Is an arrest imminent? Are you hot on the trail of an arsonist?"

"I'm sorry, Nell." His voice was curiously gentle. "I wish I could say I was. And I regret putting you in a difficult position. The police department has been working hard and cooperating with us, and we're all still coming up dry. We've got a few more things to follow up on. What can I do?"

"Tell me I can go back to my normal life. We've got a lot of documents here to process, thanks to you, and that's our business."

"So are you off the hook? If you think you've talked to everyone that you have access to, then yes, you're done. You get a gold star in your file."

"Well . . ."

"What?"

"I haven't really talked to Jennifer, except

295

briefly at that foundation event. Has any-body talked to her?"

"Obviously the police talked to her, since she knew where the collection was stored. She didn't really have an alibi for the time the fire started — she was one of the home-alone-with-a-book group. In the video we saw of the theft, none of the figures looked like a woman — she's small, and the guys shoving the fire engine around weren't. And you were with her when she got the news of the fire, right?"

"Right, at that luncheon. In fact, we were at the same table when she got the news, and she looked shocked. She and Peter were both there, and they both reacted the way you would expect. Did she say anything else to the police?"

"All she told them was that she had worked for Peter for five years, and he was very upset about everything. The police didn't ask anything else."

"And of course they didn't ask about the theft."

"They didn't know about it."

"Do they now?"

My question was met with silence on James's end, and I jumped to the obvious conclusion. "You haven't told them?"

"Nell, they have enough on their plates,

between the string of arsons and the death. And we have no proof that anything was stolen."

"No, just the strong suspicion of a couple of people like me and Marty." I didn't bring up the fact that Eric and Shelby had also agreed on first sight, but that wouldn't add much credence to the claim anyway. Besides, I already knew James agreed with me, too. "But you're pursuing it?"

"The FBI is looking into the fraud aspect, yes. Quietly."

"Doesn't it go to motive for setting the fire and killing the watchman?"

I could hear his sigh even over the phone. "Nell, the FBI has been officially involved only for a few days. I'm still reviewing the police files on this. Will I tell them about our suspicions? Probably. But high-dollar fraud would be our responsibility, not theirs."

"And here I thought you guys cooperated these days," I muttered under my breath.

"What?"

"Never mind. So, do you want me to buddy up with Jennifer and see if she'll tell me anything?" Which was a ridiculous idea — I might be a professional schmoozer, but I'd never been very good at girl talk, and prying personal information out of a virtual stranger was far beyond my comfort zone.

"We've got it covered. Nell," James said patiently, "I think you've done all you can do. We're grateful for your assistance."

"Well, I guess I should thank you for letting me off the hook. You'll keep me informed?"

"As far as I can."

I recalled that he had said we weren't going to see each other socially until this was resolved, although maybe we'd already broken that rule. I decided to make a move of my own. "When can I ask you to dinner?"

"Are you free tomorrow night?" he responded quickly.

Saturday — date night for most of the world. "Yes." I wasn't in the mood to play games. "Is it a date?"

"It is. I'll make the reservations and pick you up." Which was generous of him, considering I lived way out in the boonies. "And, Nell? If anything else occurs to you, let us know, will you? I promise I won't cancel because of that."

"Deal. See you tomorrow. I'm looking forward to it."

After we had hung up, I sat back. Part of me was relieved to be out of this mess, but another part of me knew that there was more to the story and it wasn't over yet. But now I could get back to my own job, including figuring out what to do with the massive collection the FBI had handed us. Even if we weren't keeping it permanently, it had to go somewhere, at least for a while. And I didn't think the FBI was going to move very quickly on resolving the ownership issues — didn't they have to wait some period of time for the original owners to come forward? — so that *while* could be long. We were already crammed to the rafters at the Society; besides, after what had happened to the Fireman's Museum, no way was I going to consider off-site storage. We'd just have to muddle through somehow. At least we had too much rather than not enough.

Maybe it was time to talk to the kids again. Maybe they'd discovered a time-space warp and stuck all those boxes into a parallel universe so they could process the materials at their own pace. If only.

Eric was at his desk when I emerged from my office. "Hey, Nell, you're in early."

"Lots to do, Eric, and every time I start something, something else pops up. You know that carnival game whack-a-mole? Well, that's what my job feels like some days."

"You need coffee?" he asked.

"Not right now — I thought I'd stop by the processing room and see how the sorting is going for the FBI collection. Darn, we're going to have to find something better to call it. The *stolen collection* doesn't sound any nicer, does it?"

"The *found collection?* Heck, maybe we should name it after you, if we get to hold on to it. Doesn't the Pratt Collection sound good?"

That was something I'd never even considered. It did sound rather nice, but before I could start designing tasteful brass plaques with my name on them, there were a lot of hurdles to clear. "Keep that in mind. Right now I've got to see if they've created order out of chaos yet."

When I walked into the processing room, I was glad to see that Latoya was already there, perched on a tall stool with the youngsters grouped around her, and I could swear they were all laughing. I almost turned around and left so that I wouldn't upset this happy moment, but then Alice spotted me and waved.

"Morning, Nell. Come join us and we'll give you an update."

I joined them around one of the long

tables. "Good morning, all. How are things going?"

"Just look around," Rich said, grinning. "The first pass is done. We were just discussing with Latoya how we should approach the next phase."

I pulled up my own stool and sat. "Latoya, what's your take on this?"

She turned to me, and I was struck by how happy she looked. "From what we've seen, the main emphasis is on Civil War materials. Whoever collected them had a good eye, and he chose well. Since that's the primary focus of what he assembled, I'd recommend processing that material first, as a cohesive unit. Then we can follow up with the other odds and ends."

"That sounds like a plan. Do you have any idea where you want to put them?"

"I'd like to ask Rich to sort out the Terwilliger Collection first, and then that can go back into the vault downstairs. That will free up space up here, and I think we can accommodate the rest more easily then. We may find a quiet corner for the non-related materials, at least in the short term. And, Nell? I may take charge of some of those myself — there's a cache of information on the abolitionist movement that complements my research very well."

Aha! That explained why Latoya was in such a good mood. I knew that she had originally joined the Society because we had such a strong — and uncataloged — collection of abolitionist records, which were her particular interest. She'd even wangled a four-day workweek so she could do research on the other day, although that had fallen by the wayside, at least temporarily, since we'd lost our registrar. It had never occurred to me that buried somewhere in all the FBI boxes were materials that would interest her, but I thanked the gods of collections that she had struck pay dirt. "That sounds like an excellent strategy. So Rich will concentrate on the Terwilliger papers first, while Nicholas and Alice tackle the FBI materials. Then Rich will join them after the Terwilliger papers are reinstalled?"

"That's about it," Latoya said. "And if you need any help negotiating with the FBI regarding stewardship, please ask."

"Of course. I'll leave you all to get to work. And thank you! You've done a great job in a short period, and I'm truly impressed."

I left before the moment of cordiality could evaporate. I hadn't been exaggerating: they'd done an extraordinary amount of work in only a few days. Maybe it was their youthful energy, or maybe they were trying to impress me and/or outdo each other, but whatever the cause, it was getting the job done.

The glow of satisfaction carried me back to my office and then burst like a bubble when Eric greeted me. "Nell, there's a Jennifer Phillips waiting to see you in the lobby. She said she just needs a minute."

So much for staying out of the Fireman's Museum problem.

CHAPTER 22

When I reached the lobby, Jennifer was standing and staring intently at the few books we offered for sale, in a hanging rack on the wall, without seeing them.

"Jennifer?"

She turned quickly. "Hi, Nell. Look, I'm really sorry to bother you. You have a minute to talk?"

"You want to go up to my office?"

"Oh, no, that's too much trouble. Is there a quiet corner down here? It won't take long."

"Sure, there's a room under the stairway there, where we can talk privately." I led her in that direction.

"I'm so jealous," Jennifer said. "You have so much space here! Our building used to be a firehouse and was never intended as a public space, so we've had to make do for a lot of things."

"If we thought we could get away with

putting shelves everywhere, we would, but people expect certain things when they visit us." We reached the room, and I ushered her in, closing the door behind me, then pointed her to a chair. "As I remember your museum, I think you did a wonderful job in fitting in exhibits, given your space limitations. You must have had some interesting discussions when you were planning for the renovation." Maybe it was tactless to bring up the lost collections, but that had to be related to why she was here.

"I kind of sat and listened for most of those discussions. And took notes, of course. Peter and Gary hashed out what they wanted, and I told them what I'd seen when we had tours in — what worked, what didn't."

"That can make a difference. You don't have a background in museum management?"

"No. I took the job because I needed it, and I was lucky to get it, since I really didn't have any skills back then. I've learned a lot along the way. It's a nice place. Peter's a good guy, and everybody loves Gary."

"Do you deal with the board much?"

"I take minutes at meetings, but that's about it."

"So, what did you want to talk to me about?"

Jennifer twisted her hands nervously. "Nell, this is awkward."

I was holding my breath and making internal side bets about what would come out of her mouth next. She had finally figured out there had been a theft? She was one of the rare female arsonists and had set all the fires herself?

"I need your help, or, no, well, I think Peter needs your help. He's falling apart."

Okay, that one I hadn't foreseen. "What do you mean?"

"How long have you known him?"

"I never met him in person until after the fire. I knew who he was, of course, but I wouldn't have recognized him on the street."

"So you haven't seen how much he's changed since the fire. Look, I've worked with him for over five years now. He's always been a great boss — easy to get along with, calm, reasonable. He knows he's not a world-beater, and he wasn't using the Fireman's Museum as a stepping-stone to any other post. He likes his job, and he loves firefighting. Up until the fire, I would have said that everything was great."

"And all that's changed?"

"Yes! I swear, he must have lost ten pounds since last week — I'm not even sure he remembers to eat. He's had a couple of asthma attacks for the first time in a long while. He spends time staring into space, and I have to remind him when he has a meeting to go to or something has to be completed or turned in. I swear, he looks haunted."

"I'm sure he feels terrible about what happened to the collection. I mean, to lose so much, all at once — that must be hard."

"But it's just *stuff!*" Jennifer protested. "Yes, it was a nice little collection, and the exhibits were popular, but most of it is easy to replace. In fact, we're almost back to where we were. Everybody we know in the firefighter community has chipped in, so it's not like we have nothing to put in the cases."

"And the fire engine?" I asked cautiously, curious to see what she would say.

"Well, okay, that's an important piece, but there are others around. To tell the truth, I'm kind of glad it's gone."

I hadn't expected to hear that. "Why?"

"For one thing, it took up a lot of space — space that we could use to exhibit other things, or maybe for rotating exhibits. Second, it was a real liability. You know we get lots of school groups?" When I nodded, she continued, "We always had to keep an eye on the kids to make sure they didn't start climbing on it. And since we usually rely on volunteer docents, they don't always know how to handle children. I can't tell you how many little guys I've pulled off that engine, after their group moved on to the next exhibit."

I had to laugh — hadn't James said something like that? "That's a problem we don't have here. We don't get a lot of children at all." The moment of humor faded quickly. "Was the fire engine insured?" When she nodded yes, I went on, "Does that mean you have a choice of replacing it or using the money in another way?"

She looked away. "That's a laugh. We're all living from check to check these days."

That wasn't what Gary had told me. "I thought the renovation was pretty well covered. Were there construction overruns?"

"When aren't there? And even if the city or outside donors pick up that cost, the project has dragged on and on, so we've lost a lot of admissions revenue. Usually the city has ponied up the difference, but they're feeling the squeeze now, too. I mean, if they can't pay for cost-of-living increases for garbage collectors, why should they bail out a small museum? Think about it" — she held her hands out, palms up, as if weighing the possibilities — "cost-of-living raises versus dusty fire helmets in a case. Which one are constituents going to think is more important?"

She had a point. "Jennifer, I'm sorry to hear all that, and I can understand why you and Peter are stressed out about it. Is he worried that the city or the board is going to seize this opportunity to close you down, now that you've lost your collection?"

"That's part of it, and it's a real possibility. But I think it's more than that — something's eating him up. I think he blames himself for losing the collection, and even for the death of the watchman. If he hadn't been forced to cut corners, maybe the collection would have gone to a more secure facility. I won't say it's his fault — it was the board that pushed for the cheaper solution. They didn't think it really mattered, but they're not museum people."

And maybe whatever board faction wanted to see the museum go under had engineered the destruction of the collection, sticking it in a vulnerable, out-of-the-way storage facility. It was an angle that I thought deserved consideration, based on what I'd heard from Gary and Jennifer. Could this get any more complicated? "What is it you want me to do?"

"Talk to Peter. Please? You've had some rough times here at the Society, right? Tell him that there are ways to work things out. You're his equal, and he knows you understand, because of what you've been through here. He won't listen to me."

That seemed simple enough, and certainly my heart went out to Peter. I knew what it was like to face public scrutiny, and worse, criticism, for your institution and your management of it. "Of course, if you think it will help. Should I call him?"

Jennifer glanced at her watch. "I'm headed back there now. He's out at a meeting with the builders, but he'll be back later this afternoon. Why don't I tell him you'd like to talk with him? Maybe about the collection? I don't want him to think we're planning an intervention or something. How late will you be here?"

"I can stay after closing, if you like. Call me when you know when he's coming, or have him call."

Jennifer stood up. "I'll do that. Thank you, Nell. I know this is asking a lot from you, but I really hope it will make a difference. He's been so depressed lately."

"I understand, believe me. Let me see you

out." I led her back to the front door and watched her leave.

That had certainly been interesting. As I walked toward the elevator, I reviewed what she had said. Nothing she had told me suggested there was anything more to her concern than that of a friend and coworker, and maybe someone who was worried about keeping a job she needed — if the job and the place survived. And if Peter was truly depressed, he might not even acknowledge that he had a problem, and he certainly wouldn't be likely to reach out to me for help, beyond the professional issues we had already covered. Jennifer was right: I had experience in this area. Maybe I *could* help. It looked like I might have a chance to find out.

I spent some constructive hours looking at departmental reports, sketching out a preliminary agenda for the next board meeting, and doing other essential but boring administrative stuff, so that I could feel virtuous over the weekend. Just past five Eric stuck his head in. "Do you need anything else, Nell?"

"No, I'm good. Go on home, and have a nice weekend." It was a Friday afternoon, and people usually left promptly; there was no reason for Eric to stay.

"Thanks. You, too."

I hadn't heard from either Jennifer or Peter, but I thought I'd give them a little more time. I wasn't in a hurry, and I kind of relished the peace in the building when it was empty. I could hear people calling out farewells, the elevator making its slow way up and down, and the front door opening and closing two stories below me. At five thirty the phone finally rang, and I picked it up.

"Oh, Nell, I'm glad you're still there. He's on his way over," Jennifer said breathlessly. "He just left. Sorry I couldn't call earlier, but I had trouble tracking him down. I wasn't sure if he was coming back at all. I know you'll be locked up. Can you keep an eye out for him?"

"I'll go down now and wait for him."

"Oh, thank you, Nell. I really appreciate this, and I'm sure it will make a difference."

"I hope so." We both hung up. I decided to leave my bag and jacket upstairs, since I wasn't sure where he'd be most comfortable talking, if he'd talk at all, and I certainly didn't want to look like I was ready to race out the door.

When I entered the lobby, Front Desk Bob was still there, shutting down the cash register and tidying the front desk. "Hey,

Nell — you aren't leaving?"

"Not yet. I'm meeting a friend — he'll be here in a few minutes. You go on home, okay? I can lock up after we're done."

"You know the security codes and stuff?"

"I do, don't worry. See you Monday."

Bob escorted the last stragglers out the door. There were always a few who wanted just a few more minutes for their precious research, ignoring the fact that they were holding up more than one person at the end of the day. But their admission fees and membership dues paid our bills, so I smiled and nodded as they collected their things and headed out the door. It was past six when Bob made one last sweep of the ground floor. "You want me to leave some lights on?" he called out.

"Just the catalog room, I guess. I'll take care of that later."

He returned, put on his jacket, said, "Night, Nell," and went out the door, which closed behind him with a metallic clang. I was alone in the building.

It was nice, especially because it was rare. The building itself was over a hundred years old, and looked good for another hundred — it had been built to last. I didn't want to get too far from the front door, so I could let Peter in quickly, but I drifted into the catalog room, the cork-tile floor there muffling my footsteps. The ceiling soared above me; the mismatched card catalogs huddled below, interspersed with sturdy tables. The commuter rail train rumbled far beneath my feet.

The doorbell rang and I jumped — it was always louder than I expected — and I hurried to answer it. I pulled open the heavy doors to find Peter standing on the doorstep in the gathering dusk, looking, if possible, worse than the last time I'd seen him. "Thanks for coming over, Peter. Please, come in."

He stepped inside and took in the surroundings. "I've always liked this building — there's so much space. It's peaceful. Not like my museum."

"Jennifer said the same thing, more or less."

"She's seen it?"

I debated about telling him that Jennifer had been here earlier today. In the end I replied vaguely, "She's been here."

Peter didn't seem to notice the evasion. "She said you wanted to talk to me? Did you find something else about the collections?"

"Not exactly. Come, walk with me. Have

you ever had a behind-the-scenes tour here?"

Poor Peter looked bewildered — obviously Jennifer had been cagey about the real purpose of this visit. But he didn't protest, and he didn't seem to be in any hurry. I couldn't blame him — I would certainly prefer to be here, in the solid silence, than back in his chaotic space. I led him to the first big room past the lobby. "This is the catalog room, and the research desk. Our microfilm collections are housed in a room over there" — I waved vaguely toward the left — "although the digital age is going to make them useless eventually. The card catalogs here represent a century's worth of records, although we're digitizing them slowly so we can include them on our website. On the right here is our reading room." I led him through the nearer of the double doors.

He paused on the threshold to take it in — the ceiling two stories above, the serried rows of shelves ringing the room, both at ground level and along the balcony above us, the mural over the broad entrance to the reference rooms with its local history collections. "What a handsome place this is," he said softly. "You're lucky." Then he seemed to shake himself, tearing his gaze away from the room and turning to me. "Jennifer said you wanted to talk to me?" he repeated.

"Let's find a place to sit." For some reason I was reluctant to take him upstairs — the grandeur of this room seemed to calm him. I led him to one of the long library tables, toward the back of the room, and turned on the lamp on the table. He pulled out a chair and sat, looking mystified, and I took an adjoining chair. "Peter, I don't know you well, but I'll just come straight to the point. Jennifer is worried about you. She says you haven't been yourself since the fire, and she thinks something is eating at you. She thought maybe I could help, since I've had my own share of problems regarding collections. I may be way out of line, and if you don't want to talk to me just say so, but I'd like to help, if I can."

He didn't answer immediately, and his gaze returned to the soaring space around us. I wondered if he was weighing his options: stay or go? Would he tell me to mind my own business, then bolt? I waited.

He didn't seem to have the energy to move. Finally he looked at me, his expression bleak. "She's right. I don't know — maybe talking would help, but I don't know if there's a damn thing you can do about it."

"Do you feel responsible for the fire?" I asked.

"Yes, but not the way you think. How much do you know?"

I paused a moment, trying to decide whether to be completely truthful with him. James would probably be angry if I spilled the beans about what I knew — and the FBI knew — about the fire engine, but Peter was sitting in front of me now and in obvious pain. "I know somebody pulled a fast one with your prize fire engine. I saw the newspaper pictures after the fire, and when I compared the one of the destroyed engine to the picture in our files, it was obvious to me."

Peter slumped, almost imperceptibly. Then he nodded, once. "I'm surprised more people haven't figured that out. If Gary knows, he hasn't said anything to me. Who else knows?"

"Marty Terwilliger — the engine used to belong to her grandfather, remember? So she knew it well, and she figured it out on her own. A couple more people on my staff. And I told the FBI."

Peter went still. Finally he said, "I didn't know, I swear. It was bad enough that the

317

collection was destroyed. I could live with a stupid coincidence, the warehouse fire. But someone died. I can't believe anyone meant that to happen. To think that somebody planned this stunt deliberately . . ." He shook his head helplessly.

"Do you know who?" I probed gently.

He nodded. "I think so," he whispered.

CHAPTER 23

I was waiting breathlessly for him to go on when Peter twitched like a rabbit and stopped talking. He looked at me. "Did you hear something?"

I listened a moment, but I'd been so focused on what Peter was saying that I wasn't sure if I would have noticed anything outside the room. "Like what?"

"Breaking glass?"

I really hadn't heard anything, but I was used to this old building with its odd noises. "No, but it's a kind of noisy neighborhood, and people throw things into the Dumpsters in the alley out back all the time." We both held still for several seconds, but I didn't hear anything out of place. I wondered if Peter had actually heard something or if he'd just spooked himself into thinking he had. "You have an idea what happened with the fire engine? Who's responsible?" I prompted.

He seemed to reach an internal decision, because he sounded calmer when he spoke. "How much time do you have?"

Now he was going to play coy? I struggled to remain calm and soothing. "As long as you need."

"Good. I have to go back a ways, to put this in context. You know we started planning this renovation a couple of years ago?"

"Yes. You told me when we first met that you wanted to tie it in to the tenth anniversary of 9/11."

"Right. Wait — maybe I should go back further. Or, no, let me just say that the Fireman's Museum has been bass-ackwards from the beginning. It's kind of like, a group of firefighters got together and said to each other, hey, let's make a museum! And then they did — found the place, cadged collections items from their buddies, and presto, they had a nice little museum. That was fine for the first few years. Then the Bicentennial came along, and the city had some money to spend, and they decided to upgrade the museum, give it a higher profile. Along the way they thought they should formalize the organization, so they created the nonprofit entity. All this was long before my time."

Sad to say, at the moment Peter looked

old enough to have been around since then. "Go on."

"The thing of it is, we've always been kind of a hybrid organization. Sure, there's an official structure in place, but there's always been a certain reliance on the city for support. Of all kinds, I might add. There are a lot of firefighters who lead tours, that kind of thing. No way could we afford to pay them, but we couldn't keep the doors open without them. You see the problem?"

"Yes," I said, but truthfully, I still wasn't sure how this led to arson and maybe murder.

"Okay, fast-forward thirty years or so. That's a whole generation. Traditions have changed, and the personnel at City Hall have, too. You remember Frank Rizzo?"

"The former mayor? I knew of him, but he was a bit before my time."

"He was police commissioner before he was mayor. And his brother Joe was fire commissioner when Frank was mayor — he's the one who helped formalize the museum structure. So both of them were tied to city government, right? And to the unions. Philadelphia was a different place back in those days. Then the bean counters took over — Wilson Goode, even Ed Rendell. They had to look at the business side of running the city, and things looked pretty bleak for a while."

I was beginning to wonder when Peter would actually get to the point, so I decided to nudge him in that direction. Otherwise we might be here all night. "And the Fireman's Museum became a liability?"

"In its own small way, yes. That's not to say we haven't had supporters on City Council, but there's a faction that thinks we've outlived our usefulness. They want to eliminate our funding, and if that happens, we'd die a slow death in a couple of years."

That matched what Gary had told me. "I'm sorry to hear that, Peter, but how does that get us to where we are now?"

He shook his head. "I'm not sure. I don't want to see the museum disappear, and I know there are other people who feel strongly about it, too. This may sound odd to you, but what if one of them decided to torch the collection?"

I stifled a laugh. "Don't you have that backward? How does destroying the collection improve the chances for the museum's survival?"

"Think about it. Most of the collection was cobbled together from donations from various fire stations around the city. Most of the items weren't valuable, and they're easy to replace — we've already had a lot of donations. But what's more important is that we've gotten a lot of publicity and a lot of sympathy — you know what *that's* worth. I mean, we really *are* the people's museum."

He had a point. Sacrificing easily replaceable, low-value items while attracting a lot of attention had certainly shoved the small museum into public awareness. But there was still a flaw in his logic. "What about the fire engine? Where does that fit?"

Peter fell silent, his expression pained. Finally he said, "I'm not sure. Say someone deliberately set the fire to destroy the collection. The fire engine should have gone up with it, and we would have collected some insurance on it, although not as much as you might think. Maybe that was part of the original plan. But maybe somebody got greedy and said, hey, that's worth some money — let's slip in a ringer and pull the good one out of there and sell it. Who's going to know?"

I could see that. It almost worked, too. If I hadn't happened to compare the two pictures, I would never have known. Most people wouldn't be able to do that, anyway. And if I hadn't known someone in the FBI and told him, it probably *would* have worked. "Peter, is there *anyone* you suspect?" I was getting desperate for any sort of answer.

"I've tried not to think about it. I mean, I'm not stupid — I know how few people knew where we had stored the collections: me, Scott, Gary, Jennifer, the board members. There was a board member who insisted that we use that facility, but I think he was part owner of the storage company."

"Walter Barnes?" I guessed.

Peter looked at me, startled. "Yes. How did you know?"

"I guessed. He seemed awfully nervous when I talked to him at the Bench Foundation event."

"He's probably just worried about his liability. Look, Nell, you don't have to make excuses — you did the right thing, and I know that the FBI has to look at me as a possible suspect. But I just can't imagine that any of the people I've worked with for years could be involved in something like this."

But who else was there? "I know how hard that is. But maybe whoever set this up didn't plan to kill anyone. Theft, no matter how large, is a far cry from murder. Assume for the moment that insurance fraud — or maybe that and the theft of the fire engine — was the only intended crime, and the watchman was — what do they call it? Collateral damage? — then who would be capable of planning the fire?"

He was shaking his head again. "I don't know! I mean, I see your point, but I still don't believe anyone I know could have done this."

"Sure you do," a voice said from the doorway. I turned in my chair to see Scott Ingersoll, in grubby clothes, a battered knapsack slung over his shoulder, slouching against the door frame that led to the catalog room. "Hey, Peter."

Peter stood up abruptly. "Scott?"

My mind was working furiously. How had Scott found a way into the building? Of course — the noise Peter had heard must have been Scott breaking in. I knew that our security system covered mainly the doors; there was no way we could have wired each and every window, and there were plenty.

"What are you doing here, Scott?" Peter's breath sounded raspy.

Scott ignored his brother's question. "Nice to see you again, Ms. Pratt. Although I bet you won't enjoy the visit." Scott grinned but kept his distance. Of course, he knew he had our only escape route blocked.

"It depends on what you want." I should

call the cops — except that my cell phone was in my bag two stories up, and Scott was between me and the nearest landline phone.

"You know, Ms. Pratt, it would have been a lot simpler if you'd just stayed out of this."

"Peter asked for my help in reconstructing what was in the collection." I wasn't about to mention the FBI. What could Scott want? How much had he heard of our conversation while he was sneaking up on us? I didn't know, but I had an ugly feeling I was about to find out.

"I hadn't counted on that. I figured Peter would be so broken up about the loss of his precious little collection that he'd just wallow in misery and let the cops take care of it while he collected the insurance. But, no — thanks to you, now he knows about that trade-off. You had to figure out the fire engine wasn't the right one."

Wait — how did he know that I knew? Had he overheard me tell Peter? Had someone else told — Marty, Shelby, Eric, James? I didn't think any of them would have let anything slip, and even if they had, how would it have gotten back to Scott? I tried to remember what Shelby or James had told me about Scott: he had a minor criminal record, but no one had told me the details. Maybe he was just guessing. "Why do you say that?"

"Why else would you and the police still be poking around? If you weren't suspicious, you would have handed over the records to Peter and that would have been the end of it, but you just kept right on asking questions. Looks like you were too smart for your own good, Ms. Pratt."

So it seemed. But . . . why would he know that I was still talking to law enforcement? I hadn't said a word to Peter about the switched fire engines prior to today. Which left . . . Gary, and I could find no reason to believe he was behind all this. The gears in my mind ground slowly . . .

What about Jennifer? Jennifer had engineered this meeting with Peter and made sure it was after hours when no one else would be around. Jennifer was the only one who knew we were both here. Ergo, Jennifer had told Scott. Bingo: Jennifer was the link — and she and Scott had to be in this together.

Scott seemed amused as he watched me. "Figured it out yet?"

"Jennifer," I said bluntly.

"Got it in one. I said you were smart."

How long had they been planning this? I really didn't like the idea that Jennifer had played on my sympathy and used me to lure

Peter here. She was a damn good actress.

"Scott, what's going on here? What does Jennifer have to do with this?" Peter wheezed.

"Ask your friend here." He nodded at me. "If you can get the words out."

Peter turned to me, fear in his eyes. "Nell?"

I kept my eyes on Scott. "Peter, obviously there had to be someone on the inside, who knew where the collection was and what the engine was worth. I think Jennifer's a better bet than Gary. Right, Scott?"

"Keep up the good work. Gary is exactly what he looks like — an old coot who loves to talk about fires and firemen. Now, Jennifer — she's got a head on her."

"But, why? Was it just about the money?"

"What else? Jennifer needs the money. Her husband's pension sucks — he'd only been with the department a few years when he died. The pay at the museum isn't much better. That hunk of wood and metal was worth a couple of years' salary for her, and it was just too easy to pass up. She asked me to help, for a share of the proceeds. Wasn't hard to do."

"Did you set all the other warehouse fires?"

"Maybe. What's it to you?"

"Scott, a man died there, where you switched the fire engines."

For the first time, Scott looked troubled. "Yeah, well, that wasn't supposed to happen. The guy was a drunk. We thought he'd just passed out in a corner — wouldn't have been the first time."

I wasn't sure whether I believed that Scott hadn't known where the watchman was, but this wasn't the time to debate that. "Where's the real fire engine?" I asked.

Scott all but snarled, "Look, lady, don't expect me to pull a Sherlock Holmes and tell you everything you want to know. That's bullshit. I don't have the time."

"What're you going to do?"

"Your place here is going to have an unfortunate fire, and it'll look like Peter was the one who set it. Too bad the two of you have to die. Jennifer will be all upset about sending Peter over here to talk to you, when she's had her suspicions that he was mentally unstable. But she was a loyal little employee, and she trusted her boss. Boo-hoo."

So Jennifer had set it all up. Wait, back up: *had* to die? Sorry, but I wasn't going to go quietly. "What's your end of the plan? You're supposed to do the dirty work and kill us? And why do you think you can set a fire here?"

"Oh, come on, lady — this building is full of dry old paper and books. Piece of cake. As for killing you — the fire'll take care of that."

That was convenient: he didn't get his hands dirty; the fire did all the work. What a handy rationalization. "And why is Peter supposed to have set it?"

"Why, to cover up killing you, of course. He couldn't let you keep nosing around."

"Nobody's . . . going to . . . believe that." Peter's breathing was worsening rapidly, and he reached into his pocket for an inhaler. Would anyone buy that a serious asthmatic would be able to start a fire? Of course, the fire department and the police would have two bodies, neither of whom was talking. The story Scott had presented would be the simplest solution. Would James believe it?

"Why . . . are . . . you . . . doing . . . this?" Peter struggled to say.

Scott cocked his head at his brother. "Well, let's see. Because you were little Mr. Perfect and Daddy loved you better? Because your asthma got you out of a lot of stuff that I ended up having to do?"

I watched Scott. Actually he didn't seem very invested in the reasons he tossed at his brother: they sounded like echoes of old sibling arguments. But why had Scott acted

330

now? I said, "The fire engine isn't worth that much." Certainly not a man's life.

"What would you know about it? Hey, I'm not greedy. And how often do I get to stick it to Peter here and make some change out of it?"

Maybe it was about the fire, not the cash. Maybe I was looking at a true arsonist. And maybe Jennifer had been pulling his strings all along. "Scott, you're talking about killing your *brother!*" And me, of course, but there was no point in adding that. "Do you really think the FBI and the police aren't already looking at you for this?"

"Sure they are, but I've got an alibi. I was with Jennifer the night of the fire. We're in *love.*" His eyes flickered toward Peter, who was having more and more trouble breathing. "Sorry about that, Petey, but one of us has got to take the fall for this, thanks to Ms. Pratt, and it's not going to be me."

Scott Ingersoll was one sick man. Hang on — hadn't James told me that Jennifer had told the police that she was home alone? From the way Scott drawled the word *love,* I had to stop and wonder who was pulling whose strings. Had Jennifer recruited Scott, or had he persuaded Jennifer to help him? Had Jennifer just thrown him under the bus by undercutting his alibi?

331

Did he realize that?

And this was the man who wanted to kill me? Please. I'd be embarrassed to have been outwitted by those two — except that I'd be dead. But I wasn't yet, and I wasn't giving up that easily.

"That's not what Jennifer told the police. She said she was home alone. Will the police be able to match you to one of the guys on the surveillance footage?"

For a moment Scott looked startled, but he recovered quickly. "Don't know what you're talking about, lady."

Yeah, right. I tried another tack. "We have fire suppression systems in this building, you know."

"Sure you do — old ones. I checked the specs — looked at your old annual reports, when you announced your so-called improvements. You really counting on them to save you?"

I didn't want to find out.

The bastard was still grinning at us. He was enjoying this, or maybe just anticipating the nice bright fire that he thought was coming. "And of course, there's always that handy smoke inhalation. You don't have to fry, just inhale too much. Peter'll probably go first, though. That pesky asthma, you know. I spent years listening to him wheeze at night."

Not if I could help it. *Think, Nell!* Scott was definitely bigger and no doubt stronger than I was, so I didn't think I had a chance of overpowering him physically. Peter was pretty much useless if it came to any kind of physical attack. I'd gotten that far in my thinking when Scott pulled a gun out of his pocket and waved it at me.

This was getting ridiculous. "What, Peter is supposed to have shot me? How is anybody going to account for a bullet?"

"Just some insurance." He ignored my question and turned to Peter. "Recognize it? It was Dad's. How sentimental of you, to have kept it all these years. But of course, you always really looked up to Dad."

Peter glared wordlessly at him and dropped into a chair, his breathing labored. *Come on, Nell, think this through.* Now that I knew Scott was armed, I couldn't even rush him, or I'd end up with a bullet in me. I glanced around the room: heavy tables with the lamps bolted to them, heavy chairs. I supposed I could throw books at Scott, but that seemed ridiculous. I wondered hysterically if a six-inch-thick tome would stop a bullet. Leather or cloth binding? What was I supposed to do?

And then the answer came to me: let Scott start a fire.

CHAPTER 24

Sure, it was completely illogical, but I was beginning to have a glimmer of an idea, and the only way for it to work was to let Scott do what he planned, and do it right here in the reference room. "It's not that easy, you know," I said.

"What, to start a fire? Sure it is, if you know what you're doing. Look at all the lovely paper you have here." He grinned. "And don't tell me you have recording devices and spy cameras everywhere, and a panic button in your pocket that connects you immediately to the police department. You're alone here with Peter. He sets the fire, you try heroically to put it out. Either he shoots you or he doesn't, but you both die. He gets the blame, and Jennifer and I get a nice chunk of change when we unload the fire engine, even if we have to wait until things cool down before we sell it." He barked a short laugh at his own joke. "End of story."

He'd forgotten to mention that the museum would probably go under, and Jennifer would be out of a job, but now was not the time to bring it up. "Look around you, Scott. What're you going to light?"

"Why would I be stupid enough to do it here? Even I can see the sprinkler heads up there."

If my pathetic plan was going to work, he *had* to do it here, right where we were. But how on earth was I supposed to convince him to do that? "You really think they're going to blame Peter for all the fires? I mean, look at him — he can barely breathe."

"I made sure he didn't have an alibi for any of those fires."

"Jennifer." If I got out of this alive, I was going to enjoy watching her go down.

"Yup, she's one smart cookie. She keeps his schedule, so she told me when he was going to be alone at home when all the fires started. So let's get rolling." He waved the pistol at us.

Peter struggled to get out of his chair, then fell back again.

A flicker of anger crossed Scott's face. "Get up, you jerk. We're going back into the stacks, where nobody passing by outside will notice the fire for a good long while."

Not part of my plan. I wondered if I could communicate psychically with Peter and convey that I wanted him to stay right here.

Scott waved his weapon at me. "Help him."

I moved over to Peter's chair and slid my arm under his. Which conveniently let me lean close and hiss, "Act helpless." Peter looked at me with sad puppy-dog eyes, and I realized he didn't even have to act. I hauled him out of his chair, but he was pretty much a dead weight, focusing on breathing and nothing else.

I glanced at Scott, whose face was now flushed. "He can't make it."

"Then drag him," Scott snarled.

I made a good show of it, but Peter was surprisingly heavy. Even if I had wanted to, I couldn't have dragged him anywhere near the stacks in the back of the building. "This isn't going to work. I can't move him."

Scott's expectation that we'd make it to the stacks was dimming, but now he was getting mad. He waved the gun at us. "Back there. Around the corner, out of sight from the front."

Exactly what I wanted. I helped Peter stumble slowly toward the reference room. The volumes there might be old — and flammable — but they weren't terribly valuable, comparatively. We made it to the wide doorway and turned the corner, out of view from the windows in the front. I leaned Peter up against the shelves along the wall. "What now?" I asked Scott.

Scott looked briefly around, most likely recasting his plan. "It'll still work. How old's your system? Fifty years? You even know if it works?"

He hadn't done his homework well — the systems were newer than that, but they'd never been tested. "We've never had a fire here. I don't know."

"What's in there?" Scott nodded toward the vault. "I don't see sprinklers."

"Nobody thought they were necessary in there — they figured the sprinklers out here would be enough."

"Great. Start tearing up some books."

"What?"

"You heard me. You never built a bonfire? Take a book, rip out the pages, crumple 'em, and pile 'em up." Without taking his eyes off me, he reached into the backpack and pulled out a metal can, which I had to assume contained an accelerant. "Go on, start ripping."

I started pulling books at random off the shelves. I couldn't bring myself to look at the titles; I just opened them up and started

338

grabbing handfuls of paper. I made a nice pile, with Scott's eyes on me the whole while — and I carefully positioned it as close to the vault as I dared.

"You too, Petey-boy," Scott said.

I sneaked a look at Peter, and he did not look good. He was suffering from a double whammy: the asthma was crippling him, and he was trying to deal with the fact that his brother wanted to kill him in a particularly unpleasant way. I wished there was a way to communicate to him without speaking that I'd rather have him close to me, because he was part of my desperate plan. Peter rose slowly, then pulled another book out and followed my lead. The pile of crumpled paper on the floor grew between us.

"That's enough," Scott said. "Now, pull out a bunch more books — the old dry stuff, not the shiny new ones — and toss them around. Make sure they're open and the pages are fanned out."

I was angry . . . but not angry enough to blow my one chance. At least he had let me build the pyre where I wanted to. Once the fire got started, the fire suppressant system would be activated, and that was linked directly to the fire department — I hoped. I refused to acknowledge how old — and

339

untested — the whole system was. I had to assume that Scott planned to be long gone by then, out the way he had come, and was banking on the fact that the fire would spread quickly. Would the police look any further than two bodies on the floor? The police would find me with a bullet in me, and Peter suffocated by his own asthma, presumably clutching the gun that killed me. Not a pretty picture.

"Now what?"

Scott tossed the can toward Peter, who caught it awkwardly. I could hear it slosh as he juggled it. I noticed for the first time that he was wearing gloves. Nice touch — Peter's fingerprints would be the only ones on the can. "Pour it on the papers there."

Peter looked stupidly at the can, at the pile of paper, at me. Even considering his breathing problems, he was moving suspiciously slowly. Maybe he'd finally guessed that I had a plan.

Scott sneered. "You always were useless. Step back, both of you." We backed into the corner, flanked by bookshelves. "Give me the can," he said to Peter.

For a brief moment I entertained the hope that Peter would fling accelerant in Scott's eyes, but instead he meekly tossed the can back to his brother, who caught it deftly, unscrewed the cap with one hand, and started dousing the paper. The gun trained on us never left his other hand. There was an odd light in his eyes.

When Scott looked down at the paper in front of him, I started edging toward the door to the vault, a few feet to my left, and made it partway before Scott noticed my movement and waved the gun at me. Then he grinned wolfishly. "Nowhere to run, Ms. Pratt."

I pressed myself against the books and crept closer to the door, trying to look terrified, which wasn't hard. Peter hadn't moved from the corner. Did he think he'd be safe there?

Then Scott pulled a lighter from his pocket. He looked back and forth at Peter and me. "Who wants to do the honors? You, Ms. Pratt? You, you little wimp?" He didn't appear surprised when neither of us volunteered. "Fine — I'll do it." He flicked on the lighter, then knelt by the pile of paper and touched the flame to it. It caught quickly, the loose sheets burning fast, the open books glowing at the edges as the fire began to eat into them — and following the liquid trails of the accelerant, which gave off a nasty oily smell. Old paper burned quickly, as Scott had hoped.

Scott allowed himself a moment to stare at the flames, and I wondered what was going through his mind. While he was distracted, I took a full step to my left, so I was standing in the doorway to the vault. Peter was still frozen in the corner, struggling to breathe. Scott looked up at me. "Get back here." He strode around the fire and toward me, and I took another step backward, into the vault, as if retreating from him.

But when he was close enough, instead of retreating deeper I grabbed him by his jacket and pulled him farther into the vault, catching him off balance — I guessed I had surprised him. Using his own momentum, I slung him around until he was on the inside, then hooked my foot around his and sent him tumbling backward. He looked good and mad, and bounded up again, still clutching the gun.

Then the sprinklers in the big room went off, momentarily startling him. I backed out of the room quickly, keeping an eye on Scott — and finally the metal door to the vault — the venerable fireproof vault — began to slide across the opening, just as its designers had intended.

But not fast enough — Scott was up and moving. "Peter, help me!" I yelled. For a moment I thought that Peter wasn't going to do anything, but then something penetrated his fog. He grabbed a tall heavy volume from the shelf. I did the same, and we converged on the rapidly moving door before Scott could slide out. I let Peter have first honors, and he swung and connected with Scott's hand, knocking the gun away, into the vault. I followed up with a desperate swing at Scott's head, which sent him reeling backward. The metal door ground shut, inch by inch, but too slowly. I grabbed the outer handle and shoved, closing the gap. Scott stuck out a hand, trying to grab me, but Peter whacked it, eliciting a howl of pain from Scott. And then the door closed with a clang.

Scott pounded on the metal door, yelling something inarticulate, but the door held. The overhead sprinklers continued with their deluge of water. Scott's fire sputtered and died, reduced to plumes of smoke. I was drenched in seconds. I looked at Peter in time to see him slide down the shelf of books until he was sitting on the floor, his breath coming in short pants. His face was greyish. I knelt beside him. "Thank you." He nodded. "Look, the fire system is linked directly to the fire department — someone will be here in minutes. Can you hang on?"

He nodded again.

I realized that I'd better open the front door for the fire department so they wouldn't end up destroying anything more than they had to, but then I stopped. Scott wasn't pounding anymore. Maybe he'd given up, but maybe . . .

And then I remembered.

The sprinkler system didn't extend to the vault. Instead, during an earlier remodel, it had been replaced with the halon system, more suitable for a small, enclosed space. The vault was a small enclosed space, and was surprisingly airtight. And if the halon system had gone off, triggered by the smoke or the heat, then Scott was trapped in the vault full of halon gas.

Halon gas was poisonous.

"Oh, hell," I whispered. I jumped to my feet and went back to the door. And stopped, at least briefly. Out here I was safe. On the other side of the door was a man who had just tried to kill me, and who still had a gun. And who might be dying because there wasn't any oxygen left in the room. The fire department should be here in minutes — but did Scott have minutes? How was I supposed to know? So I had a choice: let him out and hope he didn't shoot me, or leave him there to die. I chose the first option.

I grabbed the door handle and pulled. And pulled again. It didn't budge. I looked frantically for a latch or a button or anything at all that would release the door: nothing. Maybe the release switch was somewhere else in the building, but I sure didn't know where. I realized I was sobbing, although with the water still falling on my head it was hard to tell. I kept tugging ineffectually at the door until I heard the sound of sirens outside, and then I gave up and raced to the front door and hauled it open before the firemen could even knock.

They were apparently taken aback by the sight of me, drenched, grimy, and incoherent. "Fire's out, but there's a man . . . a door, in the vault . . . and EMTs . . . go, hurry, please." I don't know what they made out of that, but at least they took off in the right direction. I followed, and once inside the reading room, I pointed. When the guy in the lead looked at me, I managed to say, "Automatic fire door. I don't know where the release is. There's somebody inside."

The fireman said one word. "Halon?"

When I nodded, his expression changed. He barked some orders to his team; an axe materialized, and someone went to work on the door. I could have told them it wouldn't be easy: the building had been built too well. The dull clangs as metal met metal echoed through the room and beyond, but it took a while before anyone could force the door open, first a crack, then two guys got behind it and shoved it back into its slot.

I knew it was too late when they stopped hurrying.

CHAPTER 25

I sat in one of the reading room chairs — damned uncomfortable, I found myself thinking irreverently, maybe I should think about ordering cushions — while the firemen poked around the sodden pile of ashes, making sure the fire was out. Someone had turned the sprinkler system off, and I studied the scorched spot on the floor, the streaks of smoke creeping up the walls, and the steady drip, drip, drip of water from the shelves. Somebody had better think about rescuing all those books before they were beyond salvage. That somebody was probably me, but I was incapable of doing anything at the moment. So I sat and tried to avoid thinking at all.

I sat while the EMTs arrived and went straight to Peter, still slumped against the shelves. They found his inhaler in a pocket immediately, then started giving him oxygen before hoisting him on a gurney and making a quick exit. I thought he was unconscious, but as the gurney passed me, he opened his eyes, and the look he gave me was so bleak that it was all I could do not to turn away.

I waited while the police arrived. Initially they ignored me, conferring first with the milling firemen. I watched as though it were a play: a police officer strode across the room, spoke briefly with the fire team leader, then entered the vault. He emerged more slowly, shaking his head, and barked instructions to his colleagues. It all sounded like gibberish to me. The fireman pointed at me, and the officer started to make his way in my direction. I shut my eyes for a moment, trying to gather my strength and my wits, and when I opened them, James was kneeling in front of me.

"Nell, are you all right?"

I debated about how to answer that. Physically, yes, more or less, although I was still dripping wet and shaking. Otherwise — I'd have to say the jury was out on that.

"Nell?" he repeated, laying his hands over mine. The touch of his warm hands was startling, as if I'd forgotten that humans were supposed to be warm. I wasn't.

"What are you doing here?" My voice caught, and I coughed.

"The police said there was a fire here, and I figured it had to be connected."

"Ma'am?" That police officer had arrived in front of us. "You're Eleanor Pratt?"

I nodded. That was my name, and it seemed safe enough to admit it.

"I need to ask you some questions."

James rose to his full height of six foot whatever. "Officer, Ms. Pratt will be happy to answer all your questions, but right now she's not in any state to do so."

The officer didn't back down. "You her lawyer?"

"No." James reached into a pocket and pulled out a badge. "FBI."

I almost felt sorry for the officer.

"We still need some basic information," he said stubbornly. "Does she know who the dead man is?"

Dead. That was the word I was trying not to think about. I cleared my throat. "His name was Scott Ingersoll. The other man, the one the EMTs took away, is his brother Peter Ingersoll. Will Peter be all right?"

"Can't say, ma'am. Now can you —"

"No," James interrupted. "She cannot. She will talk to you in the morning."

They locked stares for a couple of seconds, but it was the police officer who backed down. "Ten o'clock at headquarters. You'll be responsible for her?" he asked James.

"Yes." He stood guard next to me as the officer went back to consult with his peers. Then he turned back to me. "I'm getting you out of here."

I seemed to be processing things very slowly. "My bag. It's upstairs in my office."

"I'll get it. You stay here."

"No! I'll come with you." I didn't want to be left down here with all these strangers and their questions. I struggled to stand up — my legs had stiffened. James grabbed my arm to help, but I was still wobbly when I was upright. He gave me another hard look, then said, "Keys?"

I fished in my pocket and handed them to him. He led me to the elevator, and we ascended in silence. He didn't let go of my arm; did I look like I needed to be held up? Still, I was grateful for it. Upstairs I moved by habit down the hall to my office, but when I walked through the door, nothing looked familiar, and I couldn't remember why I was there.

James came up beside me. "Where do you keep your bag?"

I pointed toward the desk, and he found it in a drawer.

"Jacket?"

"On the door."

He found that, too, and draped it around my shoulders.

There was something else important . . . "James, find Jennifer. She was in on it, working with Scott. She might even have planned it all."

"You sure?"

I nodded, and he fished his cell phone out of his pocket, then turned away to make a call. I didn't listen. I just stood there, still trying not to think of anything at all. It was hard work.

When he was done, he came back. "We're going now."

"Where?"

"My place."

"Oh." I didn't want to argue. I didn't want to make any choices. Let him make decisions; I was done with that.

We went out the back way so no one would see us. After James had settled me in the passenger seat of his car, we pulled out and drove slowly by the front of the building. The fire truck was still there, although the firemen were standing around or folding and stowing things. A police car; no, two. Two news vans. And the coroner's van pulled up. We kept going.

I shut my eyes, and when I opened them again, James was shaking me carefully, as though I might break. "We're here," he said. I looked around but didn't recognize anything. University City? He was holding the car door open, and I realized I was supposed to get out. He offered a hand, and when I took it he pulled me up from the seat. My legs were still rubbery, and everything seemed very far away.

We walked across the sidewalk and stopped at a triple-decker, climbed the front stairs, and then I stood there numbly while James opened the outer door, then nudged me through it. "Second floor," he said. I walked up a flight of stairs, carefully putting one foot in front of the other. We stopped again while he unlocked a door on the second-floor hallway and ushered me through it. We were in a room, and I could see a kitchen and a bedroom. James shut the door behind me and slipped off my jacket, hanging it on a coatrack, and he hung his beside it. I focused on the details. The room was neat, and the furniture matched. There was a nice area rug in the middle of a polished hardwood floor. There were some framed prints on the wall — I should look at them later. After . . . what?

He was standing in front of me again, and he was holding my upper arms. "Nell?"

I finally looked at him, and something

inside me broke. "I killed him." And then I burst into tears and fell against him.

I woke up sometime later to find myself lying on a couch with a blanket tucked around me. It took me a moment to figure out where I was, but the fact that James was slouched in a chair a few feet away, leafing through a magazine, was a big clue. His shirt was white, but the front of it was streaked with grey smudges — and then the rest of the events that had led up to this moment came flooding back, and it was almost more than I could take. Shutting my eyes and hoping it would all go away did not work.

"You're awake," James said.

I opened my eyes again. "You're very observant," I replied, in a croak that I didn't recognize as my own voice.

"I am, after all, an FBI agent. You hungry?"

I considered and decided the answer was yes. "I could eat."

"Good." He got up and went toward the kitchen, and I realized he was out of uniform: he'd taken off his tie and rolled up his shirtsleeves. Did that mean he was off duty? I checked my watch: it was after midnight, so I must have been out for a few hours. I still felt heartsick, but at least my brain seemed to be working again. I sat up, rolling back the blanket, and pulled various parts of my clothing up and down, trying to restore some sort of order to my appearance. Then I realized that my clothes and I had been the victims of an indoor downpour and it was hopeless, so I wrapped myself up in the blanket again. I ran my fingers through my hair, and they came away smelling of smoke.

James appeared bearing a tray with a mug of something, a bowl of something, and some crusty sliced bread. The mug and the bowl were both steaming.

"What are you, a magician?"

"You have heard of a microwave?"

"I've met a few in my day." I inhaled the aroma of the soup and realized I was ravenous. Halfway through the bowl — and half the stack of bread — I realized he wasn't eating. "You aren't joining me?"

"I ate a couple of hours ago."

I finished the bowl of soup before asking, "What happened?"

"I brought you back here and you crashed."

"Ah." I finished the bread in record time, then set the tray down on the table in front of the couch. I finally felt warmer, except for the cold lump in the center of me. "So, what now?"

"That's up to you."

"But aren't there procedures that have to be followed?"

"Tomorrow. I'm on my own time here. It's not my place to question you, not that I would anyway."

"Oh. Then I should go home." I looked vaguely around. I thought I had brought my coat and my bag. What time was it? Probably too late for a train, but . . .

James's voice cut through my mental wandering. "No. You aren't going anywhere right now."

Well, that seemed kind of abrupt. "I'm not?"

When I cocked my head at him, he said more softly, "I don't think you should be alone tonight. Marty can bring you something in the morning."

"You've talked to Marty?"

"No, I haven't talked to anyone." He kept looking at me in a way I couldn't quite fathom.

"So why am I here?" Maybe my brain still wasn't firing on all cylinders. I wasn't in custody, and I seemed to recall that the police had said James was responsible for me. What did that mean?

"Instead of police headquarters? Because a man died tonight, or last night actually, and you need time to process that. You don't need a bunch of officials yammering at you. And much as I like my cousin Marty, she's not the most sympathetic person in the world. Tomorrow's time enough to let her in on what happened."

A tiny part of me was glad — he was right about Marty. "So you're my babysitter?"

"Nell . . ." He stopped, trying to find words. "I brought you here because I was worried about you. The police would have torn you to shreds, and I didn't think you could handle that right now. You weren't in any shape to get yourself home. And I couldn't let you face this alone."

Okay, so this wasn't official, this was personal — between the two of us. We'd been dancing around it for a while, but it looked like the events of the night had pushed things to another level. Scott Ingersoll's death wasn't the only thing I had to process — and I was sure there would be plenty of official help to do that. Instead, I was sitting here looking at a man who had swooped in and rescued me from an unpleasant confrontation with the police, following a thoroughly harrowing experience; had brought me to his home, held me, and let me cry on his shoulder or chest or whatever; had fed me good food; and wasn't pressuring me for anything at all, personal or professional. I was pretty sure this was one damn unusual man.

"Thank you." The gears of my mind spun and caught. "Tell me, James, have you ever killed anyone?"

He regarded me levelly. "Yes. Twice."

"I don't want the details, but how did you feel? I mean, after?"

"It wasn't easy. In both cases it was justified. That doesn't mean I felt right about it. Taking a life is always wrong."

"Even in defense of your own?"

"Is that what happened?"

I settled back on the couch and pulled the blanket around me again. "More or less. Scott Ingersoll broke into the Society with the intention of killing his brother and me and then framing Peter for everything else. He told us that much. He planned to set a fire at the Society and make it look as though Peter had done it and I had tried to stop him, and we would both have been found dead. I think he figured he could handle Peter, but he was ready to shoot me if I didn't go along with it. He even brought along a gun that had been their father's."

"Instead he ended up dying as a result."

"Do you know how he died, James?"

"No, I didn't get all the details. I haven't talked to anyone since we came back here."

I chose my words carefully. "He died because I locked him in a room that suffocated him. He started the fire, and the fire triggered the fire retardant systems in that part of the building. In the reference room it's sprinklers, but in the vault it's halon, which can be deadly because it consumes all the oxygen in the space, which is what puts out the fire. He was the one who set the fire, but I locked him in the vault. And when I remembered what could happen, I couldn't get the damn door open again. So you might even say the building killed him."

"You acted to save Peter Ingersoll, and yourself. Not to mention the institution and its collections. What else could you have done?"

I shook my head. "I don't know — figured things out sooner?" I said bitterly.

"Nell, neither the police nor the FBI had Scott Ingersoll in their sights, not yet. You can't blame yourself for that."

"Shouldn't, maybe, but that doesn't make me feel any less guilty."

"You want me to sugarcoat it? Tell you that you did the right thing, and you'll feel better in the morning?"

"No, I don't. I just want you to tell me how to deal with the guilt."

"I won't pretend it's easy. But I'd respect you less if you didn't feel guilty about it."

"Ah." I was surprised to find that mattered to me. "Do you want to hear the details?"

"All right. You'll have to run through them with the police in the morning anyway."

I settled back into my blanket and began with Jennifer's phone call, after I'd last talked to James, and how she had suggested I meet Peter after hours, when the building would be empty. And Peter's confusion about why he was there, and the sound of breaking glass. And Scott's anger at Peter, and his contempt. There were elements of the story that obviously I didn't know, undercurrents that went beyond the recent events. Questions I wanted answered, for my own sake.

I told James about the feeble plan I had hatched, knowing as I did how the systems would work. I had hoped that even the small fire would be enough to trigger the nearer halon system, as it had. It had looked like the only chance I had, and I had taken it. I had guessed right, but I hadn't expected it to cost Scott his life.

"Where does Jennifer fit in?" James prompted.

I shook my head. "Scott didn't get into the details. I'm pretty sure they planned the theft together, but I'm not sure who was using who. Listening to Scott talk about the fire, I began to wonder if in fact he *was* an arsonist at heart. Maybe it was Jennifer's idea to take advantage of that and make some money from it, whenever they managed to unload the fire truck. I gather they were both full of resentment, but toward different things. Anyway, Scott was trying to shut down the investigation by framing Peter for all the fires."

It must have taken an hour to get through it, in fits and starts. James was quiet for most of it, inserting a brief question now and then. He didn't take notes; he just watched me, his eyes serious. I finally ran out of steam, when I came to the point when he had arrived. "I should have realized . . ."

He stopped me. "No, you shouldn't have. You've never had reason to need that fire system, right? You had no idea how it would work, or even *if* it would work. Why were you supposed to know that halon gas could be deadly?"

"But I did know — I just didn't remember

until it was too late. And I'm responsible for everything at the Society."

I could have sworn he swallowed a laugh. "Nell, you're only one person, and you're human. If you hadn't done what you did, you'd be dead and the Society would have gone up in smoke. I prefer this outcome."

"Me, too." Suddenly I was exhausted. My watch said one thirty, and I had a date at police HQ at ten thirty, and I couldn't show up looking like I did. I struggled to stand up. "I need to get some sleep." I couldn't seem to get my feet untangled from the blanket.

And then James was there again, holding me up. "You take the bed — you need it. I'll sleep out here. And I'll call Marty in the morning, and I'll go with you to the police."

"Thank you," I whispered into his chest. "For everything."

CHAPTER 26

I awoke to full sunlight, and it took me a moment to orient myself. Unfamiliar bedroom. Just me in the bed. Sound of running water from the bathroom. Okay, I deduced: James's apartment, the morning after, and any fireworks involved only the dead arsonist at the Society, not a night of passion. Scott was still dead, and the police were waiting to talk to me. And James came out of the bathroom wearing nothing more than a towel, looking quite comfortable in his skin. I gulped.

"Good, you're awake." He smiled. "Marty'll be here in half an hour. There's coffee in the kitchen."

"What time is it?" It came out a croak again, my clogged throat a reminder of last night's events.

"Just past eight. How do you feel?"

"Better. Coffee should help. What did you tell Marty?"

"I told her you needed a complete change of clothes ASAP. Nothing about the rest. She'll probably hear about it on the news and be mad as hell when she gets here, but I wasn't in the mood to explain."

Belatedly I took in the fact that I was not wearing the soggy, smoky clothes from yesterday, but rather a nice, plush terry-cloth robe with the logo of an expensive hotel. I had no idea when and how the switch had happened. I could imagine how Marty had taken James's request. And did she have a clue what size anything I wore? "I bet she was thrilled."

"I can't say — I hung up on her."

Marty was not going to be a happy camper. "Tell me you came by this honestly?" I said, holding the lapels of the robe.

He didn't answer but just grinned. He grabbed up some clothes and went out into the other room to dress, allowing me some privacy. I hoped Marty would come up with something wearable. James was right: there was no way I could brave a police interview wearing yesterday's clothes. I wandered barefoot out to the kitchen. James, now fully dressed (sigh), wordlessly handed me a mug of coffee. I perched on a high stool and sipped, studying the kitchen, which was as neat as the rest of the place. Verging on spartan, actually. "Do you spend much time here?" I asked innocently.

"I like to live simply, and I don't need much."

"Well, if your FBI career bombs, you can always hire out as a house cleaner."

He sat on a stool on the other side of the small kitchen island. "I'll keep that in mind."

"So, what happens now?"

"You tell your story to the police. If he's up to it, Peter will tell his story to them. If all went well last night, someone will have picked up Jennifer and then we'll have her side of things. Or not, if she clams up. If we're all very, very lucky, all the stories will match up and the case will be closed. Finding the missing fire engine would be icing on the cake."

I realized that I still held out hope that Peter would not face any legal issues, probably out of misguided pity. What had he known, and when? What had he ignored out of denial? "How much of this do you think you can pin on Jennifer?"

"Depends on how much she was involved. Will she play dumb?"

"She will if she's smart enough, and I think she is. She'll probably use Scott as her fall guy — she's already setting that up with the alibi confusion. I can't say I knew Scott very well, but I'd bet Jennifer was the brains behind the whole operation — he didn't seem bright enough to have thought through a plan like this, although he certainly seemed angry enough to carry it out. Sad to think of her, though — all those years doing the lowly stuff at the museum, feeling bitter about the whole thing. Scott said it was about the money for her — not enough money from her late husband, and then having to accept what amounts to a handout in the form of that museum job. I wonder how and when she and Scott connected. Peter told me that Scott used to work security at the museum."

"We'll find out, I'm sure, now that we know what we're looking for. More coffee? Food?"

"Please, to both. And it seems pretty likely that Scott was behind those other fires. He said something about Jennifer making sure that Peter didn't have an alibi for those times. I'm sure Scott enjoyed the practice."

We were sharing fresh cups of coffee and toasted bagels when Marty banged on the door. James went to open it, then stood back as she barged in, looking like the proverbial wet hen, but blessedly carrying a garment bag. She took one look at us — particularly me in my fluffy robe and not much else — and said acidly, "You called me out at dawn because Nell here needed a change of clothes after a nice roll in the hay?"

"It's a little more complicated than that, Marty," James said. "Coffee?"

"Yes, and an explanation. Good morning, Nell. Did you have a nice evening?"

"Not exactly. I take it you haven't seen the paper yet this morning?" When Marty shook her head, James and I exchanged glances, and he nodded at me to continue. I began, "Peter Ingersoll's brother Scott broke into the Society last night. He tried to start a fire, and he was planning to kill Peter and me so we could take the blame. I managed to trap him in the vault, and he died when the halon system kicked in, triggered by his own fire."

For once Marty was rendered speechless. She looked at James, who nodded. Then she looked at me, her eyes wide, and bounded toward me and grabbed me in a hug. I was startled, to say the least — I had never seen Marty hug anybody — and half my coffee sloshed over the countertop. Marty finally released me and stepped back. "Are you all right? Well, of course you are, because you're sitting here in front of me. What happened? What are you doing *here?*"

"Slow down, Marty. I have to be at the police station by ten thirty, and I have to shower and get dressed, but I think that leaves time to give you the short version."

Once again I explained why Peter had been at the Society last night, and what had happened once Scott arrived. Marty's face grew grimmer and grimmer, and lines I didn't realize she had grew deeper. "So he died? In that room?"

I swallowed. It was going to take me awhile to get used to that. "He did. I hadn't realized how quickly halon could act, and how toxic it could be."

"Thank God we moved the Terwilliger Collection out of there!"

I took one look at James, and we both burst out laughing, leaving Marty staring at us in bewilderment. "What?" she said.

I finally managed to say, "I'm glad to see your priorities haven't changed. But I know what you mean — at least the papers that were in the room are safe. I can't say as much for the books in the reference room."

"Oh, crap — I hadn't even thought of that," Marty said. "We're going to have to do something about that ASAP. I don't suppose you have a disaster plan for this kind of thing?"

I stared blankly at her until she said,

"Yeah, right. No plan — why am I not surprised? The most important thing is to stabilize whatever got wet, and the Society hasn't got any space left to handle that, much less any space that's got the right temperature and humidity controls. So, that means we need professional help, and fast. I know somebody at the Northeast Document Conservation Center — I'll give them a call and see how fast they can get here. We'll have to get a rough inventory of what's in the room, but it's more important to get them treated. Too bad Nicholas isn't up to speed on the catalog so he could tell us what should be in that room, but I think we can manage. Thank goodness it wasn't the best stuff. And it's lucky that we're closed today, so we'll have today and tomorrow to sort things out. Do you think we'll be able to open on schedule?"

"Marty, I don't know. I wasn't paying much attention to the damage to the building at the time."

Marty looked contrite. "Of course you weren't. I'm sorry, again."

"It's okay — you only just found out. Actually I don't think the structural damage is that bad, but once we get the books sorted out, we'll have to get a crew in to clean up. And replace the halon system in the vault with something newer." And less deadly.

"Oh, damn, you're right. And we'd better call the rest of the board and let them know what's going on before they hear it on the news — I assume there will be news? Shoot, of course there will — a fire *and* a death. And we'd better put our own spin on it for the next round in the press today. At least Saturday's usually a slow news day. Can you handle an emergency board meeting today? Tomorrow?" She was off again, barely stopping for breath.

I had to break in. "Marty, right now I need to get dressed. You call the board, so at least they'll know what's happening. If we can get a majority together tomorrow, we can meet then. I'll leave all the rest in your capable hands. If you'll be at the Society this afternoon, I'll come by after I'm done with the police. But, James? I'd like to talk to Peter, if I can. Can you arrange that?"

"I think so. You go shower, and I'll check on all the other stuff."

I fled to the bedroom, taking with me the clothes Marty had brought. I had no idea where they'd come from, since I outweighed her and there was no way her clothes would fit me, but she'd guessed well as far as sizes went.

369

Showered, dried, and even wearing makeup — Marty had been remarkably thorough, so I wouldn't have to face the police looking like a ghost — I returned to find them bickering amiably right where I'd left them. James caught sight of me first and stopped talking. Marty eyed me critically and said, "I chose well, didn't I? Shoes okay?"

"Yes, everything's fine, Marty, and thank you. Where on earth did you come up with the clothes on such short notice?"

"A friend of mine runs a high-end consignment shop near Rittenhouse Square. I borrowed her keys. You're getting some great bargains there."

I cringed at the thought of having to pay her back for what she'd brought — definitely a cut above my usual wardrobe. Maybe I could write it off as a business expense. Or bill it to the FBI? After all, my clothes had been destroyed in the line of duty, sort of. "Any updates while I was in the shower?"

James got in the first word. "Jennifer is in custody — the police found her before the news got out and brought her in for questioning. They have enough to keep her for a bit while we sort out the details. Peter is holding his own, but he's still in the hospital. He's asking to talk to you."

"And I'm meeting the cleanup agency at the Society at noon," Marty added.

"I'm impressed. You two work fast," I said. "What're you going to tell the board, Marty?"

"That the Society's intrepid leader valiantly fought off a vicious attack by an arsonist and saved the day."

"A bit over the top, don't you think?" I protested.

Marty sobered. "Maybe. But it's true, you know — if you hadn't done what you did, things could have been a lot worse."

Except for Scott, I thought, but didn't give it voice.

"Nell, we should leave now," James said. "We don't want to keep the police waiting."

"You're still coming with me?" I asked.

"If you want me there — not that I have any doubt that you can handle them yourself."

"I want you there."

We exchanged smiles, until Marty snorted. "Time for that stuff later. Now we need to get moving."

James drove to police headquarters at the Roundhouse and accompanied me in, then shepherded me through the ranks of officialdom until we reached the interview. His badge dispelled any issue of his presence,

371

although he stayed silent in the background as I told my story. And told it again. I had nothing to hide, and since I had actually been an invited participant in the investigation, thanks to James, it was easy to stick to the facts. I refused to guess *why* anyone had done anything; I was certainly curious myself, and I hoped that Peter could fill in some of the biggest holes. But the basic outline of events was simple enough: I had asked Peter to meet me at the Society at Jennifer's request; his brother Scott had broken in (the police had found the broken window at the back of the building); and Scott had tried to burn down the Society, or as much as he could, and had planned to kill Peter and me along the way. I had to include the story behind the fire engine switch, although I regretted that Peter would have to deal with that, too. In the end, the police detective thanked me and asked that I come by to sign a statement in a day or two. He escorted me out to a waiting area, but James stayed behind to exchange a few words with him. It looked as though things went smoothly, because they parted with hearty handshakes. As well they should, for together — with my help — they had just solved both the recent string of arsons and the suspicious death of Allan

Brigham, plus a few crimes they hadn't even been looking for. A good day all around for Philadelphia law enforcement.

I felt drained by the time we made it back to the street, but I wasn't done. "Can we talk to Peter now? Will the police mind?"

"Nell, I'm beginning to feel like a mother hen here. You need to get something to eat before you fall over. Then you can talk to Peter — I've fixed it with the police."

"And I need to see what Marty's up to at the Society. Then I promise I'll go home and sleep for a week."

He guided me to a small restaurant just off Market Street, and we ate a pleasant if forgettable meal. Our minds were not on the food, and we seemed to be wandering through a minefield of things we didn't want to talk about right now, including murder and mayhem and . . . us. But I found I was curiously content letting him take charge, which surprised me. I had always fancied myself the independent type.

"Which hospital?" I asked as I finished my coffee.

"Jefferson — it was the closest ER. We can walk."

And so we did, and I stood back and watched as James flashed his badge and got us past the reception desk and the nurse's station and into Peter's room, where he was lying with his eyes closed, looking like a medieval effigy, even to the grey color of his skin. The plastic oxygen cannula snaking around his head kind of spoiled the image, though.

I approached the bed and said softly, "Peter?"

He opened his eyes, and his expression lightened when he saw me. "Nell! You're all right?"

"I'm fine, Peter." I patted his hand.

"And your building?" he asked anxiously.

"Minor damage. A few books lost. Nothing irreplaceable." And then I was struck by the awful realization that he might not know what had happened to his brother. "Peter, do you know about Scott?"

Peter nodded. "He's dead, isn't he? I guessed as much. Every time I've asked a nurse about anything, they've put on a smile and told me not to worry. It's all right, Nell — there was nothing else you could have done. He brought it on himself."

He looked past me and saw James, and his face fell. "I've talked to the police, you know, but I thought Nell deserved to hear the whole story from me," he told James.

I intervened quickly. "Peter, James is here for me, not in any official capacity. If you want him to leave, that's okay."

He waved a weak hand. "No, it's all right. I want to get this out, even though it makes me feel like a fool. I should have seen it coming."

"Are you up to it? I was worried about you yesterday."

"I'm sorry — it was pretty rough. Everything that's gone wrong at our museum, and then Scott showing up like that, and the fire — it all just hit me at once. I'm sorry I couldn't be of more help to you. When I got here, they gave me some heavy-duty medication to get my lungs open again, and I feel much better. Please, sit down." I pulled the only guest chair — a hard and slippery plastic number — closer to the bed and sat down. James elected to lean against a wall.

Peter seemed to be fumbling, now that he had his audience. "I don't know where to start," he said.

"Can you explain why Scott . . . did what he did?" I prompted gently.

Peter nodded. "I told you, my — our father was a firefighter, and a good one — you know, lots of heroic rescues and that kind of thing. Loved giving statements to the local press, clutching a wet kitten. I thought he was God when I was growing up, and more than anything I wanted to be like him. Unfortunately I couldn't — this damn asthma. Dad pretended to be understanding, but then he pinned his hopes on Scott."

"Scott was younger?"

Peter nodded again. "A couple of years. But he was everything I never was — strong, athletic, cocky, great with girls. The thing is, no way did he want to follow in Dad's footsteps. He had his own ideas. He and Dad had some really nasty fights, and sometimes Scott moved out of the house for a while until Dad cooled down. Dad would just look at me and shake his head." Peter stopped, his chest heaving.

"Peter, you don't have to do this now," I said. "Let me guess — everybody hoped that things would work out between you when you two grew up, but Scott couldn't let it go?" Peter nodded. "When you were growing up, did you ever think Scott liked to set fires?"

Peter shook his head vehemently. "It never occurred to me. I mean, Scott wasn't stupid, or even destructive. Sure, it would have pissed Dad off, but Scott did that just fine by making what Dad would have called *inappropriate lifestyle choices*. He refused to go to college. He wouldn't get a steady job — he even mooched off some girlfriends.

He got into fights, a lot. He had a minor criminal record."

"And you lost contact with him?"

Peter shrugged. "For a while. I cut him out of my life. I had to — he wasn't changing, and I was moving on. I couldn't help him, and he didn't want me messing with his life. Then at Dad's funeral a few years ago, he showed up late, wearing jeans. It was kind of insulting, but he didn't make a scene or anything, and I appreciated that he'd come. Then I realized that he was all I had — our mother's had Alzheimer's for years — and we needed to reconnect."

From what Peter had just said, Scott sounded like an average guy gone wrong — stuck forever in some adolescent phase. Whether he was an arsonist was another question, one that I couldn't answer. Maybe Celia could figure it out.

"It must have worked, if he ended up working at your museum," I said.

"I thought so. I guess I was wrong."

"When did Scott and Jennifer . . . get together?"

"It didn't take long, once he started working at the museum. They really hit it off, and I didn't interfere. I actually thought Jennifer might be good for Scott — steady him, you know. Then I had to lay him off, when the collection went into storage — there wasn't anything left in the building to guard. Jennifer didn't say much about him after that, but I guess they were still together."

Shrewd woman. "Would she have been easy for Scott to manipulate?"

"Jennifer? I doubt it. More likely the other way around. She's tough, and she's practical. When I hired her for the museum, it was really as a favor to the union — she just couldn't make it on her husband's pension. She didn't have much in the way of office skills, but she learned fast, and she didn't mind doing whatever I asked. She's been a big part of the museum."

Too bad that Peter was going to have to come to grips with the fact that she wasn't going to be his good right hand at the museum anymore. If he even had a museum to go back to. At the rate things were going, I wasn't sure about that.

But Peter was already ahead of me. "You're thinking about the fire engine, right? I know you must think I was stupid, but I couldn't bring myself to suspect anyone at the museum, and of course I didn't want to believe that either Jennifer or Scott was involved. Or Gary. These were people I trusted. Maybe I should have told the authorities, but I wasn't sure, and everything else was in such a mess, I couldn't face it. I had a feeling that you knew, because you'd seen the same thing in the pictures. I just didn't want to be the one to blow things open publicly. Sorry, Nell — if I'd done something sooner, maybe Scott wouldn't have . . . gone after you and me."

And Scott had paid for Peter's reluctance with his life. No matter where the blame was laid, Peter was going to have to live with that. If he'd spoken up sooner, maybe Scott would still be alive.

A nurse chose that moment to bustle in to check her patient. She cast a baleful glare at James and me. "I'll have to ask you to leave now. This man's not out of the woods yet."

I caught James's eye and nodded. We'd done enough damage already, and there was nothing else we needed from Peter now. "Of course. Peter, you get some rest, and try not to worry." As if that were possible.

Peter smiled weakly. "Thank you for coming, Nell. I'm sorry you were dragged into all this."

So was I, but it wasn't his fault. "It's okay, and it's over now. Good-bye, Peter."

I left the room, and James followed. When we reached the elevator, I said, without looking at him, "I probably broke seven kinds of laws about interfering in a federal investigation, and I've screwed up any further interviews. Right?"

"Probably," James agreed amiably.

"I don't care. I doubt that the police can prove that Peter knew what was going on, and when he figured out some parts of it . . . well, he's got his own burdens now."

"I agree. I'll try to keep the police off his back."

We got off the elevator and reached the front door. "Can you drop me at the Society?"

"Do you really need to do that now? Why not just go home and unwind?"

I stopped on the sidewalk and turned to face him. "Yes, I do. The place is my responsibility, and I want to see how bad the damage is so I can talk to the board and decide when we'll be able to open to the public. You don't really want Marty to take over completely, do you?"

His mouth twitched. "She does get things done, you know."

"Yes, but I'm the president, even if she did shove me into that position. Any decisions that are made should be mine."

"I'm not going to talk you out of it, am I?"

"Nope."

CHAPTER 27

It was oddly reassuring to know that I could out-stubborn an FBI agent. We retrieved his car, then James drove me the few blocks to the Society. He parked, but when I climbed out, he did as well. "You're coming in?" I asked, surprised.

"Yes. Call it reviewing the crime scene, if you want. And I'll let Marty beat me up for keeping her out of the loop, if it'll help."

It probably wasn't worth arguing about, so I didn't. Actually I thought it was kind of sweet of him. Was he worried that I wouldn't be able to handle being back in the building, confronting the vault where Scott had died? I was pretty sure I'd be okay, but it was nice that he had my back. I walked to the front of the building and then faltered. Everything looked the same from the outside, but I realized I *was* afraid of what I would find when I opened the door. And what I would feel.

But I had no choice, if I was going to live with myself. I squared my shoulders and marched up the stone steps, stopping at the top only long enough to retrieve my keys so I could open the door. I stepped into the lobby and stopped again. I could hear voices farther back — presumably whoever Marty had called in to clean up; Marty must have been letting them in. I could smell a lingering odor of smoke and something chemical. The usually glossy tiles of the lobby were scuffed and smudged — all those firemen and EMTs tramping around, no doubt. I could feel James behind me, silent, like a body guard. He was going to let me find my own way, and I was grateful. I started moving again — through the lobby, through the catalog room. I paused at the nearest door to the reading room and made a conscious effort to blot out my feelings. I needed to do a damage assessment and determine the remedies. Period.

There were a couple of people pulling books off the shelves, inspecting them, and making notes, with Marty keeping an eagle eye on them. Marty noticed us standing there. "Well, there you are! Hi, Jimmy."

"Marty," I said. "What's the damage?"

She got serious, fast. "The sprinkler system works by zones — thank God it wasn't an all-or-nothing situation, like in the old days. The fire triggered the sprinklers in the reference room only, so the damage was limited. The fire was out fast, but a few thousand books got soaked, and I don't know how many will be salvageable."

I nodded. "I don't need to tell you that most of what we keep in the open stacks here are general reference, so they can be replaced if need be. Can we get an evaluation of what the cost of restoration would be versus the cost of replacement?"

"Sure can," Marty said. "The stuff in the vault, now — what little there was — is fine, since that's the way the halon system is supposed to work. The old metal door will have to be replaced, of course, and the floor tiles in that corner of the reference room, but since it's concrete underneath, there's no structural damage. Oh, and the police showed me where the guy got in — a broken window in the back of the building. Overall I think we really dodged a bullet. Oh, sorry — I didn't mean that literally."

I assumed the police had found Scott's gun and taken it away. "It's okay, I know what you mean. It could have been so much worse."

I didn't hear anything, but James pulled a phone out of his pocket and stepped away to talk. After a moment he came back. "The police are going to talk to Jennifer again, and I want to be there. I'll come back for you later, give you a ride home." Before I could protest, he was gone.

"Let's go check out that window problem," Marty said, grabbing my arm and all but dragging me toward the back of the building. She let go only when we'd reached the area near the back loading dock, where I could see a scattering of glass shards on the floor.

"We should call a glass place," I said.

"I already have, and they're on their way. What I want to know is, what the hell was going on?"

"What do you mean?"

"Well, let's see. Why were you here alone with Peter Ingersoll, one of the prime suspects in an arson-murder? Why did a gun-toting arsonist show up and try to kill you? And how did you end up at James's apartment?"

"This may take some time. Pull up a seat." There weren't any chairs handy, but there were several sturdy wooden packing crates, so we sat, and while we waited for the glass repair person to show up at the back door, I gave Marty the details of everything that had happened, since she'd heard only the outline earlier. She was appropriately shocked.

"Peter's brother? He was carrying on with that secretary person, what's her name?"

"Jennifer. It sounds like it. Or maybe Scott and Jennifer were just using each other for financial gain, or in Scott's case, revenge. I don't know. We'll see what Jennifer has to say. But I still believe Peter. He may have suspected that something fishy was going on with the fire and the fire engine, but he didn't want to admit it, even to himself. I hope the police aren't too hard on him."

"Serve him right. It's always best to face things head-on — that's what I do. And I thought you did, too."

"I try."

"Then will you please take a look at what you're doing with James?"

"What?" I really didn't have the time and energy to fend off Marty's efforts to manage my personal life, even if it did involve one of her relatives.

"You just spent the night with him." Before I could sputter a protest, Marty held up a hand. "Okay, given the circumstances I'm sure that there was nothing remotely like hanky-panky going on. But I've never known him to step up and look after anybody that way."

Oh. Well, yes, there was that. I'd been so stunned that I hadn't been able to think, but he had swooped in and taken charge, and I had been and still was grateful. I should have realized that caretaking of that sort was not part of the standard FBI investigative package. Of course Marty was going to feel she had a stake in this, because she had introduced us.

"Nell, I may be nosy," she went on, with what for her passed for softness, "but I've known Jimmy since he was bratty little kid. I also know that he's a competent adult and he's good at what he does. So are you, to both. Don't let that get in the way of the two of you."

How had I ever ended up in this position? Trying to run an unwieldy, cash-strapped institution; facing repairs for a fire and all the related questions from law enforcement, insurers, and even my board; and now being lectured by Marty — board member, colleague, and maybe friend — about my love life? It just wasn't fair, and for the second time in twenty-four hours I wanted to cry. For all that I was putting on a brave front, deep down I was still pretty shaky. But Marty wasn't about to hold me the way James had, and I didn't want her to; I had to deal with this on my own.

And, damn it, she was right. James and I had been dancing around our apparently mutual attraction since the second or third time we'd met, and we'd both been careful to maintain a professional distance. Well, it was time to admit that was nonsense. Physical attraction — that came and went. But no one had ever stepped in and taken care of me the way James had last night, and this morning.

"Marty, you're right."

Apparently my quick capitulation had startled her. "I am? You mean I've wasted all this time thinking up good arguments when I didn't have to?"

"Yes. Look, the last twenty-four hours have been hell, and I know there's more to come. But that kind of puts things in perspective, because I don't have either the time or the energy to play silly games anymore. And it makes me sad to see how people screw up their lives for all the wrong reasons." Like Scott Ingersoll doing everything he could to thumb his nose at dear old Dad. What a waste.

"Nell, you make me proud to know you. I promise I'll stay out of it from here on out. Now, let's get the immediate problems taken care of, like having the window repaired before some other lowlife crawls in."

We went back to the reference room and helped the emergency conservation crew to inventory the books, dividing them between those that could be saved and those that had to be tossed. I supposed I could have called in one or more staff members, but I wasn't ready to share the news with them yet — I thought I owed the board an explanation first — although I'm sure they and members and others were clogging the phone lines and email in-boxes with questions. But I preferred to deal with something tangible like soggy books, and it didn't take a lot of expertise to decide a book could never be brought back to usable form and should go off somewhere to be recycled or burned or whatever. It was a horrifying number, but less than I had anticipated. And it was only a tiny fraction of what the Society held.

It was getting dark when James came back. I was drafting an email to the staff on my laptop, explaining briefly what had happened and what they should expect on Monday, when I looked up and found him slouched in the doorway, watching me.

Marty saw him, too. "I can stay here until this crew is finished, Nell. You must be wiped out," she said. "I'll try to get the board here sometime in the afternoon tomorrow, if that works for you. I'll call you in the morning when I've got that sorted out."

The weight of the day came crashing down, and I realized I was exhausted. I hit Send and said, "Sounds good to me." I stood up and stretched to loosen up my spine, and recalled that some of the scattered aches and pains came from other recent events, like wrestling with a criminal. I wondered if there were bruises to match.

James straightened up and walked toward me. "You ready to go?"

"Yes. Home?"

"I'll drive you."

And that was the extent of our conversation until we reached my house. It wasn't an uncomfortable silence, but I felt a bit out-of-body. Nothing seemed quite real; the world wasn't the same one I had awakened to yesterday.

At my house he helped me out of the car and walked me to the front door. "You're coming in?" I said as I unlocked the door, although it wasn't exactly a question.

He smiled. "Of course. We had a date, remember? I brought dinner — it's in the car."

"You know, I don't deserve you." I smiled back.

"Yes, you do."

I wasn't sure how to answer that, so I said nothing. I walked into my house and almost expected it to look different: it seemed ages since I'd been here. James went back to the car and reappeared moments later carrying a couple of bags. When had he had time to find food, what with interviews and paperwork and all that stuff?

After I'd shut the door behind him, I found myself saying something stupid along the lines of, "I think I'll change." I was still wearing Marty's smart outfit, and I thought I should take care of it, since it was better than most of the stuff in my closet.

"I'll deal with dinner," James said, heading for the kitchen.

Upstairs I avoided looking at myself in the mirror. I was pretty sure the dark circles under my eyes were expanding by the minute, and when I carefully pulled off the layers of clothes, purple bruises emerged — and I felt every one. I was in no mood to be entertaining or witty, or even coherent, but I didn't think I could send James away if I tried, and I didn't really want to. I finally pulled on some of the loosest, softest, oldest clothes I owned. I wasn't going to impress him in a ragged college sweatshirt, but I didn't think it mattered.

Downstairs again, I found that James had located plates and silverware and set my table, and I could hear the microwave humming. Takeout, then, but high end — I had recognized the bags. He ferried something to the table and asked, "Wine?"

"Please." I assumed he didn't expect me to string together logical sentences, so what could it hurt? He emerged from the kitchen again with a large bowl filled with some kind of pasta that smelled incredible even from across the room, and set it on the table before pouring me a glass of wine. "Sit." I sat.

The next few minutes were devoted to intense consumption of wondrously flavored carbohydrates, accompanied by that first glass of wine. Then the pace slowed, and I helped myself to a second glass from the bottle James had so kindly left on the table.

"The police let me sit in on their interview with Jennifer while you were at the Society with Marty," James said without preamble.

"Oh? What did she have to say?"

"Something along the lines of, *Scott seduced me and persuaded me to give him the whereabouts of the collection — I had no idea what he was going to do,* et cetera."

"And of course she didn't ask why he wanted to know," I followed sarcastically.

James nodded. "So she says. After all, Scott's not around to contradict her."

"Did she know Scott was an arsonist?"

"Not that she'd admit. It would be hard to prove. When we showed her the surveillance footage, she admitted that it was her brothers' trucking firm that hauled the fire engine away. But she'll find a way to blame Scott for that, too — he's been working for the brothers on and off, since the museum laid him off. Everything is Scott's fault — and he's not here to defend himself."

"Ah," I said. "So if she knew her brothers were involved, and she knew they were switching machines, she must have known about the fire? Does that make her an accessory in the death of the watchman?"

"Maybe."

"Have you rounded up her brothers?"

"Of course. They are, as they say, singing like birds. And since they're across state lines, it's actually a good thing the FBI is in the mix here."

"You know, I never thought to ask where the other fire engine came from — the one that burned."

"One of the brothers said they came across it in a hauling job. It was a mess, in pieces, but they figured if it was in a fire no one would notice."

"So odds are good that the museum will get their original fire engine back? If there's a museum for it to go to." That made me sad and glad at the same time.

"Eventually, if Peter's up to managing the place."

"That could be a problem. I get the feeling that if Peter doesn't come back, the city might seize the opportunity to shut the place down. Which would be a shame."

James was silent for a few beats, staring into the depths of his glass. Finally he said, "Nell, I'm so sorry you got caught up in this. I'm sorry I brought you into it."

I looked at him directly. "I wanted to help. It's not like you sent me into enemy territory to spy on anyone. You asked me to find out what I legitimately could about a peer institution and the people associated with it. I probably would have checked that out myself, just out of curiosity, once I recognized the switch in the fire engines, or would have when Marty pointed it out, too. I couldn't have let that go without saying anything to you or the police. You had no way of knowing how it would turn out."

"I still regret putting you in that position."

"Well, don't," I said tartly, taking another

sip of wine. "I make my own decisions, and I was glad that you asked for my help."

"Ah." He looked at his plate and pushed a few noodles around. "Thing is, I'm sorry I put you in that position because I care for you a lot, and when someone attacks you I want to smash his face in before I shoot him twelve times."

At last we'd gotten down to it. I felt giddy with . . . relief? Exultation? "I feel the same way about you. Well, minus the beating up and the shooting part. But what really got to me was the way you just came in and held me together. James, nobody has ever done that for me before. It made me realize that maybe I could possibly lean on someone — you — without giving up anything of me. Does that make sense?"

He nodded solemnly. "It does."

"But you've really perfected that stony agent face! I have no idea what's going on in your head most of the time."

"You're pretty good at stonewalling yourself."

He was right, and I knew it. "I know. And I'm sorry. I've wasted too much time pushing you away. And you didn't have to scrape me off the floor, take me home, feed me, and give me pep talks to keep me going, but you did. And I liked it. I *really* liked it, and that surprised me. *You* keep surprising me. I want to know more."

"That can be arranged."

"I'm glad to hear that."

He looked at me for a moment, then stood up and came around the table to my side and held out his hand. I took it, and he pulled me up — and into his arms.

We got to know each other quite a lot better.

CHAPTER 28

James and I were enjoying a leisurely breakfast consisting of whatever I could find in my cupboards — not much — when Marty called.

"He still there?" she began.

It wasn't worth protesting that I had no idea what she was talking about. "Mm-hm. What's up?"

"I managed to corral a quorum of the board for three o'clock this afternoon. Most of them were squawking like chickens after they'd seen the news, but nobody was answering the Society's phone. I explained that you had gone into seclusion to recover."

Shoot — I should have thought to leave a message on the machine, but I'd been just a little distracted. "Any problems?"

"Nothing you can't handle. I got a ball-park estimate for cleaning up the mess in the reference room, both the books and the space, so we can throw that at the board and let them argue about pennies."

I saw James tiptoe down the hall with his cell phone at his ear. I admired the line of his back as he went.

"Yo, Nell — you still there?"

"What? Oh, yes, of course. Do I want to know how much the cost will be?"

"No. But it's not like we have a choice. It has to be done. So I'll see you at three. Say hi to Jimmy for me."

James had returned and was watching me with a smile. "Marty, right?"

"Yes. She says to say hi to you. Do you ever get the feeling she's pulling the strings here?"

"Marty? Maybe. Under that plain exterior beats the heart of a true romantic. So, you're meeting with the board today?"

"Yes, at three. We need a damage-control strategy, putting a positive spin on this whole mess, as far as possible. *But look, only one person died! It could have been more!* When nobody should have died at all."

"It's not your fault. That's your mantra for the day. If you hadn't done what you did, it would have been far worse. Oh, and I've got some news that should distract them."

"Good news? Because I really don't want to hear any bad news at the moment."

"I'd say good. The police have found the fire engine."

I felt like clapping my hands like a small child. "That's wonderful! Where?"

"Jennifer's brothers hadn't gotten around to moving it far — they stuck it in one of the warehouses they use in Jersey. Once they heard the FBI was involved, they gave it up fast. I think they figured they could handle local cops, but not the feds. And I have a feeling that the city will think twice about shutting down the Fireman's Museum, now that there's been so much publicity. Maybe you and Peter can plan a grand reopening — with the fire engine."

"Maybe. He's going to have to replace Jennifer. It's not going to be easy to find someone who can do everything for the lousy pay the museum offers."

"He can ask Gary O'Keefe to help with recruitment. I'm sure he could sweet-talk someone into doing it."

"Good idea. I'll suggest it. So I guess I have a couple of hours to spare before I have to leave for the city. You have any idea what we could do?"

"Yes."

I like a man who knows his own mind.

Two thirty found me fidgeting in my office.

I'd checked the cleanup progress when I came in, and things looked as good as could be expected after a fire and a flood. At least, as Marty had said, the damage had been limited to the one room, and the lost books were not irreplaceable. And we'd proved that our fire retardant systems worked, a small crumb of good news. I'd rather not have found out.

At quarter to three I went downstairs to the lobby. Marty and I had decided to start by giving the board members a quick tour of the damage and get it out of the way — I couldn't guess what horrors they were imagining, based on the news headlines.

Lewis Howard, a grizzled old buffalo of a Philadelphia lawyer and board chair, was one of the first to arrive. He greeted me with what appeared to be sincere concern. "Nell, my dear, the papers would have you at death's door, and the Society in ruins. I'm happy to see both of you looking so fit."

"Thank you, Lewis. The press does tend to exaggerate, don't they? I'm glad you could make it on such short notice, but I thought we should be proactive in address- ing some of the events of the past few days."

"Of course, of course," Lewis rumbled. Then he spied a colleague. "Excuse me, m'dear, but I need to have a word with

Thomas." He lumbered off, and I turned to a new arrival. At five past three Marty and I shepherded our small flock through the catalog room and reading room until we found ourselves clustered in a ragged semicircle around the battered door of the vault. I cleared my throat, this time not because of smoke but because of the lump that had grown there, and addressed the group.

"Gentlemen — and ladies — I'm sorry we had to convene this hasty meeting, but as you all know, there was a fire and a death here on Friday. I wanted to explain . . ." and I launched into a sanitized version of the events, from the warehouse fire to the connection with the Fireman's Museum, to the string of arsons in the city, which had ultimately led to the death of Scott Ingersoll. No one commented while I spoke, and they gave me a fair hearing. When I drew to a close, there was a moment or two of silence.

I wasn't surprised that Lewis Howard was the first to speak. "So it was through your quick thinking, and your familiarity with all aspects of the building, that you were able to derail this man's plan?"

"Yes." I found myself wanting to elaborate, to apologize for somehow bringing this violence into this building, but I restrained myself; Marty had been coaching me on managing the board.

Lewis swept the group with his gaze. "Then I think we owe you a collective vote of thanks. Had it not been for you, the losses could have been catastrophic."

"Yes," I said, "but —" Marty's hand on my arm stopped me; Lewis wasn't finished.

"Martha tells me that she has already obtained estimates to repair the damage and replace the items that were destroyed," he went on. "I think that we may safely assign that first priority. Was there anything else that we need to discuss?"

What? That was all? No mention of Scott's death? No censure for getting myself involved in yet another mess? "There is one more matter. Subsequent to the thefts we discovered here last fall, the FBI has entrusted us with cataloging *all* the items they recovered in their successful prosecution of the case. We've just hired a new registrar as well as an intern who I've assigned to the FBI cataloging project. The FBI's payment for our services will more than cover their time. And finally, there is some chance that we may be able to keep some or all of those items that remain unclaimed at the end of the process."

"Definitely a silver lining to that unfortunate episode." Lewis checked his watch. "Do we need to vote on anything? If we need a formality, I make a motion that we allocate sufficient funds to make necessary repairs and replacements, and that we accept the FBI's request that we assist them in their efforts to return the items they have recovered to their rightful owners. Do I hear a second?"

There were several. Ayes? They were unanimous. "Then we are adjourned. Thank you, Nell, for your good work."

Five minutes later Marty and I were left alone in the building. "What just happened here?" I asked, still feeling a bit stunned.

Marty grinned at me. "The board just gave you a huge vote of confidence. Seriously, we came out of this better than we could have hoped, officially. Who knows — maybe this collections assessment thing will turn into a steady gig with the FBI. We could use the money. You want to go out and celebrate?"

I smiled. I did — but I also wanted some time alone. Or maybe just alone with James. "Maybe later. I've got a lot to think about. I'll be in tomorrow morning."

"You'd better be — we need you here."

"Thanks, Marty. For everything."

"Including Jimmy?" She grinned.

I didn't want to give her credit for that, but I could be generous. "Everything. Persuading the board to take a chance on me. Backing me up through all the catastrophes. Trusting me. And maybe just a little for James."

"You've earned it all, Nell, and you deserve it. Besides, it's never dull around here with you in charge."

The employees of Thorndike Press hope you have enjoyed this Large Print book. All our Thorndike, Wheeler, and Kennebec Large Print titles are designed for easy reading, and all our books are made to last. Other Thorndike Press Large Print books are available at your library, through selected bookstores, or directly from us.

For information about titles, please call:
  (800) 223-1244

or visit our Web site at:
  http://gale.cengage.com/thorndike

To share your comments, please write:
  Publisher
  Thorndike Press
  10 Water St., Suite 310
  Waterville, ME 04901